CW01432745

SAFEGUARDING SORREL

A STEAMY, SMALL TOWN ROMANCE

SHELLEY MUNRO

MUNRO PRESS

Safeguarding Sorrel

Copyright © 2024 by Shelley Munro

Print ISBN: 978-1-99-106345-8
Digital ISBN: 978-0-473-33036-1

Editor: Mary Moran

Cover: Kim Killion, The Killion Group, Inc.

This book is a work of fiction. The names, characters, places, and incidents are products of the writer's imagination or have been used fictitiously and are not to be construed as real. Any resemblance to persons, living or dead, actual events, locales, or organizations is entirely coincidental.

All rights reserved. No portion of this book may be reproduced, scanned, or distributed in any manner without prior written permission from the author, except in the case of a brief quotation embodied in critical articles and reviews.

Munro Press, New Zealand.

First Munro Press electronic publication August 2015

First Munro Press print publication January 2024

DEDICATION

For Paul, my partner in crime and fellow adventurer.

DEDICATION

INTRODUCTION

SORREL *BITTER* THYME SEEMS destined to spend her entire life at the Children of Nature compound. Not an ideal situation. She dreams of so much more—a better future, one outside the cult where she can experience freedom.

After working long hours, she's close to achieving her secret goal. She's perfected the Dream Cream, which enhances orgasmic pleasure, and it's time to approach Fancy Free management with her invention. Easier said than done! Sneaking around the cult leader who will steal her idea if he learns of the financial potential is tricky and rife with problems.

Jake Ramsey, a Special Air Services soldier on sick leave,

agrees to go undercover in the cult to help local police close a case against the leader. Fun times when a beach holiday with a sexy babe would suit him better. Plain and dumpy Sorrel is his inside contact and not what he expects.

Their partnership works well. A rapport blooms, and kisses meant to cement their cover, take on new possibilities. Jake uncovers secrets, and their loving heats up, passion coalescing into more than camaraderie. Then danger stalks Sorrel. What began as a favor is now deadly serious—a game Jake must win to keep Sorrel safe.

Contains an alpha male soldier intent on protection, a determined ugly duckling heroine who dreams of freedom, and a cult leader with his eye on financial security and revenge.

NOTE TO READERS

Readers first met Jake Ramsey in Innocent Next Door (www. shelleymunro.com/books/innocent-next-door). These days, he is a changed man after his experiences at war. He's injured and feeling sorry for himself until his friend suggests he accept an undercover assignment in the small country town of Sloan. Jake thinks Louie is pulling is leg, but no, the assignment is to go undercover in a cult.

My series collide in this story. If you're interested, you can read Luke and Janaya's romance in Janaya (www.shelleymunro.com/books/janaya).

Richard and Hinekiri's romance in Hinekiri (www.shelleymunro.com/books/hinekiri)

James and Alice's romance in Fancy Free (www.shelleymunro.com/books/fancy-free).

CHAPTER ONE

SLOAN, A COUNTRY TOWN IN NEW ZEALAND

SORREL THYME PEERED THROUGH the scratchy bushes, desperately trying to ignore the sand flies making a meal of her bare arms. This had to be one of the world's most uncomfortable ways to score a job interview.

The man and woman she was spying on started to kiss—a passionate no-holds-barred kind of kiss. Horrified, she watched hands steal beneath clothes, gulped as busy fingers squeezed and caressed.

The amount of flesh on display increased, and she squirmed, heat whooshing through her body to explode in her face. Talk about embarrassing. She wasn't sure what to do, where to look. Alice and James Bates, the owners of the Fancy Free condom company, didn't have a mere picnic on their minds. Oh, no. They were busy tearing off each other's clothes, right in front of her.

Aghast, she squeezed her eyes shut, her skin crawling from exposure to the bugs. It was the only way to explain the edgy sensation blooming inside her, prickling across her skin, irritating her breasts.

The sharp evergreen scent of the totara and manuka trees wafted to her, refreshing and aromatic. Her stomach let out a feisty rumble of complaint, and she jerked in panic. The bushes concealing her rustled, and her eyes flew open. She froze, horror filling her at the risk of discovery.

Alice and James continued their amorous activities. Sorrel's breath eased out. She caught a flash of pale breast. At least they were too far away to hear her stomach clamoring for food. Placated by the thought, she eased her weight into a more comfortable position. The bush played a musical tune against her robe, and a branch cracked beneath her right foot.

"What was that?" Alice's voice carried across the clearing.

Sorrel bit back a moan of dismay, her gaze darting this way and that to determine the damage. If she didn't move, didn't answer, perhaps they'd decide a restless bird loitered in the trees. *I promise to leave the instant they settle again.*

Please let them continue. Maybe she'd manage to retreat with her dignity intact.

This was a bad idea. A stupid one. How she'd ever thought—

"Who's there?" James was on his feet now, putting his jeans to rights and staring in her direction. "I know there's someone there. You might as well come out."

Intent on self-preservation, Sorrel sprang to her feet, adrenaline kicking in big-time. She cried out as cramp struck in a painful surge, staggered two steps. Her robe snagged tight on a bush. Held fast, she panicked, yanking fabric free, frantic to escape.

Then he was on her, tackling her from behind. She hit the ground. A pained grunt escaped, the air exploding from her lungs. A hand closed around her leg, and seconds later, his weight held her in place.

"Let me go." She flailed. Ineffectually, as it happened. James Bates was one big dude.

"Who is it?" Alice called.

"A woman."

He shifted his weight, and Sorrel could breathe again. She sucked in a huge draft of air and gathered herself, ready to flee.

"Not so fast." James grasped her upper arm and yanked her around to face him. His bright blue eyes held an edge of anger that had her quaking in her sandals. He dragged her into the clearing where Alice stood with her arms crossed protectively over her chest.

Sorrel couldn't meet their gazes. She straightened her robe, brushing off the dry leaves and dirt. Her hands trembled while panicked thoughts buzzed through her mind like a swarm of bees in a tizzy about honey theft.

Job interview.

Not going well.

This was a bad, bad idea.

With escape looming large in her mind, she slid a furtive glance to her left.

"You're from the Children of Nature cult."

Give the man a prize. Sorrel twisted her hands together, her grubby robe brushing her bare legs. She had others the same, albeit cleaner, hanging on the rack in the shared wardrobe at the single women's quarters. The white robe was a dead giveaway of her status.

Cult member.

Woman.

Trapped.

"Yes." She aimed for a crisp tone. Instead her reply emerged young and scared. Terrified, which was nothing but the truth because the noose was already around her neck. Day by day it tightened, threatening to choke the life from her.

"Why are you spying on us?" Alice's brown hair stood in tousled peaks, her face pale beneath its sprinkling of golden freckles. "Is this a new angle—another campaign to smear Fancy Free?"

Sorrel swallowed, still prepared to flee the second James loosened his grip. But her legs trembled, her knees threatening to crumple like flimsy paper, not up to the job of holding her weight. She'd give anything to turn back the clock ten minutes. *No.* She had their attention—the opportunity she'd schemed and plotted for. It was time to embrace courage.

She sucked in a fortifying hit of tree-laced air, striving for calm. "I wasn't spying. I have no intention of hurting your company or...or haranguing you about the evils of condoms and birth control." *Better.* Her voice quavered only a fraction this time.

"You were spying through the bushes," James snapped. "Do you have a camera?"

A startled laugh burst from her. "Where would I get a camera? I have no money. I didn't mean to spy. Really, I just wanted to talk to you."

"Most people use the phone," James said.

"You don't know much about Children of Nature, do you?" Sorrel owned the clothes on her back—her sole possessions—and even then she wasn't sure she always received the same white robes back from the communal laundry.

"What did you want to discuss?" Alice's tone carried a generous helping of suspicion.

"I've invented a cream. It's similar to a...an aphrodisiac. It enhances sexual pleasure. I want to sell it to your company, in the hope I can raise enough money to strike out on my own and leave Children of Nature." Once she'd started, the words poured from her, one almost running into another in her haste to get them out. "But you can't tell anyone I've offered it to you. You can't tell or they'll steal it from me. You have to promise. You have to promise me you won't tell."

"Shush," Alice said, visibly calmer now. "Have you eaten?"

"I..." Sorrel's stomach let out an embarrassing rumble, forcing the truth from her. "No."

"James, release the girl." Alice offered a kind smile, which settled some of Sorrel's unease. "Come and have something to eat. You can describe your product while we have our lunch."

"I thought we were going to have a private picnic." James scowled, his brows drawing together in displeasure. His longish dark hair gave him a disreputable air as did the stubble on his face.

Alice reached out and ran her fingertips over his cheek. "I'll make it up to you tonight."

"Promise?"

The clear intimacy between the couple brought discomfort, and Sorrel shuffled from foot to foot, debating whether she should grasp this opportunity or try to make an appointment for a later date.

"With a cherry on top." Alice winked at her husband. "Come." She grasped Sorrel's hand and tugged her to their tartan picnic blanket. "Do you work in the Children of Nature store?"

"No." Sorrel's mouth compressed into a tight line. She used to take her turn working in the store and had enjoyed interacting with the town's people. But that had been before Brother Rick had taken over the running of Children of Nature from his father. That had—

She broke off her thoughts. "No, I make the soap and other products to sell in the store."

"The cult won't let you leave?" James asked, his eyes narrowed on her as if she were untrustworthy and out to take advantage of his wife. She'd seen the way he looked at Alice, as if she was the most important thing in his world. As a teenager she'd wished someone would gaze at her in that—

Again she put a brake on her thoughts. Thinking of what-if wouldn't help her situation. She had to make her own luck.

"It's difficult to leave if you lack money or contacts in the outside world."

"Sit," Alice said. "Here, you can have my glass. I'll share with James."

Gingerly, Sorrel kneeled and settled herself on the edge of the blanket. Now that she had their ear, fear writhed through her—a ravenous beast. She'd tested her product on herself, but what if her tingly cream didn't work on other women?

"I need to do more tests," she blurted.

"Of course you do." Alice handed her a glass of homemade lemonade and a chicken sandwich. "Eat first, and then we'll talk."

"Who stops you from leaving the cult?"

Alice laughed lightly. "James, do let the girl eat before you decide to grill her."

"They're not trustworthy." James scowled at her. "None of them."

Sorrel's shoulders slumped. "It's all right. I understand your doubts. I'll find another way." Despite her hunger and her disappointment, she placed the sandwich back on the plate and set down the glass of lemonade. "Thank you for listening to me. I'm sorry I interrupted your private time together." She stood and turned away, defeat a heavy sack on her shoulders.

She could hardly blame them. Children of Nature held regular protests outside Alice and James's company, Fancy Free. They organized petitions and talked to everyone who would listen about the evils of condoms—the very product Fancy Free manufactured.

"Wait. You want out." James glanced at his wife in clear speculation. "How far are you willing to go to leave the cult?"

Gasping, Sorrel drew herself up tall, or as tall as a five-foot-three-inch woman could and scowled at him. "I don't do group sex."

Turning away once again, tears of failure smarted at her eyes, but she held her shoulders square and departed. She'd have to find another way, and soon before Brother Rick implemented his plans to partner every woman above twenty-five with a man. There was no doubt in her mind he'd make good on his threats, and her twenty-fifth birthday was a mere two months away. Stars! She couldn't pretend enthusiasm for sex when pregnancy would trap her in the compound.

"We don't participate in group sex, either," Alice said in a wry tone. "One man is more than enough for me to handle. Wait." She jumped to her feet and ran after Sorrel. "Please stay."

Sorrel hesitated, unsure. She cast a doubtful glance over her shoulder, her steps slowing.

"Please, tell us about your cream. Please." Alice smiled in encouragement and led her back to the blanket. "What's your name? You know ours so you have us at a disadvantage."

"Sorrel Thyme. I know your names because I've been part of the picket line outside Fancy Free a time or two." She lifted her chin in faint challenge when they scowled at her words. "It's a change from making products for the shop."

"Glad our condom business offers you rest and relaxation," James muttered.

Alice elbowed her husband and smiled at Sorrel. "Share our food. Tell us what help you want from us."

❤ · ❤ · ❤ · ❤ · ❤

JAMES BARGED INTO THE Sloan police station, skirted the front desk and strode down a dim-lit passage. He tapped on the second office door, and opened it before anyone answered. "Luke, I might have found a way into the cult for you."

14

Luke Morgan, one of Sloan's cops and James's best friend, removed his feet from the top of his desk and stood in one smooth motion. "Let's take this out of the station. I could do with a coffee."

"The cafe isn't private."

"We'll get coffee to go and wander down by the river. I think better on my feet."

Fifteen minutes later they strolled along the bank of the river. Leaves crunched under their boots, sun streamed from overhead and a brisk wind rustled their hair.

"Talk," Luke ordered.

"One of the young cult girls approached me and Alice yesterday. She wants out of the cult."

"Why doesn't she just leave?"

"From what she told us she was born there. According to her, once they're in, it's difficult to leave without resources. Any money they earn goes into a central pot. They're not encouraged to leave. She told us their long-term leader died six months ago. His son has taken over and he has new ideas regarding the direction of the cult."

"Six months ago is about the time the farmers started complaining of missing cattle," Luke mused, interest sparking in his features.

"Yeah, the thought occurred."

"How is that going to help us get inside?"

"I thought Sorrel—that's the woman we met—might know of a way we can get someone inside, and once our man is in, she can help to smooth his path."

Luke nodded. "That's a possibility. Where can I meet her? When?"

James paused once they reached the bridge. He stared at a group of six ducks, quacking loud demands for food. "Do you have another plan?"

"No, other than going in with guns and shooting the weirdos. That's my stepmother's suggestion."

James spluttered out a laugh, the shake of his head flopping his dark hair over his eyes. He shoved it aside with a careless hand. "Hinekiri is a handful."

Luke snorted. "Where do you think my wife got it from? Janaya takes after her aunt. Yeah, I've thought about planting someone in the cult to spy for me. I have a guy, one of my cousin's friends who needs something to keep him busy. He's a special services soldier on sick leave. My cousin reckoned he'd be perfect since he looks scruffy. Feeling sorry for himself, according to Louie."

"You've given this some thought. Sorrel told us she'd try to get away this afternoon after she delivers new supplies to their shop. She can't meet us in a public place. Any suggestions?"

"We can intercept her once she leaves the shop. If you see her beforehand, ask her," Luke said. "We'll meet her wherever she feels safest. I don't want to make her life any more difficult than it is now. She obviously feels she can't leave if she approached you in a clandestine manner. Ring me with details once you're set, and I'll be there. If I can't make the meeting for some reason, I'll send Janaya. Tell her that, will you?"

"Alice promised she'd meet her. Sorrel indicated a meeting with a man would raise suspicion. One of the other cult women is bound to notice and report back to the men running the place."

"Makes sense. What's your impression of the woman?"

"Solemn and plain. Not much to look at, and a bit on the dumpy side."

"Yeah but is she telling the truth? Could she be setting us up?"

James sipped his coffee. "No, I think she's genuine in wanting to get out. She was jumpy. Kept looking over her shoulder, and she doesn't think much of the new leader. You met him?"

"Yeah, he's charming but slimy with it. You know the sort. I can see him being the controlling type. What was Alice's take?"

"She wanted to help and was ready to take Sorrel home

with us then. I'm not such a soft touch."

Luke shot him a swift glance. "She might be genuine."

"Maybe. Maybe not." He checked his watch. "I'd better go. We have a board meeting this afternoon. I'll call you the minute she gets in touch."

· ♥ · ♥ · ♥ · ♥ · ♥ ·

CHILDREN OF NATURE COMPOUND, Sloan

"Excuse me." Sorrel reached for a tray as she waited for the last of the men to move along the meal line in the Children of Nature dining hall. The aroma of fresh, yeasty bread and a savory soup drifted from the nearby kitchen. Hunger clawed at her, but she kept her eyes off the women serving the meals.

Instead, her gaze flitted around the hall. It was a large rectangular room, filled with a dozen trestle tables. Each table seated twelve people, and most of them were already taken.

A robed man, ahead in the line, turned to glare at her. "What do you want Sister Bitter? We're not done eating yet."

The men and women sitting at the nearest table stared in open curiosity. They nudged one another, some of the men sniggering.

"You'll have to wait," another ordered. He eyed her dumpy figure, a smirk forming. "It won't hurt you to wait. You need to lose weight."

"Of course." Sorrel took a step back, glancing down at her feet in submission. *Bastards*. Bullies the lot of them, and Brother Rick encouraged them to pick on her. She hated the changes since he'd taken over, the way the men treated the women as inferiors.

"Bitter, aren't you almost twenty-five?" one of the men asked. "No one will want to fuck you. You're too fat and ugly."

Sorrel knew better than to show any outward reaction. It would goad them to greater cruelty. She should be used to the way they treated her with disdain because of her appearance, yet, stars, it hurt. They thought they were so clever, taking the literal meaning of Sorrel and using it to taunt her.

Bitter.

Bitter Thyme.

The wit who'd rechristened her Bitter thought the new name fit so well, he'd told everyone, and the wretched nickname had stuck.

"Go," the first man said. "You must have chores to perform."

Sorrel blinked once, twice. Tears stung her eyes, but she

refused to let them fall. It would give the men another weapon to taunt her.

Keeping her head bowed, Sorrel turned away from the food, ignoring the hunger pangs twisting her stomach. She'd set herself on this path and mustn't falter now.

Without thinking of her destination, she found herself back at the workroom, across the other side of the compound, where she made soap and creams and various other items to sell in the shop in town. Dried herbs and flowers hung from the ceiling in tight bunches, their colors faded while their scents perfumed the air with lavender, rose, rosemary and marigold.

Today she was making lavender bath bombs and bath salts. Her stomach let out a rumble, the pangs of hunger so bad they were painful. She hurried to the sink and poured herself a glass of water, hoping to trick her stomach into thinking it was full. She was halfway through a second glass before a prickle of awareness identified another presence in her workroom. Stomach churning, she turned to face the new arrival.

One of the women.

Some of the tension lifted from her shoulders. "Can I help you with something, Sister Marigold?"

Sister Marigold, the elderly woman who was in charge of the cult shop, glanced over her shoulder before entering.

"I brought you something to eat." She extended a piece of fresh bread and a hunk of cheese. "It's not right, the way they treat you and make you miss meals. It's not right."

The tears were back again. This time the emotion was gratitude instead of anger and fear. One small act of kindness was all it took.

"I don't want you to get into trouble." But she couldn't stop herself from reaching for the single slice of fresh bread. The lack of butter or jam or a bowl of soup in which to dunk it mattered little.

"It's a risk I'm willing to take. Most of the other women agree with me. When you deliver the stock for the shop and the lunches for the women working there, you'll find an extra one for you as often as I can manage it." She glanced over her shoulder and leaned closer on noticing two robed women heading in their direction. "Make sure you eat your lunch before you get back to the compound."

"I...thank you."

"Quick. Eat before someone comes. Where are the supplies for the store? I'll help you load the handcart."

No longer protesting her hunger, she crammed the bread and hard cheese into her mouth, chewing rapidly. The faint yeastiness of the bread burst on her taste buds, the nuttiness of each bite following swiftly and contrasting with the sharpness of the cheddar cheese. It was the best thing she'd tasted for weeks.

"Thank you," she whispered.

Sister Marigold's cheeks colored. "Enough of that. You have friends among the women."

Feeling infinitely happier, hunger pangs assuaged for now, Sorrel pushed the handcart through the gates of the compound.

One of the men studied her straining figure. "Are you sure you can manage, Sister Sor—Bitter?"

"Let her go." The second man jerked his head. He was younger, taller, his manner superior, a duplicate of the other cult males. "Make sure you're back before dusk."

"Of course." She kept her tone agreeable, not raising her gaze to meet either of the men's. Women were fit for raising children and doing the work around the compound. Nothing more. Inside, her seething anger grew. Somehow, someway, she *would* get away from the cult or die in the trying.

She shoved the handcart along the track, the creak of the wheels an accompaniment to her thoughts. She needed to meet with Alice Bates and find a way to eat the meal Sister Marigold had arranged for her.

The ruts on the track created the usual difficulties, but she manhandled the cart over and around, trying to make the trip to town quicker than normal to give her longer to undertake her own business. She slowed the handcart as she wheeled past the factory, pausing on the footpath to let James Bates pull his vehicle into the factory driveway. He saw her, his head dipping a fraction in acknowledgment.

When she reached the store almost three-quarters of an hour after leaving the compound, a film of perspiration coated her skin. Ignoring her discomfort, she pushed the cart around to the rear of the store and knocked on the door.

"Good, you're here. I'm starving." Sister Jasmine was young and blonde with a curvy figure.

"I'll unpack your lunches in a moment."

"Let me help you with the supplies," Sister Jasmine said. "What have you brought us today?"

Even though Sister Jasmine was popular and slept with many of the brothers, she retained her sweetness. Sorrel couldn't help but like her, but she couldn't agree with Sister Jasmine's aim to fulfill her purpose as a woman and have children.

Brainwashed.

Most of the people who lived at the compound were under Brother Rick's spell. They never hesitated to obey his demands.

Damn, what was wrong with her lately? *Put this stuff out of your head and focus on the important things.*

Freedom.

"I made lavender bath bombs this morning. Here's a box." Sorrel handed them over. "I've made some carnation body lotion and there's plenty of sea salt and peppermint soap in there. I know that's been popular."

"Super. Do you have some sample sizes?"

"Of course." Sorrel followed Sister Jasmine into the rear of the store. She set the boxes down and went back for more. Soon the handcart was empty and the women had their lunches.

"I'm off to collect eucalyptus leaves to use in my soap. They're on the other side of town, so I'll have to hurry because I need to be back at the farm before dusk." Not too much information? Sorrel paused to check the women's expressions, but none of them bore an ounce of suspicion. "Is there anything in particular you need me to make this week?"

"The lavender soap is popular, and we're almost out of the rose-scented cream," one of the women said. Her gray hair was braided and hung down her back, almost reaching past her bottom.

"I'll make more this week," Sorrel promised. "I'll see you again later in the week."

"I'll ask Brother Rick if you can come more often. The products are selling well. We need more."

"I can't make more and deliver them too."

The woman reached over and patted Sorrel's hand. "I'll talk to Brother Rick. Perhaps he'll assign you an assistant or maybe someone else could make the deliveries."

Alarm surfaced in Sorrel, but she bit back the hasty words forming on the tip of her tongue. She merely nodded and waved goodbye.

There were spies everywhere within the compound. She couldn't trust anyone—no matter how kind they were to her. An assistant around her workshop would make her plans for escape more difficult. It wouldn't help her ongoing experiments with her special cream either.

Aware of the passing time, Sorrel pushed her handcart through the town to the stand of eucalyptus trees. Hopefully James had alerted Alice to her arrival in town.

Once she had the eucalyptus in sight, she glanced over her shoulder. She was alone. With trembling hands she reached into her handcart and pulled out a packet of sandwiches.

She unfolded the brown paper and almost moaned at the wonderful scent. Roast beef. She hadn't had meat for months. There was never any left on the occasions they allowed her to eat.

She bit into the bread and chewed, despite the urge to gobble it down. A small plastic bottle of homemade lemon drink and an apple rounded out her lunch, and she savored every bite.

The sound of a vehicle approaching made her burst into action. She frantically wiped the crumbs from her mouth and thrust the bottle under the empty packages in her handcart.

Then, she turned to face the music, prepared with excuses. Her shoulders slumped with relief on recognizing the woman who climbed from the car. A second woman, tall and blonde, and one she'd seen with Alice before, climbed from the passenger side.

"I need to collect eucalyptus leaves to take back to the farm with me. Can we talk while I pick?"

"That's fine. Have you met Janaya? She's married to Luke Morgan, head cop here in Sloan," Alice said. "Janaya, this is Sorrel Thyme."

"Pleased to meet you." Sorrel forced a smile at the beautiful blonde woman. Now that Alice had arrived, trepidation danced a Highland fling through her thoughts. What if this went pear-shaped? What if someone ended up getting hurt? Brother Rick was capable—no, she couldn't think that way. "I've brought you a sample of my cream." After a furtive glance around the area, Sorrel raised her robe and retrieved a small tub of cream from a concealed pocket. She handed it to Alice. "I can make more."

"The user rubs it where?" Alice asked.

"Breasts and nipples, inner thighs and labia. The clitoris. There's nothing in it to hurt or cause an allergic reaction, but I haven't used the cream internally. External use seems enough to cause increased sexual awareness and desire. It should make a woman's natural lubrication increase." Sorrel was proud of her matter-of-fact explanation. Her cream was a great product—she knew it—and she was counting on her expertise with herbs, flowers and natural cosmetics to gain her freedom and escape from Children of Nature.

"Great. I can't wait to try it. Normally I'd get you to sign documents, but we'll have to work on trust this time. I give you my word that if this product is something we can use I'll help you to leave the cult and give you the full credit you deserve. Janaya, you're witness to our verbal agreement."

"Can I try some too?" Janaya's violet eyes glowed with interest. "It sounds fun."

"Is there enough in the tub for more than one person?"

Sorrel nodded, excitement and relief pumping through her now that she'd taken this step.

"We wondered if you could do something for us in return," Janaya said.

"Me?" What could she do for these two women? They

looked as if they had everything.

Janaya stared at her intently, her eyes beautiful and mesmerizing. Bright purple flames. "My husband wants to get a man into your cult. How easy is it for someone to join?"

Sorrel gaped at them "Do they have a head injury?" Stars, she was trying to get out of the place.

Alice laughed. "No, it's a serious question."

"The cops want a man undercover at the compound?"

"Yes." Alice nodded.

"Yes," Janaya confirmed.

"Why? What's wrong? No, wait." Sorrel held up a hand. "I'm better off not knowing."

"Is it possible to join?" Janaya fiddled with the end of her blonde braid while scrutinizing her as if she were a big black bug. "How does a person join the cult?"

"Most people visit the compound and look around. If they're impressed by what they see, they gift their property—their money and valuables—and move in. That's the simple answer."

Janaya pursed her lips. "And the complicated answer?"

"Brother Rick is the new leader. He hasn't taken in new people since he's become leader, but a decent amount of money might change his mind."

"Interesting." Alice made a humming sound. "How

decent?"

"Maybe four or five thousand. It will depend on Brother Rick. This man—who is he? What are the cops looking for? What's going on at the compound?" Curiosity got the better and questions tumbled out of her.

"You haven't seen anything illegal?" Janaya eyed her with a probing gaze, as if she was measuring every word and gesture.

Sorrel shook her head. "I spend my time making soaps and lotions to sell in the Children of Nature shop. If I'm not making stuff in my workshop I'm collecting herbs or flowers. I need to collect leaves now. I can't be late."

"Show us what you need, and we'll help," Alice said.

Sorrel dug out her clippers and started gathering leaves from the lower branches. The sharp scent of eucalyptus filled each breath and coated her bare hands.

With the women's help, her handcart was soon full of leaves.

"So you think our guy shouldn't have any difficulty joining Children of Nature?" Janaya asked.

"Brother Rick will interrogate him about his reasons for joining, but if he has money..." She shrugged in the guise of finishing her sentence.

"Good. We can work with that," Janaya said.

"My cream?" Sorrel was more interested in her future.

"How long will it be before I know your decision?"

"I'll trial it and get back to you. A few weeks maybe. If I see potential in the idea, we'll get you to come to the lab, and we'll work on the recipe, refining it if necessary."

"A job?"

"Or, if you prefer, we could buy the rights to the recipe outright," Alice said. "But we're getting ahead of ourselves. When are you delivering new stock to your shop?"

"I go Mondays and Fridays, but they're saying they need new stock more often. I'm finding it difficult to keep up with demand."

Alice nodded, her manner thoughtful as she considered the matter. "We'll watch for you and attempt a meeting if it's doable."

Sorrel nodded, not trusting herself to speak. Her hands trembled as she fastened elastic cords across the foliage to keep it in place during the trip back to the compound. "Thank you," she managed. "I need to go." She pushed the handcart up the incline without another word, excitement bursting free in a wide smile once she was sure neither of the women would see. She'd taken the first step, and now all she needed to do was trust in herself because she'd invented a dynamite product.

CHAPTER TWO

Jake Ramsay had done some crazy shit in his time, but this idea was plain weird even for him. He stared at Louie Lithgow, one of his best friends who he'd served with in the SAS, New Zealand's elite military unit. His gaze slid to Louie's cop cousin, Luke Morgan, while he waited for one of them to break and crack a smile. This had to be a joke at his expense.

Didn't happen.

He continued to stare at them without blinking. "You want me to what?"

"I need someone undercover at the cult before the local farmers take matters into their own hands. Innocent people will get hurt," Luke explained.

"Why is it my problem?" Jake wanted to bite back the

words as soon as they left his mouth. He was a soldier. It was his job to protect.

"Luke needs your help." Louie kept his expression impassive. "You're not doing anything apart from watching TV all day."

Jake's top lip curled. Louie hadn't mentioned the plethora of empty bottles littering his kitchen counter. "Haven't you noticed my limp? I'm not fit to work. They're telling me I have another three weeks of recuperation at least."

"That's the beauty of this assignment," Luke said. "The way you look now is perfect. With your long hair and scraggly beard you'll fit right in. All you need to do is poke around a little and report back if you find any evidence of stock rustling."

Jake frowned. "I thought cults were into drugs, kidnapping and brainwashing."

Luke laughed. "Not this one. My father caught younger members selling special cookies to high school students, a few minor offenses, but that's all."

"Then why do you suspect them of cattle rustling now?" Jake asked.

"Change of management. The old leader died and the son has taken over."

Jake's interest was caught in a way it hadn't been since

his last assignment. "Suspicious circumstances?"

Luke shrugged. "It's possible, but I haven't heard any rumblings."

"All right. Suppose I decide to help you out—how do I get in? I'm sure they don't accept anyone who strolls up to the gate."

"Gaining entry might prove a problem, but if you sell it right—tell them you're back from an ashram in India, and you're looking for a place to settle in New Zealand. Tell them the idea of living at a farm and the slower pace of life appeals to you."

Jake suppressed a snort. Slow sounded great. Anything would be better than the sniper fire and bombs of Afghanistan. Besides, he was tired of his own company. His friends, Nikolai and Louie had wives now, other responsibilities. He didn't see them as much. Hell, maybe having something to focus on would put a stop to Greg's ghost, dogging his heels, not that he intended to mention his fun companion to anyone.

"Do you have more questions?"

"No, I'll do it," Jake said. "I'll give it my best shot."

· ♥ · ♥ · ♥ · ♥ · ♥ ·

CHILDREN OF NATURE COMPOUND

Sorrel saw the new guy arrive, and unlike everyone else at the compound, she suspected what his presence meant.

Clandestine surveillance. Secrets and sneaking around.

They'd moved quickly after talking to her. She hadn't even had her second meeting with Alice yet.

He was tall, over six foot, and he wore his dark hair tied in a ponytail at his nape. A faded navy-blue T-shirt covered his chest while jeans, faded at stress points, garbed his lower half. Despite his thinness, he was a big man, and he held himself proudly, meeting the gazes of the men at the gates without hesitation. At least it appeared that way. A bushy black beard hid a large portion of his face.

Aware she'd grab attention if she was found staring, she hurried to her workshop and started a batch of soap. She'd already distilled the oil from the eucalyptus leaves, and she intended to use it to scent the soap today. She measured and stirred, her mind drifting, the heady bouquet of eucalyptus filling the air.

Would Brother Rick let the man join? And what sort of man was he? A soft snort emerged. He'd behave in the same manner as the other men and treat her with contempt. He'd call her Bitter because he was playing a part.

The day passed, and despite the pangs of hunger, she kept going, making a batch of marigold cream, a chocolate body scrub and another batch of soap, this one decorated with delicate pink rose buds.

She timed her arrival at dinner in order to walk in with the other women. Luckily, the men seemed busy, clustered around or near the new guy. For the first time in weeks, she managed to eat a full meal, and her stomach thanked her for it. She sent warm, fuzzy thoughts to the new guy—whoever he was for causing the distraction.

♥ · ♥ · ♥ · ♥ · ♥

ONE WHIFF OF MONEY, and they'd welcomed him with open arms. Much easier than dodging bombs. The robes weren't so shit-hot though. It was gonna take a while to get used to the breeze flapping around his legs.

"Brother Jake, do you think you'll be happy here?" Brother Rick queried. He was a slim man with short brown hair, a few inches short of six foot, but he had a presence about him. Sly intelligence lurked in his brown eyes.

Luke Morgan had described him as charismatic with a side of sleaze. Got it in one. The man's smile edged up until he flashed a mouthful of white teeth, yet it never reached his eyes. This was a professional smile, one to inspire confidence, yet Jake wasn't stupid enough to fall for the tactic. An Oscar-worthy performance. That was what Brother Rick would receive in exchange for his fake smile and phony interest.

"From what you've told me I believe I'll settle in here very well. Of course there's a place in the South Island that might also suit. I believe you said I could stay here for a week or two while I make up my mind?"

"Of course." Brother Rick's pleasant expression never faltered, although the brisk note in his voice told Jake he'd pissed off the younger man. "What made you return to New Zealand?"

"I caught a bug in India, had a bad run of dysentery." Jake made an affected motion with his hand. "My illness brought on a bout of homesickness, and I decided it was time to return to New Zealand. I've been back a month now, staying with a friend in Auckland. It's taken me a while to recover." Aware it was best to keep it simple, Jake stopped talking.

"Why here?"

Ah, the man was still wary. "My preference is a quiet life in the country. I enjoy working with herbs. I understand you have a shop in the town where you sell soaps and other stuff." Jake prattled as he'd never prattled before. Nikolai and Louie would've bust their guts, laughing themselves silly if they'd heard him. "Perhaps I could employ my talents in that direction, if you require my help there, of course."

"What duties did you carry out at the ashram in India?"

"I helped look after the guests who came to the yoga retreat. I arranged meals and cleaned the guest rooms."

"I see."

Jake doubted the smug bastard saw a thing, which was perfect.

"You're welcome to stay here while you're making up your mind. They will make space for you in the single men's quarters. We will, of course, have to charge you for the length of your stay."

"Of course." Jake kept his expression impassive, but he knew a man out for a buck when he saw one. "I expect to pay my way while I'm making up my mind. I'm willing to work at whatever chores you decide to set me. I have to say, I'm very impressed with the setup you have here."

Brother Rick inclined his head with the hauteur of an aristocrat. "As it happens, Bitter Thyme, the woman who makes the soaps needs to increase her production. She would welcome an extra pair of hands." His mouth curled up in a secret smile, which made an alarm fire to life in Jake. He was pretty sure the Thyme woman was the one who wanted out of the cult.

If Brother Rick was on to her, Jake needed to tread

warily. No prob. After navigating a minefield this would be no sweat. He'd be out of here, lying on a beach with a beer and a babe by next weekend.

"I daresay I can take on other chores if I dislike the work?" He lifted his brows in query.

"We encourage our people to aid where they wish. You're welcome to help with the livestock or in the gardens as you choose."

"Thank you. Is there someone available to give me a tour or is it all right to wander around the compound on my own?"

"You're free to explore, but I'm sure everyone will be eager to show you around or answer questions if you ask."

"Thanks again," Jake said. "You've made me feel very welcome."

A bell rang in the distance, the tinny sound echoing through the valley.

"That's the dinner bell," Brother Rick said. "We tend to eat early. Come. Sit at my table tonight. Meet some of the men who help me run the compound."

"I'd enjoy that." Jake found himself limping alongside Brother Rick as they made their way to the dining room.

He noted the groups of robed people wandering toward the large building to one side of the compound. Men and women wore white robes, although Brother Rick and some of the men had maroon stripes set in the loose sleeves.

The air whistled past his pursed lips as he took in the two men still at the gates. Security. Why did they need people manning the entrance? What were they afraid of? Maybe this wouldn't be as easy as he hoped. It would take time before the members of the cult started to think of him as one of them. At present he was a novelty. The weight of their gazes struck him as he limped at Brother Rick's side.

Jake entered a large hall, set out for communal dining. The men strode straight to the food, the women serving them first despite women waiting in the line. Jake hid his reaction thanks to his training, bit back the incredulous comment at the tip of his tongue.

It seemed women were second-class citizens around this place.

Most of the men were of middle age—forties to fifties—but there were also ten men who were younger, and they were the ones with the maroon stripes on their sleeves. Brother Rick appeared around thirty.

The food was good and plentiful, and Jake enjoyed every mouthful of the roast beef and vegetables. A wry thought that he might be eating the neighbor's stud bull brought amusement. A bit late to worry now. He set his knife and fork across the empty plate, surprised by his good appetite. He picked up a glass of water and drank deeply. For the first time in weeks, he wasn't craving a beer or a whisky. Louie was right. It seemed his problem was lack of purpose.

Brother Rick finished his meal and stood, his booming voice bringing an instant hush. "As you know, we aim for self-sufficiency. We're also in favor of natural methods in all things. We're against birth control." He gestured with his hands.

"Bad, bad birth control," the men and women shouted at him.

They clapped enthusiastically, and Brother Rick paused for quiet. "Exactly. Children are a blessing."

With his chair tilted a fraction to the right, Jake was able to scan the faces of the men and women in the hall. He cataloged the various expressions. Most of the men grinned. Some of the women too, but he noted apprehension on a few faces.

Luke had told him the cult members often picketed the condom factory, Fancy Free, but apart from this public protest, they kept pretty much to themselves.

"In five nights we'll hold a gathering. I expect everyone over the age of twenty to attend, but participation isn't compulsory for those under twenty-five. You are adults and may make the decision as you see fit."

A burst of excited chatter filled the hall. Reactions varied from open excitement to...to...fear. Jake frowned.

What the fuck was the man talking about?

Brother Rick held up his hand in a sign for quiet. The noise died away. "Nursing mothers may attend if they wish, or they can volunteer to watch the children. The kitchen will make a batch of bliss cakes, and the brewer intends to open his cellar. We will trial a batch of his beer."

More enthusiastic shouts met this announcement.

Bliss cakes? What the fuck? Again Jake studied the various reactions to the announcement. Which one was Sorrel? Was she this Bitter Thyme person or someone else?

Brother Rick held up his hand again. "I'll be away for three days. I intend to travel to Auckland and spread the message. Brother Felix and Brother Tyrone will be aiding me, and I hope to bring back new recruits."

Another roar of approval swelled throughout the hall.

"That is all." Brother Rick beamed. "We leave tonight. I'll see you at the celebration."

The men at Jake's table stood, leaving their plates where they sat. Jake followed suit, although he noticed the people at other tables carried their used plates and cutlery to a central point.

Brother Rick stopped by a neighboring table, filled with women. "Sister Bitter, clear our table. I've heard the store needs additional stock. Do you have products ready to go to the shop tomorrow?"

Jake noticed the woman didn't glance at Brother Rick. Her gaze remained on her hands while she answered in a calm voice.

"The next delivery is Friday. There isn't enough stock for a trip to the shop yet."

"I've noticed your laziness." Brother Rick kept his voice even, yet it held undertones of intimidation. "Work through the night. Make sure you have enough stock to deliver to the shop. Increase production. The new man is interested in herbs. He can help you tomorrow."

"Yes, Brother Rick."

This chubby, colorless woman was Sorrel. For some reason Brother Rick detested her, but the man had made Jake's job easier. With a positive identification, he wouldn't need to blunder around, wasting valuable time to find the right woman.

Brother Rick marched from the room without looking left or right. At the door, two of the men followed him while the others ambled in the direction of the recreation room. Jake memorized the two men, leaving with Rick. Brothers Felix and Tyrone were around the same age as Rick and wore robes with maroon bands on the sleeves. Both had shaved their heads, and if they'd worn jeans and T-shirts, they would've fit a thuggish category. Not even the robes disguised their beefy builds.

Jake stepped outside, welcoming the coolness of the summer breeze. He glanced back over his shoulder and noticed the woman—Bitter—was clearing the table. None of the other women were helping, and Jake wondered why. Pity swelled inside him, every instinct to assist her.

But the fact everyone was ignoring her, told him something else was amiss. He'd talk to her later, once she returned to her workshop. Meanwhile, he'd reconnoiter, wander the grounds, and poke his nose into the buildings—get the lay of the land and ferret out the strengths and weaknesses of the compound in regard to security.

Luke was waiting for his report.

Hell, maybe he'd even get lucky and find a pen full of cattle. He lifted his nose and sniffed. When he caught a whiff of animal, he ambled in that direction. The sooner he found viable proof, the sooner he was out of here. The beach, beer and babes beckoned.

·♥·♥·♥·♥·♥·

SORREL HUSTLED FROM THE table to the kitchen and back as she cleared the tables. The other men, taking their cue from Brother Rick, left their plates and walked away too.

The women didn't help, although their sympathy buffeted her in silent waves. Brother Rick made no secret of the fact of his dislike, but she had no idea why he detested her so much. She hadn't acted rude or done anything else to attract his animosity.

She'd been close to Brother Samuel, the first leader of the cult and Brother Rick's father. Maybe Brother Rick was jealous of their close relationship. But no, it couldn't be that. Brother Samuel had treated everyone equally.

She scraped and stacked the plates, sorted the cutlery and glassware all the while thinking and worrying how to produce enough stock for the shop. Maybe bath salts. They were less time consuming to make, and she had adequate supplies of perfumed oils to make different types. They had a glut of fruit in the orchard. She could make a batch of natural face masks. They'd need refrigeration, but the Sloan women appeared willing to try new products.

By the time she'd finished, almost an hour later, she had a plan of how to make enough stock to fill her handcart. And if she had a helper tomorrow, even if he only chopped or stirred ingredients, it would free her to make extra products. She might even have time to make more of her cream.

She hurried across the compound, her worn sandals

slapping the dry track made by many feet over the years.

A large form separated from the shadows without warning.

"Oh." She clapped her hand to her thundering heart, backing up before realizing she was in no danger.

"Forgive me. I didn't mean to startle you." Concern furrowed his forehead, and the sentiment echoed in his brown eyes. His dark brown hair was loose and shaggy now, tossed into spikes and unruly waves by the breeze, his beard crying for a trim. Up close, he towered over her and the robe hung on his thin frame. Despite his size, once she'd identified him, her heart settled to a more normal beat.

"I was miles away." She settled into a brisk walk and spoke over her shoulder. "I must go. I have a lot to do tonight."

"I've come to help."

She halted and turned to face him. "But Brother Rick said you should start tomorrow."

"Brother Rick isn't here to reiterate otherwise." He thrust out his hand. "My name is Jake Ramsay."

Sorrel stared at his hand before she took it. His palm, large and warm, wrapped around hers, squeezing a fraction but not to the point of pain. A bolt of sensation streaked up her arm, and her breath caught. She had to swallow before she could speak again. "Sorrel Thyme."

He cocked his head a fraction, still retaining her hand. "Why do they call you Bitter?"

"A joke." A flash of heat swept her face and settled in her cheeks. "My name means Bitter. One of the women had a book of baby names. The men checked my name, and now Brother Rick and the others call me Bitter." She shot him a swift glance before focusing on her feet again.

He released her hand. "Nothing better to do. I've explored most of the compound buildings already."

Unsure of what to say, she started walking again, plunging toward her workshop. She opened the door and stepped inside, flicking on the lights—thank goodness for the generator—to illuminate her domain.

Jake stepped inside and closed the door behind him. She was aware of him at her back, large and masculine and out of place in her workshop full of herbs and flowers. She was certain this was the man who was acting as spy, although she wasn't stupid enough to ask for details.

"Can I look around?"

"Of course. I'll start making a batch of bath salts." She watched him prowl the interior, his gaze intent and alert. Despite his frail appearance he reminded her of a caged big cat, bearing the same watchful air and prepared to pounce at a moment's notice.

She pulled out a large mixing bowl and measured cups of baking soda and citric acid. She stirred the mix with her wooden spoon. Once that was done she added rose oil and stirred it until combined. A few drops of coloring and the final touch—some dried rose petals.

And still the man prowled, poking and prodding at windows and checking the walls.

She gathered small jars and started to spoon her mixture into them, fixing the lids firmly with the ease of practice, despite the faint tremor of her hands. She wasn't used to big men in her space. Stars, she wasn't used to any men in her domain.

From the corner of her eye, she saw him search the containers holding her stock. He'd better have clean hands. She'd bean him if he contaminated her supplies.

"What are you looking for?" she demanded, her nerves at breaking point.

He remained silent, merely shook his head and placed his finger to his lips in a gesture for quiet.

"Pass me the labels please." Sorrel pointed, and he complied.

While she wiped the jars and affixed labels, he continued his explorations. Definitely the spy, but what was he looking for? No one came in here apart from her. She slept here a lot of the time because it was easier than stumbling across the compound in the small hours of the morning. The last thing she wanted to do was run into one of the men and have him interpret her presence as an invitation for sex.

"I think we're okay. What do you want me to do?"

"My handcart is in the lean-to out the back. I need these jars packed into the boxes and loaded into the handcart ready for me to deliver them tomorrow morning."

He followed her instructions, not fumbling or breaking anything, and soon she relaxed, giving him another job in order to save her time.

"Tell me about the compound," he said in his husky voice. "Why should I move here?"

She looked at him then, startled by the question. Was he not the spy? Luckily, she hadn't questioned him further. "Did Brother Rick not give you a tour?"

"He described the facilities, but he was busy and didn't have time to give me a personal tour. He gave me leave to explore on my own."

Sorrel hesitated. What should she tell him? She hated the place and couldn't wait to leave. It was all she dreamed of—departing the compound and making her own way in the world. Material possessions weren't important. All she wanted was enough money to live a life of independence.

"It's a good place."

"You're lying through your teeth."

It took her a few seconds to register his words, and when she did, she stared at him in shock. "I...I..."

"It's all right. Luke Morgan sent me. I'm here to watch and learn. I'll help you all I can."

Her knees buckled, and she had to grip the corner of her worktable in order to remain upright. Relief struck first—the knowledge she wasn't alone. Suddenly she couldn't see, and she realized tears had welled in her eyes, blinding her temporarily. Sniffing, she brushed them away with the back of her hand.

"Thank you," she whispered.

"I've volunteered to help you here, but I don't know the first thing about herbs. If anyone asks me questions, I'll blow my cover for sure."

She laughed then, and this time managed to hold his gaze, although it was difficult to look at a man in such a direct manner. The brothers took this as an affront and a challenge. It attracted attention. Better to keep her head down.

"Ask me all the questions you want. It will be pleasant to have someone to talk to."

"Why does everyone avoid you? Why do they let Brother Rick treat you as a slave?"

"They're frightened," Sorrel said. "A few months ago

49

someone tried to stick up for me, and he disappeared one night. Brother Rick announced that Brother John caught him stealing supplies. They turned him out, shunning him. No one has seen him since."

"You think Brother Rick had him killed?" Jake's alert eyes narrowed, the focus on her so powerful her gaze automatically shot to her feet, her belly lurching with anxiety. "Look at me, damn it. I'm not going to strike you. I've never hit a woman in my life."

Sorrel swallowed. "The man they turned away was a gentle soul. He wasn't the type to steal. He was pure and always had a good word for everyone. There's always a first time."

"First time for what?"

"To hit a woman." Again she couldn't maintain eye contact.

His hand shot out, and she flinched, half expecting a blow. Instead, he gripped her chin and lifted her face. She stared, swallowing while a host of butterflies stampeded inside her stomach, charging around like a herd of crazed cattle.

"I'm here to help. No one will hurt you while I'm here, but you'll have to assist me in return. I need to know the ins and outs. What the hell did Brother Rick's announcement mean? I get it's some sort of celebration, but other than that, I'm clueless. Fill me in on the details. Help me understand the inner workings of the place so I can decide how to attack this mission."

Her shocked mind fastened on his last word. "Mission?"

His lips kicked up into a crooked grin. It echoed in his eyes and turned his expression into one of boyish charm. It made her wonder how he'd look without the beard. "See, I've slipped into soldier talk already. I need you to help me to prevent other mistakes."

"You're a soldier?"

"Yes."

"I won't tell anyone," she promised.

"Good. Now we'd better get working on these things you need to make. What's next?"

Her mind full of hope, she started him on peeling fruit to make the face masks. She chopped and measured and dreamed of freedom.

"This celebration," he reminded her. "What's it for?"

The fear returned, and she concentrated on measuring one scant cup of Fuller's earth. She leveled it precisely, even as heat crawled up her neck and into her face. From experience she knew the patches of color would be ugly and startling against her blotchy skin.

"Sorrel?" His voice held curiosity, a silent demand for answers.

"The purpose of Children of Nature has always been to encourage the growth of children in a natural environment. We're against birth control, which means there are a lot of children." Somehow, the heat in her cheeks intensified. She measured another cup of Fuller's earth and tapped it into her mixing bowl.

"And?" he prompted, his stillness unnerving.

"Brother Rick wants Children of Nature to prosper. He arranges gatherings where couples—people—come together for the purpose of procreation." She chose her words with care and managed to get them out before she choked on them.

She shot him a swift glance, noted the furrow between his eyebrows and his eyes. Those eyes would feature in her dreams tonight. They were a deep, dark brown and intense. When he looked at her it felt as if he saw every secret. His gaze stripped her of pretense yet made her feel safe too—secure in a way she hadn't felt for months. The inky-black lashes surrounding his eyes were lush, the kind women desired but were often bestowed on the male of the species. A tremor shook her, a spear of heat darted through her lower belly. She swallowed, alarmed by the unusual sensation.

"Let me get this straight. Brother Rick arranges gatherings to encourage sex between the adult members of the cult."

"We're not a cult," she said automatically.

"Brother Rick is organizing an evening of sex complete with drugs and alcohol to lower the inhibitions of those who are less welcoming of the idea. He's organizing an orgy."

Sorrel pressed her lips together, gave one swift nod.

"And everyone over the age of twenty-five is expected to participate."

Another nod.

"Jesus," he ground out. "How old are you?"

"Twenty-four. I turn twenty-five this year."

"Jesus," he muttered again. "They can't even get him on underage sex. Has it always been like this?"

"No. Brother Samuel died without warning, but it was well known he was grooming Brother Rick as his successor. No one disagreed when Brother Rick took over running of Children of Nature."

He blew out a sigh. "Okay, what do you want me to do next?"

She gave him instructions, and they worked together as if they'd always shared the workspace. He never balked at her instructions, and she enjoyed having someone else around.

"How did you develop your products?" he asked

without warning.

Her embarrassment had settled, but his words had the heat building to dangerous levels again. "My mother used to run the workshop and taught me everything she knew. I experiment and make my own variations. I guess a lot of it is instinct."

He glanced at the closed door and, reassured they were still alone, leaned closer. "The product Alice mentioned—how do you know it works?"

"I tested it," she snapped, irked with him now. She glanced at him and caught the faint quirk of his lips, the unholy gleam of laughter in his eyes. "If I told anyone else about my product, I'd lose any hope I have of freedom. If Brother Rick learns this, I won't stand a chance of leaving."

"We'd better make sure he doesn't hear then." He paused. "You can use me as a test subject."

"What?" Her gaze flew to his, consternation battering her over the head, tugging the tips of her breasts and pooling in a flood of heat between her legs. The sensation came close to the one she experienced while testing her cream.

"I'll look after you, Sorrel. I'll make sure no one stops you from leaving. Even if your product doesn't work, I'll help you."

"It works." Sorrel gripped the wooden spoon in her hands so hard the healthy color fled from her knuckles. The compassion in him, the truth shimmering behind his words brought buried emotions to the fore. She wasn't used to people offering help and support. "You know nothing about me," she whispered, and at the reminder, fear slithered through her mind again, stealthy and slinking through the shadows.

He reached over and squeezed her forearm. "I know you."

Sorrel forced a smile, a nod. Somehow, she didn't think leaving would be as easy as she wished, as easy as Jake made it sound. Brother Rick was clever and cunning. His disapproval of her was no secret to the others, and they took their signals from him. No, now that she'd set her plan into action she needed to take extra care. The one person she could count on and trust was herself.

Chapter Three

A FUCKIN' ORGY. MAN, he hadn't seen that one coming. Wasn't sure how to handle it. He *was* over twenty-five and sure as hell didn't want to get anyone pregnant.

"These gatherings. What does Brother Rick do to the people who refuse to attend?"

She shot him a quick look with those big blue eyes. The woman wasn't much to look at with her short, dumpy stature. The robe hid a multitude of sins but couldn't hide the small breasts that went with her rounded stomach. Her hair was mouse brown and hung down her back in a thick braid. Her features weren't plain, but she suffered from acne or some sort of unfortunate rash. Most of the compound inhabitants avoided looking at her if they spoke to her. Not that it would have helped because her timid disposition and the way she focused on her feet instead of her surroundings made her even rounder and more unattractive.

"No one refuses."

He tried again, searching for an out. "Surely not everyone agrees or wants to have sex."

"The first gathering was successful, by all accounts. Many of the women are with child."

"I see." Fuck no! He didn't see at all. Drugs and alcohol added to the recipe weren't such a far stretch from date rape. There were a few days until the gathering. Maybe he could wrap up this case before then. "Do you want these loaded on the cart too?"

"No, these ones need refrigeration until the morning. I'm not tired yet. I'll have time to make a batch of soap as well. Why don't you go to your quarters and get some sleep?"

"What time are you making the delivery?"

"Early. Maybe the women who work in the store will help me carry the extra stock that won't fit in the handcart." Her words lacked conviction.

"Do you have a van to transport your products?"

"We have a truck. Brother Rick doesn't allow us to use it." The lack of inflection told him this was a sore point.

The way he saw it Children of Nature was a cult, pure

and simple. Brother Rick was a despot ruler treating his subjects as he saw fit. The more Jake learned, the more he loathed the man. Damn it. Sorrel might be the one everyone bullied, but if she left, Brother Rick would pick on someone else. That was the nature of the beast.

"You have two handcarts. I could load that one and go with you."

Her blue eyes widened. "No, Brother Rick will—"

He cut in with a curse. "I don't give a flying fuck what Brother Rick thinks. He's not going to be here. He left an hour ago with his buddies." Jake had heard a vehicle depart while he was loading the handcart. "If he has problems, he can come to me. Besides, I need to make contact with Luke."

"What about your limp?"

"It's not too bad. I'll survive."

"Oh." She licked her bottom lip, a slow stroke of her pink tongue.

He stared, captivated by the sight. Hell. He shook himself. He should have had a woman before he entered the cult. Things were bad if even plain Sorrel Thyme made him hot.

"All right," she whispered.

Jake pulled out the second handcart and loaded more stock. One of the carts was almost full. He entered the workshop again, pausing to savor the scent of the flowers she was crumbling into the pot she'd placed over the burner. The lavender reminded him of hugs from his granny during his childhood. "Are you sure you don't want me to do anything else for you?"

She jumped and dropped her spoon into her pot. She made a sound of disgust and shot a belligerent scowl over her shoulder. "Will you please stomp your feet as you enter my workshop? The way you prowl everywhere makes me nervous."

A grin formed before he even thought about it. "Yes, ma'am."

"Sorrel."

His grin widened. "Yes, Sorrel."

"Go," she ordered. "I leave at seven-thirty. Make sure you break your fast first."

Still smiling, Jake left Sorrel to her witchy potions. Once he reached the open space of the compound, he emphasized his limp. *Easy, now. Harmless and incapacitated.*

Now that darkness had set, most people retreated indoors. Masculine laughter drifted from the male quarters, but he turned in the opposite direction. He wanted to check out security during Brother Rick's absence.

Two men on the gates. They were both older, and one was sound asleep, on the verge of snoring. The second peered into the darkness, a fraction more alert.

Jake added weight to his steps, spied a stick and stamped on it. The sharp crack jerked the snoring man awake.

"Hello there. I'm out for a walk before I turn in." Jake allowed a heavy sigh to escape. "I'm afraid I've overdone it today. Do you mind if I sit a while to catch my breath?"

"You're the new guy," one of the men said. "Where are you from again?"

Jake went through his ashram tale. They'd have difficulty checking his story since the ashram Luke had selected rejected phones and other methods of modern communication. Once someone entered the ashram they were cut off from public contact. Part of the treatment, according to the literature Luke located from somewhere.

"What happened to your leg?"

"Accident. Tangled with a motor vehicle while crossing the road. The doctors say it will improve, but I'll always have a limp." Also the truth—the part about the doctors and the severity of his injury, anyway. The thought brought a wave of depression. Deep down he suspected he'd never make it back to active service. Soldiering was all he knew. His future lurked as unsubstantial as mist, and the loss of purpose ate at him.

"That's too bad," the security man said. "Still, fresh air and good food will put you right."

Jake nodded. The food was good. He'd soon put on the weight he'd dropped after his injury and subsequent hospitalization. Hopefully he could work on his fitness too. The doctors had instructed him to walk as much as possible. There wasn't any other option here.

"Why the gates and guards? I wouldn't have thought your compound would require tight security." Jake scanned the gates and the fences as far as he could see through the gloom, assessing the compound security.

"New measures," the snoring man explained. "We have valuable stores of food plus stock and equipment here. Times are tough and some people might look on us as a soft touch."

"That's true," Jake said. "I hear it's not uncommon for companies to close down and put everyone out of work."

The more alert of the two men gave a decisive nod. "That's what Brother Rick told us."

"It helps that those men who volunteer to undertake security duties are in the first group to choose women at the gatherings." The other man gave a sly wink, his smirk smacking of crafty.

They both chuckled, the sound rife with sexual hunger. Jake's hands balled to fists, luckily hidden in the folds of his robe. These two old coots should know better. The gathering was an orgy. Jake wouldn't have minded if the coupling was between consenting adults, but Brother Rick was making attendance compulsory. Add in the so-called bliss cakes plus booze and attendees had little to no control of their actions.

"Sounds interesting. I'm looking forward to my first gathering." Somehow Jake managed to get the words out without choking. "Well, I think my legs might make it to the men's quarters now. How long are you on duty?"

"Another couple of hours. It's not so bad."

Jake raised a hand in farewell and limped away. He'd spent part of a day here, and already he wanted to punch some of these men. He hoped he'd discover proof for Luke soon because he wanted to see some of these bozos behind locked bars.

· ❤ · ❤ · ❤ · ❤ · ❤ ·

THE NEXT MORNING JAKE helped Sorrel with the handcarts, pushing the largest one down the rutted track. Used to lugging a heavy pack for hours on end through difficult terrain he shouldn't have experienced difficulty. To his chagrin, by the time they reached the town sweat dripped off him. The little lady glowed, her face covered with red splotches, but she'd kept up without difficulty.

"I'll help you unload." His tone was brisk, despite his exhaustion. Nightmares of Greg's death had replayed in his mind through the early hours of the morning. Over and over, and no matter what he'd tried, the result had been the same. His friend bled out because he hadn't done enough.

"Why don't you wander through the town and explore?" she said in an undertone. "No one will think anything of it. They know you're thinking about joining Children of Nature. It makes sense you'd explore the town and speak with the locals."

"I'll help you unload," he repeated.

"The women at the shop will help me."

"How long will it take you?"

"An hour at least."

Finally, he gave her a clipped nod and limped away. He turned toward the river and prayed he'd bump into Luke.

His aimless amble took him past a flower shop, a women's wear shop and a cafe. He spotted Luke sitting at one of the outside tables with his father, Richard. They had a coffee in front of them, and both wore their cop uniforms. Hell, the contact part had always been the iffy part of the plan. He could hardly wander over to chat with them.

He continued with his slow limping progress along the road, turning down the path that ran along the riverbank. When he came to a bench, he took a seat, stretching his legs out and closing his eyes.

How the hell had he found himself in this mess? It was gonna look bloody odd if he refused to take part in the gathering.

"Mind if I share this bench with you?"

Jake's eyes popped open, chagrined because he hadn't even heard the woman walk up to him. "Free world," he barked.

Her violet eyes twinkled in her pretty face while her blonde hair bounced in a flirty ponytail. "My, my, I'm certain that's not suitable cult behavior." Her lips curled upward while she took in his appearance, her teasing voice making his eyes narrow.

"Who are you?"

"Janaya." She glanced around the vicinity, and once she confirmed they were alone, she spoke rapidly. "I'm Luke's wife. He thought it would be better if you met with women rather than men. He recruited me to meet with you to avoid raising suspicion. Maybe Hinekiri if I can't make it. Hinekiri is married to Luke's father, Richard. Do you have anything for Luke?"

"Nothing much. They've allowed me free rein to

wander the grounds. It was too late to explore much last night. I hope to see more this afternoon. I've talked to Sorrel Thyme."

A smirk formed on Janaya's lips.

"What?" Jake demanded.

"The cream she invented does everything she says and more."

He felt an instant of surprise then nodded as a sense of pride took hold. "I'm pleased for her. She works hard, and they give her slave status."

"Alice wants to do a few more tests before she gives her the good news."

"Can I tell her the initial tests are favorable?" Jake didn't understand why it was so important to him for Sorrel to gain the freedom she wanted.

"Sure, no problem. Anything else I should tell Luke?"

"Things have changed a lot since Brother Rick took over from his father."

"Hmm." Janaya appeared thoughtful. "Any whispers of Rick hastening Samuel's death?"

"No, but I'd love him to find him guilty. He makes the hair at the back of my neck stand on end. He's a bully, and I wouldn't be surprised to learn he's using cult funds to enjoy himself. He left the cult and drove to Auckland with some of his fellow brothers. Indicated he intended to recruit new blood."

"Do you know where he went?"

"No, but I have the number plate for his truck." Jake rattled off the number, and Janaya scribbled it on a piece of paper then slid it inside her bra for safekeeping. "There's something else." He informed her of the coming gathering.

Janaya's brows shot upward. "That's only a few days away. What are you going to do?"

"I'm gonna investigate the fuck out of this case and try to find something to implicate the cult."

"And if you find nothing?"

Jake let out a muttered curse, honesty propelling him to admit the truth. "The chances of finding anything so soon are nil. Brother Rick would hardly give me run of the place if evidence is out in the open." No, anything to implicate them would be hidden, which meant weeks rather than days undercover. "Any ideas?"

"What about Sorrel?"

"Have you seen her?" Jake felt shitty the moment the words left his mouth. "She's not my type."

"But at least you seem to admire her. It sounds as if you're trapped. If you stay, you'll have to take part."

"Maybe I can fake it."

Janaya let out a snort. "How?"

"Fucked if I know."

Jake pondered the gathering all the way home.

"Is something wrong?" Sorrel asked.

"I'm worried about the gathering. Unless I come up with a good idea, I'm going to be in a position where I have to participate. I don't want to raise Brother Rick's suspicions."

She sniffed. "Isn't sex what most men want?"

"I enjoy sex as much as the next guy," he snapped, the disdain in her sniff rattling his cage. "But that doesn't mean I think this is right." Could pretend to be sick, maybe improvise on the night. He hated to let this bastard win and leave Sorrel without options.

"It's not right. Do you think I'm thrilled with the idea of knowing if I find a man I can stand, he'll have sex with others? I'm tired of sharing. One man, one woman is what I want, and I won't settle for anything less."

The fire in her voice echoed in her cheeks, and she actually looked pretty. Jake studied her closely. She didn't have as many spots on her face today.

Jake considered the problem and offered the one suggestion he'd come up with—even though it wasn't ideal. "What if you and I hooked up together? Would that work?"

Sorrel came to an abrupt halt. She turned to him, her

eyes big and blue and startled. "You're offering to have sex with *me*?"

"No, I figured we could fake it somehow. Maybe take it private."

She shook her head. "The last time Brother Rick told everyone to stay inside the communal room."

"Maybe we could wait until everyone gets involved, distracted."

"I don't know. I figured I'd shut myself in my workroom."

"We could always start something beforehand." Jake thought out loud. "Before Brother Rick gets back. Yeah, give him something solid, something he doesn't expect and throw him off balance."

"I am not having sex with you. Or anyone else," she said hurriedly. "No matter what Brother Ricks says when I turn twenty-five. If I get pregnant, I can't leave."

"You could still leave."

"How? Who's going to help me?"

"You still have your invention."

"The moment Brother Rick learns I'm pregnant, he'll shift me to another part of the compound. All the pregnant women are kept together and have different duties. They have an honored place within Children of Nature. All the things I have in the workshop would be given to my successor."

"If that's the case, he won't be able to complain if you're involved with someone. Could you kiss me? Let me touch you without flinching? Could you keep up the pretense of a relationship in front of the others?"

"Did you see James or Alice? Did they mention the progress on the tests?" She started pushing her handcart again, her steps hastening to the compound.

"Don't change the subject." Then he took pity on her. "As far as Janaya knows, they're still testing, but she loved your cream, and initial tests are promising."

"Do you think they'll try to cheat me?"

"Who, Alice? No." At least he didn't think so. All the people he'd met so far—the normal ones who lived in Sloan outside the compound—seemed decent. "Consider my suggestion or, better yet, offer up a workable alternative."

She scowled but remained silent. They arrived back ten minutes later, the two men on the gates opening them to let them through.

Jake spotted the truck first. "Brother Rick is back early."

"It's better if he's not here," Sorrel said in a tight voice. She pushed the handcart into the shelter and stalked into her workshop.

Jake followed, closing the door behind them. "Do you

have any family here at the compound?"

"My mother died a few months after Brother Samuel. She had some sort of a stroke."

"Hell, sorry. I didn't know. You have other brothers and sisters?"

"No. I was the only child my mother managed to carry to full term." She flicked her braid over her shoulder. "I thought I'd make some candles. The women in the shop said the batch I made a few months ago sold in a few days."

Jake turned her to face him. "Your mother was close to Brother Samuel."

"Yes." She tugged away from his grip. "They spent their free time together and shared a bed."

Something in her voice gave away an unspoken fear. "Do you think Brother Rick had something to do with your mother's death or his father's passing?"

"No, I..." She twisted her hands together. "I try not to think about it too much."

"Tell me how they died. I need all the ammunition I can find to help you."

"I told you my mother died of a stroke." Her voice hitched, but she carried on gamely. "She'd had a minor stroke the previous year that left her with a slight paralysis on one side of her body. The Sloan doctor thought this one was a massive stroke."

"And Brother Samuel?"

Sorrel frowned. "His death was sudden. One week, he was fit and healthy, and the next, he was bedridden with convulsions and vomiting."

"What was the official cause of death?"

"Poisonous mushrooms. The poison destroyed his liver. Two young children died at the same time. Sister Andrea was adamant she wasn't responsible for the poisonous mushrooms in her pie, but popular rumor says that was the cause."

"Did they discover where the mushrooms came from?" Jake's mind twisted the pieces of information and came up with suspicions. "Is it possible Brother Rick murdered his father? And why does Brother Rick loathe you so much?"

"Who knows? Brother Samuel called Brother Rick for a meeting about a month before he died. After their meeting there was tension between them, but murder? I can't make up my mind on the subject."

Jake considered her words, saw her confusion. She didn't know, but maybe his questions would prod her memory and she'd remember something to help his investigation.

Outside heavy footsteps sounded, the scuff of gravel, and he acted on instinct. He hauled Sorrel into his arms and laid one on her.

He'd barely registered the surprised O of her lips, the uneven firmness of her curves when the door flew open, striking the wall. Sorrel jumped, but Jake maintained his hold on her and lifted his head to face the interloper.

"Did you want something?"

Brother Rick gaped at them before recovering. He chuckled in a suggestive manner. "That, I did not expect."

Jake narrowed his eyes. "Did you want something?"

"I heard from Sister Marigold at the store. They need more stock. You'll have to do another delivery tomorrow morning."

"Fine," Jake said.

Sorrel pinched his forearm beneath his robe. Hard. "Of course, Brother Rick."

Jake wanted to punch the smirk right off the man's face. He resisted because he felt the nip of Sorrel's callused fingers again, and she was right, damn it. He'd flatten the guy's nose another time.

Instead, he released Sorrel and hobbled over to the other side of the workshop. With a pained grimace, he dropped onto a stool and made a point of rubbing his leg. "Walked too much today. Did you conclude your business earlier than you expected?"

"Yes," Brother Rick gritted out, a flash of temper replacing his slimy smile.

"I'm sorry it was unsuccessful." Jake noticed Sorrel's flinch even though he was across the other side of the workshop. He also read the warning in her blue eyes. Unfortunately, she was right. He shouldn't draw too much attention to himself or make Brother Rick curious enough to poke at his background. Luke sounded confident his cover would stand scrutiny, something his stepmother had done. Hacking and such, but he still didn't want to risk discovery.

"The truck broke down after I dropped off Brother Tyrone and Brother Felix. It's going to cost a bit to fix. I was lucky to make it back to the compound." Brother Rick's gaze went to Sorrel. "I'm pleased with the increase in your production, but the women at the shop still need more. Some days they sell out of stock."

Sorrel lowered her gaze, but not before Jake caught the flash of fury in her blue eyes. "Of course, Brother Rick. With Brother Jake's help I was able to deliver double the amount of stock today. We took two handcarts this morning."

"Excellent. I'll leave you to your work." His lips curled into a sneer. "Work," he emphasized, and he stepped from the workshop, not bothering to close the door behind him. Obviously politeness was women's work.

Jake glared after him. Interesting he'd left two of the

brothers behind. Jake wondered how they'd get back to Sloan. A bus, perhaps. Sorrel was working as hard as she could, and he doubted she could physically produce more, given the number of hours she worked and the size of the workshop. "That man is a prick. The more I get to know him, the more I want to flatten his nose."

"You shouldn't rile him. He's dangerous."

Yes, she was right, and he knew better. Everything about this assignment rubbed him the wrong way. He stood and walked to the door, forgetting his limp for a few steps. With a soft curse, he shoved his head into the game again, paused at the door to note the locations of the various people in sight. From his observations to date, everyone took care to remain apart from Sorrel and her workshop. He closed the door with a gentle *snick* and turned to her.

"Are you going to tell me why you have so much padding under your robe?"

She gaped at him before erupting in a flurry of movement. "You heard Brother Rick. I need to start work on the candles."

Jake paused, stared at her stiff shoulders as she grabbed supplies from her cupboards. She was right, but this conversation was merely shelved. Now that he studied her closely, he was starting to notice other things such as the spots and rash that was in a different place from yesterday.

Sorrel Thyme had secrets, and he intended to ferret them out.

·❤·❤·❤·❤·❤·

DAMN, DAMN, DAMN. THE man had taken her by surprise, springing at her in his catlike manner. He was playing a part, she reminded herself. Her hand trembled a fraction as she placed the beeswax into the tin to melt. "I need these molds set out and the wicks trimmed to the correct length." She indicated the silver molds for the tea light candles. Her hand steadied, and she continued to work, showing him what to do while she started mixing the ingredients to make more bath bombs.

"Maybe Brother Rick should look at raising the prices in the shop."

"The women set the prices. I'll talk to them. It sounds as if we'll be making another trip to town in the morning. You can relax on the bench near the river and rest your leg while I supervise the unloading of the carts."

"Thanks," Jake said. "Will we have enough stock by then?"

"I think so, although I'll have to work late." Her stomach let out a lusty rumble of complaint since she hadn't taken time for breakfast.

In the distance the lunch bell rang, summoning everyone for the midday meal.

"Are you going to stop for lunch?"

"No, Brother Rick doesn't allow me to have more than one meal a day, not when he's around the compound."

"Why?"

"I refused to attend the last gathering, citing my age, and he decided to punish me for my decision."

"I'll bring you something back."

"No, the last thing I need is Brother Rick focusing on me more than he does already." She'd have to leave the compound soon. Brother Rick was making things more and more difficult for her. No, she'd keep her head down and keep the promise she'd made to her mother. She was doing this for both of them.

Jake shot her one of his looks—the combination stare and glare that sliced through her and crept into her mind, learning things she wanted to keep hidden. He couldn't have glanced at her for longer than a few seconds, but he made her vulnerabilities surface. He scared her with his intense eyes and his dark good looks.

"All right. I'll be back in half an hour. Line up some jobs for me. Could you organize one of the younger girls to help for a few days? It might lessen Brother Rick's questions if there is someone else here with us—at least for a few hours."

"Good idea. Ask for Sister Andrea when you collect your meal. Tell her I require one of the older teenagers to help for three hours each afternoon this week. She'll send someone suitable if she agrees. I'll make some space so we'll all fit in here without tripping over one another."

Jake moved toward her, and she pressed up against one of the counters to enable him to pass. Instead of limping toward the exit, he halted in front of her. His dark eyes gleamed as he studied her. His arms slid around her shoulders, and he tugged. She lurched, off-balance and landed against his hard chest, letting out a soft *oomph*.

She would have spoken, but his mouth trapped her words, leaving her instinctive protest unspoken. His lips moved against hers, the warm stroke of his tongue surprising her into opening her mouth. Immediately, he took possession, deepening the kiss, tangling tongues and leading the sensations rioting inside her into unfamiliar territory.

Warmth seared her body, and everything seemed louder, brighter, moving in a strange slow motion. Her thoughts mutinied in abandon, the rich masculine scent of him tinged with faint citrus filled each breath. She found herself clinging, her fingers digging into bulging biceps.

And still he kissed her, explored her mouth and nibbled

at her lips until she trembled and was aware of every part of her body. The linen strip rubbing against her breasts, the fit of her plain cotton panties and the abrasive rub of her cotton robe against her arms and legs.

When he lifted his head, she stared at him, heart hammering against her ribs. His eyes seemed darker than before, but there was no mistaking the masculine satisfaction shining in them.

He rubbed his thumb across her bottom lip, the faint drag making her want to groan aloud.

"I'll see you in half an hour."

Somehow she managed to formulate a question before he wrenched open the door. "Why?"

"This is the best way to keep you safe. I can't let you leave yet, because we need your help, but I promise, Sorrel, Brother Rick is not going to grab you, no matter what sick thoughts fill his warped brain. We need to practice so everyone believes we're together. I don't want any slip-ups in this plan."

Then he was gone, leaving her with trembling legs and heat still coursing through her energized body. He intended to kiss her again, touch her. She pressed her fingers to her lips. They felt swollen and sensitive. A dart of heat tore across her skin to pool between her thighs. One kiss from Jake and everything she'd known about sex was cast adrift and consigned to nothingness.

Shaking herself from her stupor, she dragged a table from the storage room where she kept her handcarts and set it outside in front of the workshop. Jake wouldn't mind being outdoors, since it would allow him to watch the comings and goings while he was working.

And it would give her some breathing space while she gathered her scattered wits.

Jake Ramsay was a disturbing man, a dangerous man. In the silent battle of him against Children of Nature she had little doubt who would emerge the winner. The man was too clever for his own good, too observant.

Yes, Jake Ramsay was a dangerous man.

Despite her disordered thoughts, Sorrel managed to mix two batches of bath bombs, the scents of cinnamon and cloves, vanilla and a hint of sandalwood soon flooding the workshop. She was pressing them into molds when someone tapped on the door. It opened seconds later, and a young girl peered inside.

"Sister Andrea told me to come and help you." Her long hair was confined in the same braid most of the women wore, but wisps had escaped, lending a charming and casual untidiness to her appearance. Her light blue eyes and rosy cheeks combined with an up-tilted nose gave her the look of a pixy. Sorrel couldn't help her return grin.

"Perfect timing, Sister Bernadette. I need this mixture pressed into the molds." Sorrel demonstrated and watched the girl until she was satisfied she would do a good job. "Perfect."

The girl pulled a green apple from her pocket. She glanced over her shoulder, through the door she'd neglected to close. "Brother Jake told me I should bring you an apple because you didn't have time to take lunch today."

"Thank you." Sorrel wiped the apple on her robe, saliva building in her mouth. "I am hungry." Damning Brother Rick, she bit into the apple, the small act of rebellion making her munch down with relish. The tart juices sprang onto her taste buds, the crunch of the crisp flesh bringing satisfaction. No doubt she'd pay for the transgression, but it was worth it.

She ate the apple in quick bites and tossed the core into her bin. She set a large pot over the heat and started on a batch of soap. With the others helping, she'd have time to make a new batch of her cream.

"I'm back," Jake said. "What should I do?"

"I have a bucket of overripe mangos that they couldn't use in the kitchen. They'll work well for face masks. Could you peel the fruit and take the flesh off the stones? I'm allergic and try to limit my contact. It's such a nice day I've set up the table outside."

Jake gave a quick nod and handed her a piece of homemade bread. She glanced at Sister Bernadette, but the girl was busy at her task. With a tremulous smile, Sorrel accepted the bread and thrust it into her pocket.

"Thanks," she mouthed. "Do you want me to show you how to stone the mangos?"

"I think you'd better." Once they were outside, he spoke in an undertone. "Good idea putting me out here. It will give me a chance to watch everyone, see the comings and goings from the compound."

"That's what I thought." She demonstrated what she required him to do and left him to it.

Sister Bernadette peered into the bowl Sorrel was mixing. "What are you making there?"

"It's a special hand cream that's good for those who suffer from arthritis." She lied smoothly, having used this excuse in the past.

Sister Bernadette leaned closer and sniffed. "It smells nice. What's the scent?"

"Ylang-ylang, ginger and sandalwood, mainly." *And a few other secret ingredients.*

"Can I try some?"

"Of course, although it's not for everyone because some people experience a bad reaction. It causes tingling—a pins-and-needles sensation—in some people." Sorrel wondered if she should worry about the smoothness of her fibs, although like all the best liars, hers held a smidgeon of truth. The cream had started as a cure for arthritis. It was her mother who'd had the brainwave.

"Why do you make it then?"

"Because arthritis is extremely painful and the cream works for some people."

"Brother James?"

"Yes." Sorrel scraped the side of her pot and blew on the spoon. A quick spot test on the back of her hand told her the cream was at room temperature. "Give me your hand." She rubbed a little of the cream on the fleshy part below Sister Bernadette's thumb.

After a few seconds, the girl jerked her hand away, her eyes widening. "It's tingling."

"If it's too painful—wash it off."

"That's weird," Sister Bernadette said. "Brother James uses this on his hands?"

"Yes."

"The poor man. I'm going to help him with his meals if I see him struggling."

"I'm sure he'll appreciate that." Sorrel turned off the heat and set her spoon aside. "Let me show you how to make potpourri sachets."

By the time the dinner bell rang she was quietly satisfied with the items they'd produced. There was too much for the two handcarts, which meant she could start stockpiling. She'd worried about how she'd manage to make more of her cream, but she'd be able to work on another batch during the evening. No one would think anything of her working long into the night since she had done it often in the past.

"Can I go now, Sister Bitter?"

"Of course. You've been a big help."

Pleasure suffused Sister Bernadette's pixie face, making Sorrel want to sigh. She was so beautiful. The moment she reached the legal age, the men would pounce. She'd be pregnant and trapped before she could blink.

"You've worked so hard. Let me give you a sachet as a thank you."

"Thank you." With a wave Sister Bernadette skipped from the workshop. She heard the girl stop to chat with Jake then silence fell.

"Do you want me to pack away the table?"

"Please, then you can go to dinner."

"What about you?"

"I'll go and wash up while the ablution block is quiet."

"You'll miss out on dinner."

She shrugged, not bothering to tell him she missed a lot

of meals. She'd had an apple and some bread. It was more than she ate most days.

"I'll save you something."

"Thanks, but no." Sorrel imagined Brother Rick's irritation. "If I'm too late, it will be my fault. At the moment all I want is a hot shower and to wash my hair."

"Perhaps I'll come with you."

Alarm flared in her. She preferred to bathe at this time of the day if she could manage because there were fewer prying eyes around. "No."

"Very well. I'll meet you back here after dinner, if I don't see you in the dining hall."

She gave a clipped nod and relaxed once he'd departed. Jake might be here to spy on their group, but it didn't mean he needed to learn her secrets too.

CHAPTER FOUR

THE WOMAN WAS UP to something. Even if he hadn't seen the guilt rush into her face, he'd have known because of his gut instincts screeching at him. Just as they were telling him Brother Rick was up to no good.

He'd have to risk leaving Sorrel alone later tonight to prowl the compound, but there was no way in hell he'd fail her in the same way he'd let down Greg. As he entered the dining hall, he scanned for Brother Rick and his particular friends—the ones who'd left the compound the day before.

They weren't present. Possibly they were late, but they didn't arrive while Jake moved up the meal line. Roast lamb tonight. His image of cults as full of hippy vegetarians had done an abrupt U-turn since his arrival.

The question was where they obtained their meat.

When he reached Sister Andrea at the head of the line, he asked, "Is it possible to save something for Sorrel, a meal I can take back to the workshop? She needs to work through the dinner hour."

The woman gave him a cursory glance then shifted her gaze to someone behind him. Her mouth pulled to a prune-like purse when a raucous laugh blasted through the dinner clamor. Brother Rick was in the building. She turned her attention back to Jake and gave a decisive nod. "Heard the gossip. About time someone started looking after the girl. Come to the kitchen door before you go back to Bitter—Sorrel's workshop. You need to go out of the dining hall and turn right, taking the passage to the first door. Ask for me once you get there. Don't speak to anyone else."

Jake nodded at her terse instructions and moved on before the next person in the line reached Sister Andrea. Maybe he'd do a little subtle probing regarding the meat when he went to pick up Sorrel's meal.

With his dinner in hand, he glanced around for a spare seat. The tables with men were all full, so he took possession of one of the chairs with a group of women. At his arrival they fell silent. Their expressions ranged from astonishment to outright glares.

"Am I not allowed to sit here?" Jake forced a smile, one of his most charming. "I promise I won't bite."

One of the younger girls recovered her powers of speech first. She batted her eyelashes in his direction. "Maybe we enjoy men who bite."

"Sister Lisa," one of the older women admonished.

It did no good since the rest of the women giggled. The flirtation spread from Sister Lisa to the rest of the younger girls, and Jake belatedly realized he should've kept the charm zipped. Attention wasn't good when he intended to skulk around the compound unnoticed.

"Is the gossip true?" Sister Lisa leaned over, allowing the bodice of her robe to gape. "Did Brother Rick walk in on you and Sister Bitter kissing?"

Bloody hell. Jake picked up his knife and fork, holding his anger close. If any of the women bothered to check his hands they'd notice the bloodless knuckles. None of the men or women called Sorrel by her name. It was always Bitter. No wonder Sorrel craved freedom.

"I knew it couldn't be true," Sister Lisa said. "She is very plain."

"She has a good heart." Jake fumed while eating his dinner. He wanted to say a lot of things. He uttered none of them. Instead he pondered the questions he needed answering. "I'm interested in learning about the farming side of Children of Nature. What animals do you have here?"

The women basked under his attention. Their fawning made him uneasy, slightly unclean. Their roving gazes brought edginess. Maybe he'd take a shower after dinner to cleanse off the drool.

"We have sheep and pigs. We keep chooks and sell eggs at the market," one of the sisters told him.

"What about cattle?"

"No," Sister Lisa said. "Our acreage isn't enough to support larger stock. We don't have cattle or horses. I sure wish we could get some alpacas. They're so much cuter."

"Maybe we should suggest alpacas at the next community meeting. The fleeces make beautiful clothes," one of the women commented.

Jake let the talk drift over him. He'd learned the cult didn't own cattle, which begged several questions. Where had the beef they'd eaten for dinner the previous evening come from? Had they paid for it?

The cult prided themselves on self-sufficiency. Of course they might trade.

"What's for pudding tonight?" one of the women asked.

"I heard it was sticky date pudding and custard. I'm off to see if the rumor is true," another declared. The rolls of fat beneath her robe rippled as she waddled past.

Jake eyed her for a few seconds longer, wondering how come she got to eat when Brother Rick wouldn't let Sorrel have three meals a day.

He finished his meal and took his dirty plate to the collection point. Deciding to pass on dessert, he left the dining room. The door to the kitchen stood open, a blast of steamy heat slapping him in the face when he stepped inside.

"Here you go, Brother Jake." Sister Andrea handed over a square box.

"Thanks. Do we grow all the produce and meat here at the compound?"

"Yes, we're totally self-sufficient. We do a little bartering with the local farmers. That's where Brother Rick obtained the beef we had for dinner last night."

"And very delicious it was too." Bah, lies. Beef was expensive, especially the finer cuts. Besides, what could the cult exchange that was equal value? His mind drifted to bliss cakes and drugs. He could hardly imagine the farmers Luke had described dealing in drugs, although stranger things had happened. "Thanks again for this." With a wave, he turned away, making sure to limp.

Back at the workshop, Sorrel was making another batch of soap. Her hair was damp, and she'd tied it back in a high ponytail instead of her normal braid. She'd changed robes since this one lacked the splatters he'd noted before he left for dinner. There was a strange smell, sort of metallic and verging toward unpleasant. After shutting the door, he moved closer, no longer limping since he was out of sight of everyone else.

"Sister Andrea packed a dinner for you." He thrust the box at her. "I'll stir the soap while you eat."

Shock flashed across her face. She stared at him, her blue eyes wide and unsure before her gaze darted to the box. Slowly, she reached out to accept it, her stomach letting out a rumble of hunger. Her expression turned sheepish. "Thanks."

The look of vulnerability flickering across her face tugged at him, made him angry and off-balance. Why did they treat her no better than a dog turd when she worked hard to support the cult's financial needs? There were individuals who didn't think the same way in private, yet if they were in the company of other cult members, they followed Brother Rick's lead like well-trained sheep dogs.

He stirred the pot with the soap, dragging the spoon across the bottom as she'd shown him earlier. "This is almost melted. What do you want me to add?"

She swallowed a mouthful, dabbing the corner of her mouth with a linen cloth. "Measure out three cups of oatmeal and one tablespoon of the vanilla perfume oil."

Jake followed her instructions, sniffing at the mixture in the pot. This wasn't the smell. "This looks integrated. Should I pour it into the molds?"

"Please. Don't fill the molds all the way to the top. Leave a few millimeters so we can add some toasted oats for decoration."

Jake took the pot off the heat and poured it into the square molds she'd already set out. His friends would tease if they could see him, but he kind of enjoyed the process of making things.

She finished eating but remained seated instead of taking over. "Good. Now sprinkle enough of the oat mix on top to cover the soap. Yes, that's right. Perfect."

Once he'd finished, he set the pot aside in the industrial-size sink, ready for washing. He cleaned the workspace as she'd shown him and put the tubs of raw ingredients back on the shelf. "What else are you going to do tonight?"

"The bath salts seem to be going well. I'll make a quick batch of chocolate bath salts and call it a night."

When she stood and moved past him, he caught a whiff of the same metallic stench. "Why do you color your hair?" The minute he uttered the words, things started to click—the turn of a lock as a puzzle slotted together in the correct manner. A rush of success, of intrigue and curiosity simmered in him, and he hesitated in light of the knowledge although he suspected the reasons for her subterfuge. "Come here."

Sorrel stared at him, shock striking her as she acknowledged the order. He knew. He'd guessed her secret.

Panic bloomed then, and the hard, rapid knock of her heart trying to claw out of her chest. She took half a step toward the door.

"Sorrel."

"What?" Alarm yanked her from her normal subservient manner. He knew. The question was what did he intend to do with the knowledge.

"Come here."

A repeat of his order, and she found herself obeying before her brain processed the instruction and issued an alternative. She came to an abrupt stop.

"No problem," he said, this time his voice silky, a little menacing.

Oh stars. He couldn't turn on her. He couldn't impart his knowledge to Brother Rick. He couldn't. But she knew human nature, knew him for a soldier. Would he offer up the information in order to get closer to completing his undercover assignment?

He stalked the distance separating them, and terror

multiplied inside her like a virulent strain of bacteria. She certainly felt ill, the dinner she'd eaten churning in the pit of her stomach. Self-preservation roared to life. She took a rapid step back to find herself trapped against one of her workbenches. He was on her in seconds, his large frame blocking her departure, his arms caging her in place.

"Wh-what do you think you're doing? I need to go to the restrooms."

"I don't think so, sweetheart." He leaned over, reducing the space between them. Her pulse raced, but she couldn't avert her gaze, trapped as she was by his dark gaze. For a moment, she thought he intended to kiss her again. She listened, but couldn't hear the approach of footsteps, couldn't hear the arrival of rescue.

Jake continued to stare, his chest pressed against her breasts. She could feel him, even through her robe—the heat of his bigger frame, the hard muscles. Although the man was on the thin side, he was strong. Already with regular meals, the healthy air and exercise had made a difference.

Stars, not helping. "This isn't funny, Jake. Let me go."

"Ah, sweetheart. You're full of secrets, aren't you?"

"What do you mean?"

His head dipped again. Her eyes fluttered closed, and she tilted her head up a fraction. She shouldn't want him to kiss her. It was wrong, yet she craved his lips on hers again, had thought about him during her shower. The urge for physical contact ate at her, the desire to feel normal, like Alice and her husband James.

Time passed, and still, his lips didn't touch hers. She swallowed and opened her eyes enough to peek through her lashes. She discovered him studying her intently. His grin widened, and he sniffed her hair.

"What are you doing?"

"Nothing." He pressed a kiss to her forehead, and while she gaped at him, he kissed her lips. Unlike their first kiss, this one contained no preliminaries. A hot, hard masculine mouth feasted on hers, his tongue slipping between her lips and taking the contact deeper into sensual territory. His taste roared through her. His touch as he pressed her against him, locking his hands against her hips. She moaned, gasping for breath yet not wanting him to stop.

When he lifted her head, his eyes glittered. "What color is your hair?"

"Huh?"

"You're covered in padding beneath your robe. Your face is blotchy in a different place than it was earlier and your hair smells of some sort of dye. You're deliberately making yourself look ugly. I presume it's to keep under of radar of the men here in the compound."

"You have no idea what it's like living here."

"You could have left."

"I'm trying to leave. I have to get it right the first time, because I'll never get a second opportunity."

"So you put up with everyone mistreating you. You miss meals because Brother Rick wants to punish you for whatever reason. All that so you get your precious freedom."

"You're a man. You have no idea of the pressure to conform."

"We're going to get you out of here. I've promised you already, and I mean to keep my word. Are you done here for tonight?"

"I suppose the bath salts can wait until tomorrow." He still hadn't released her, not that she wanted him too.

"I want to explore more of the compound. If you come with me, we can tell anyone who catches us we've gone off for some privacy. The quicker I find what I'm looking for, the sooner we can both leave."

"You're taking me with you?"

"I'm not leaving you here." Jake's grasp tightened on her hips. His head dipped, and he kissed her again. This time was slow and deliberate, and she felt the echo in her sex. By the time he lifted his head, she fought for breath, and her entire body hummed with pleasure. For the first time, a man tempted her, and she didn't know if she should deck him or draw him closer for another kiss. He pulled away and offered her his hand. "Are you ready to act the courting couple?"

"Where do you want to explore first?"

"We'll wander to the tree line. I want to check the boundaries on the north side of the compound. Sister Andrea told me the beef was bartered with one of the local farmers. That's a lie. According to Luke Morgan none of the local farmers have dealings with Brother Rick or anyone else here at the compound."

"I heard Brother Rick arrived with the beef last week. He had farming equipment too." She lowered her voice as they wandered closer to some of the compound members. Jake started exaggerating his limp again, and she slipped her arm around his waist as if she were helping him. "Do you think it was stolen?"

"I haven't heard any mention of missing farm equipment, but I'll ask next time I talk to my contact. The farmers are more concerned with their missing stock." Jake spoke next to her ear, his warm breath distracting. He subtly guided her in the direction he wanted to walk.

"Everyone is staring."

"Let them," Jake said with unconcern. "Is there room for me to sleep in your workroom with you?"

Sorrel stopped walking. "What?" She'd wanted to test the latest batch of her cream. She could hardly do that with him in the same room. "Why?"

"Now that I've started paying attention to you the men will start to wonder what I see in you. You shouldn't be alone. Don't trust anyone."

"I don't need a minder."

He hesitated then nodded, despite his misgivings. "As long as you're careful, I suppose it will be all right. It's possible I'll still learn something in the men's quarters."

With a glance over his shoulder, he led her into the trees. He was pretty sure someone—probably one of Brother Rick's close friends—would follow them. They needed to set the stage first. Once he was sure they were out of sight, he surveyed their surroundings. He was as sure as he could be no one was ahead of them.

"Why hasn't anyone noticed you're dying your hair?"

"My mother suggested it a long time ago. She knew it was too late for her to leave the compound, but she wanted me to get out if I could. She'd enjoyed the life here with Brother Samuel, but she knew I wanted something different."

He stopped walking and turned to face her. His gaze slid to her lips and lingered. He shouldn't, but he wanted to kiss her again. And he desperately wanted to see the body under the robe. Damn fool. He needed a woman. Yeah, that was all this was—the urge to scratch an itch. "So this has been a long time in the planning."

"I told my mother I would continue the plan we concocted. I promised her," she added.

If there was one thing Jake understood it was promises. Guilt slashed him at the thought. He'd sworn to Greg he'd get him out, get him to medical help.

"I promised I'd help you and I will," he said tersely. "But you need to trust me."

"I don't know you."

Her words stung, even though they were true. She was taking a big leap of faith trusting him as much as she had already. "I'm all you have. You have to trust me." Urgency throbbed in his words. "Brother John, at least I think it's Brother John is following us. We're going to give him a show so he can go back to Brother Rick and report."

She stiffened. "What sort of a show?"

Jake glanced around and spotted a small clearing. Perfect for what he had in mind. He drew her toward it, tugging lightly on her hand while resuming his slow, tortured limp. Once they reached the grassy area, he urged her down. She flinched as he loomed over her, her eyes widening.

"This isn't a good idea."

"Why? You frightened because you're starting to enjoy it?" Ignoring her building scowl, he dipped his head, snaring her lips before she could voice another objection. For a few taut seconds, her lips remained stiff. Unyielding. Irked by her lack of response, he put his heart into the kiss, pushing his tongue deep, thrusting them both into a world where sensation ruled and thoughts steered to sexual.

A grunt of satisfaction escaped him when she relaxed and curled her arms around his neck.

"I'm going to touch your breasts," he whispered on lifting his head. "Or what I can feel beneath that padding. The next time we're alone together in a safe place you're going to answer my questions, sweetheart."

"I'm not your sweetheart," she muttered and nipped his bottom lip.

Her sharp teeth should have hurt, but instead a knife of pleasure arced to his dick. Damn, what was it about this woman? She was filling his thoughts when he should be concentrating on sneaking around and catching Brother Rick and his cohorts stealing cattle.

Because they *were* stealing. If not cattle, then they were up to other types of mischief. His soldier's senses told him so.

He rolled on top of her, holding her in place with his weight.

Sorrel gasped.

"No struggling," he murmured. "Brother John is spying on us, and I'd hate him to report back to Brother Rick that something is amiss between us. The last thing we need is rumors flying around the compound saying our relationship is a pretense."

Her fingernails dug into his biceps, a pointed reminder she wasn't entirely with his program. After a harsh breath, she went limp beneath him. Hiding his satisfaction, he took the opportunity to kiss her again, one of his hands slipping under the neckline of her robe.

She froze. "What are you doing?"

Ah, as he suspected. No padding in this area, but instead a tightly bound strip of fabric. The knowledge brought curiosity, and his cock lengthened. The sole reason he could think of for a woman to make herself look ugly and unobtrusive was if she were worried about attracting too much attention.

He lifted his head, shot a swift glance in the vicinity where he'd last spotted Brother John and saw he'd either gone or relocated. Fine. It wasn't a hardship to feel-up Sorrel Thyme. Jake settled in to do a decent job of kissing her. His hands wandered while his lips mapped her face, her mouth and her neck. He breathed in her scent, mostly masked by the stench of whatever substance she'd put in her hair, and went with the flow of arousal.

He took his time, even though darkness was falling.

"What is that digging me in the stomach?"

"Have you had sex before?"

She hesitated. "Once, a long time ago."

"Then surely you recognize the thrust of a cock." He was curious regarding her sexual experience.

Her wet tongue lashed across his earlobe, then traced the outline of his ear. A shiver swept him, and unable to help himself, he ran his fingers over her hip and down her leg, stroking back and forth, testing the flesh beneath her robe. He shifted his hips, thrusting against her before the thought registered.

"A modern marvel," she whispered, pausing in her worrying of his earlobe. "You have two cocks."

A bark of laughter escaped him. "I have a torch in my pocket."

"That's what I felt the first time. I didn't think I could have that effect on a man, not until I felt the second."

He stopped then, lifting his head to peer at her through the gloom. "If that's the truth, then why have you bothered with your disguise?"

She kissed him this time, thrusting at his shoulders at the same time with enough strength to take him by surprise. They rolled with her landing up on top of him. "That's better," she said in satisfaction. "I couldn't concentrate with two cocks poking me."

A chuckle burst free. "You're not into sex with more than one man. I thought that was the modern woman's fantasy. To have two men focused on her pleasure."

"Not me. All I want is to leave this place."

"Then you'll think about a man?"

"No," she replied without hesitation. "Not straightaway because I need to focus on my goals."

"I might take that as a challenge." Hell, he did take that as a challenge. He wanted to peel away the layers hiding her real personality, her true form. He wanted to know what her natural hair looked like without the god-awful smelly stuff she'd combed into it.

"Don't," she warned. "Once I hear back from Alice—if I hear back from Alice and the news is positive, I'm going to ask her if I can work for Fancy Free. She mentioned a job."

Jake nodded, reaching up to cup her face with his hand. "I hope the news is good."

He let her kiss him again, enjoying the hell out of her lips and tongue brushing his. With each kiss her confidence grew, and he loved experiencing her shy looks and innocent attempts at playing the siren. If she wasn't careful, she'd get hooked on him. Jake smiled inwardly. Hell, maybe he'd let her.

"We can go now." If they kept up the groping, he was gonna embarrass himself. His cock was hard enough to use as a hammer.

"Go where?"

He lifted her off him and rolled to his feet. At the back of his mind, he realized his left leg felt better than it had for weeks. The walking was helping more than the long gym sessions he'd subjected himself to before he'd come to Sloan. Jake paused to listen, satisfied when the sole noise was the *baa* of a distant sheep.

"Jake?"

"We're going to continue our walk. I need to check the boundary line." With sure steps, he led her in the direction he wished to go. Despite the growing gloom, his eyes picked out a distinct path. "Do you know where this goes?"

"It goes to the top paddock. I come up here sometimes to pick leaves to use to decorate my candles."

"Good idea. Make sure you pick up a few leaves on the way, in case someone stops us."

Once the path widened enough for them to walk abreast, he curved his arm around her lumpy waist. When she moved closer, allowing him the liberty without complaint, he smiled. He might not be out with the team because of his injury, but his military friends, Nikolai and Louie were right about a change in routine helping to jerk him out of his mental funk.

Nothing leaped out at him, not that Jake had thought he'd find incriminating evidence. It was too obvious, and he figured Luke and Richard Morgan would've checked the boundary fences with the other properties already.

When they'd almost reached the main compound, Jake reached for her hand. "Are you sleeping in your workshop tonight?"

"Yes, it's safer for me. I don't want the other women looking at me too closely."

Jake nodded, aware of the dangerous game she was playing. "I'll escort you back before I go to the men's quarters."

Habit and instinct made him conduct a quick check of the dark workshop corners to ascertain no one was lying in wait for her. "No bogeymen in the corners."

"I didn't think there would be."

Jake went to her and tipped back her head with his fingers. "You're close to your goal now," he whispered. "No complacency." He kissed her slowly and thoroughly, leaving them both breathing hard by the time he finished. "Promise you'll lock the door after me."

"There's no lock. Nothing is locked in the compound."

Jake nodded. "What about the room Brother Rick uses as an office?"

"I don't know. I keep away from Brother Rick as much as possible."

"Understandable. I might do more checking tonight. Put a chair under the door handle so you have a warning if anyone tries to snoop around while you're asleep."

"Yes, sir. And I'll scream loud enough to wake the dead if anyone scares me."

"You do that," Jake said.

Jake left Sorrel and walked across the open ground of the compound toward the single men's quarters. On reaching the buildings, he ducked into the shadows and paused, cocking his head to listen. Although he could hear voices, they were nothing out of the ordinary. From his observations, most of the men spent their evenings listening to music, gossiping and letting the women wait on them.

After deciding no one was scrutinizing his actions, he wandered to Brother Rick's office, a small building to the side of the main ones. The lights were out, and after another quick pause, Jake tried the door. Locked. He circled the structure, checking the windows. They were locked too.

Brother Rick had something to hide.

Jake considered a forced entry, but a night when Brother Rick was away from the compound would make better sense. Jake slipped back toward the men's quarters.

It was dark now, the moon shining enough light for him to see without turning on his torch. Most of the men were still in the communal rooms, so he turned in that direction. He needed to pick up snippets of gossip.

He stepped inside the room, and each of the men turned to look at him.

"Where have you been?" Brother Rick demanded.

"Sister Sorrel and I went for a walk. She wanted to collect some leaves and dried twigs to decorate her candles."

Brother John snorted in disbelief. "At this time of night?"

"Sister Sorrel has been working all day making products for the shop. Tonight was the first opportunity to collect supplies." Jake waited to hear what they replied to that. Brother Rick was working her hard, and he wasn't sure why. If Sorrel knew, she wasn't telling.

"Her name is Bitter," Brother Rick said. "Bitter by name, bitter by nature."

Jake counted to five under his breath. He wanted to defend Sorrel but kept his mouth shut. *One day*, he promised himself.

Jake walked past Brother Rick and took a seat. The men

started to talk again, murmuring between themselves.

Someone came to sit beside him, and Jake turned to find Brother John smirking at him. The man had a thin, narrow face and a pointy chin. Combined with the hints of red in his hair, he reminded Jake of a fox.

"I saw you and Bitter. I'd fuck her in the dark too. That way it's easier to pretend she's not so ugly." He nudged Jake on the arm. "How was she? I bet she was desperate for it. The quiet, snooty ones usually are."

"Were you following us?"

Brother John leered. "Didn't witness much leaf collecting."

Jake straightened. "Follow us again, and I'll push your nose down your throat." He followed up his threat with a steely glare.

Brother John blinked. A tide of color swept into his face, highlighting his high cheekbones. "We don't believe in violence."

"You gonna tell Brother Rick on me," Jake taunted, probably unwisely.

"You're here on a trial basis."

"That's true, so you'd better be nice to me or I'll decide to move to the South Island group."

Brother John rose to his feet and left without another word.

"You shouldn't tangle with him," one of the elderly men said. "The boy has a mean streak."

"Thanks for the warning. I shouldn't have baited him. I'll apologize to him in the morning."

"Won't do any good." The elderly man tugged on his white beard. "The boy holds his grudges. He's been that way since he was a toddler."

"Have you lived here for a long time? Would you recommend Children of Nature as a good home?"

The elderly man glanced over his shoulder, leaned a fraction closer. "This used to be a good place to live. Things changed after Brother Rick took charge."

"In what way?"

"We used to all be equals, but now the men run everything and make the decisions. Some of the women are no better than slaves. They do the cooking, the cleaning and bear children." The elderly man paused, his brow knitting in a fierce frown. "Then there's this gathering business. It's not right the way they treat the women."

"Did you attend the last gathering? From what I heard most of the men enjoyed it."

"They enjoyed the sex and the alcohol." The man snorted. "Their behavior was disgusting. Animals behave better."

"You were there."

"Aye, I was there. I was no better than the others. The next morning I woke up with one of the young girls and was disgusted with myself. Young man, don't partake of the food or drinks supplied on the night. I'm sure it was drugged. That's the only explanation I have. I didn't touch the alcohol some of them drank. The young girl wouldn't have slept with me willingly. Not an old coot like me."

"I thought the men and women under twenty-five weren't required to attend."

"That's the official line, but their attendance is looked upon favorably. The youngsters who attended have received material rewards—better tasks and new, more private quarters."

"Where does Brother Rick sleep?"

"He commandeered the old farmhouse after Brother Samuel died."

Jake nodded. "Does anyone share it with him?"

"His three friends share the house, and occasionally they have female company."

"Anyone in particular?"

"No, not really. They share it around. Brother Rick keeps that part of his life private. If any of the women gossip, they're cast aside. One of the sisters used to be a favorite. She mentioned his new furniture and the wide-screen television up at the house and hasn't been invited back."

Jake's brows rose. "He has a TV?"

"Among other mod-cons," the elderly man said dryly.

"Interesting." He needed to get into the house to see for himself as soon as Brother Rick left the compound again.

The women arrived bearing a late-night snack, and two young women served tea and hot chocolate plus shortbread biscuits.

Jake took a cup of hot chocolate and biscuit with a polite smile.

An hour later the men started to drift off to the sleeping quarters. Jake decided he might as well retire, too, because Sorrel intended to do another delivery early in the morning.

Jake went through his bedtime preparations and kicked off his sandals. One by one the men stretched out on their single beds and the lights flicked off. Jake shouldered off his robe, hanging it on the wall peg near his bed. He stretched out, searching his plan for flaws. The quicker he caught out Brother Rick, the sooner he could leave this wacky place.

The walking left him physically tired, but he felt better than he had since his last mission ended abruptly in an injury. A wide yawn took him, and he closed his eyes, slipping easily into sleep.

· ❤ · ❤ · ❤ · ❤ · ❤ ·

SORREL TOOK JAKE'S ADVICE to heart and, after removing the junk off her mother's old chair, she managed to shove it under the doorknob. As he said, it wouldn't hold out a determined man, but she'd receive warning of anyone trying to enter.

That done, she checked the windows. She'd allowed them to collect dust on purpose, a suggestion from her mother when they'd first started working on the cream together.

"The less the others know of our private business, the better," her mother had declared. "There's such a thing as too much sharing."

Once she was positive no one was spying on her, she retrieved the cream from the hidey-hole her mother had shown her under the floorboards. This was a new batch she'd made earlier in the day, and she was looking forward to the testing.

Sorrel organized her bedding and switched off the lights, plunging her workshop into darkness. The familiar scents of her dried herbs and flowers made the pitch-black friendly and free of creeping ghosts to play on her mind.

She'd enjoyed today, working alongside Jake and Sister

Bernadette. It made her feel...normal. It gave her a glimpse of life on the outside, working at a job during the day and returning to her home in the evening. Her mother's stories of her years before the compound, the parties, the days of work. Going shopping. A sigh escaped. It was difficult to imagine spending an afternoon wandering aimlessly through one shop after another.

She dropped to her pallet, suddenly experiencing hesitation. No, she needed to fully test the cream. The chair would give her enough warning to dress. With years of practice, she tugged her robe over her head. She unfastened the bulky padding from around her waist and set it aside. Then she unwrapped the linen strip binding her breasts and her baggy cotton panties. Naked, she stretched, enjoying the caress of fresh air across her skin, the prickle of her breasts as they reacted to the cooler temperature.

Anticipation stirred both mind and body as she reached for the cream.

Masturbation is a sin. The words echoed in the back of her mind, and she smirked into the darkness. Her mother had refuted the horrified words of the elderly sister in private to Sorrel.

"It's the best way to learn your body. How can you tell a lover what you want if don't know yourself?" her mother, ever practical, had asked her.

She'd made sure Sorrel knew about sex, but even so her one time at age eighteen had been a disappointment. Listening to her mother, she'd made sure she picked a day in her cycle she was unlikely to conceive, but the bumbling Brother Gabriel had been so excited he'd come prematurely after one clumsy, painful thrust.

In hindsight, she'd been lucky. Brother Gabriel, who had later died after falling out of a tree, had told the other boys she was terrible in bed. Her mother had spun this into a good thing.

"You'll have more options if you avoid pregnancy. I love you, Sorrel, and I have no regrets for having you, but if I hadn't become pregnant, I'd have done things differently. Children of Nature was the only way I could see of keeping you and staying safe."

And she and her mother had planned a way for Sorrel to leave if she wanted. It had been a secret her mother hadn't even shared with her lover, Brother Samuel.

Sorrel reached for the tub of cream and removed the lid. She dipped her finger inside and sniffed to savor the different notes of the bouquet. The initial floral scent deepened to musky and mysterious as it absorbed her body heat. Slowly, she traced a circle around one nipple. Awareness surged through her, a delicate creep toward pleasure, but she wasn't sure if it was the cream or residual feelings she'd experienced from getting close and sexy with Jake.

The instant a vision of Jake bloomed in her mind, hot pleasure spilled through her. She returned to teasing her nipples, her thumb skating against the side of one breast. Using the cream as a counterpoint to the friction of her work-roughened fingers, she continued to stroke until her nipples were hard nubs, signaling lustful messages to her pussy. She swallowed, her mind full of Jake, his rare yet enticing smile and the hard pressure of his hands on her body as he'd kissed her.

She collected another smidgeon of cream on her forefinger and delved between her legs. Heat unfurled inside her and tiny tingles coalesced into something more, better. Soon her fingers moved in long, luxurious strokes down her slit and skated her clitoris.

A gasp escaped as Jake's visage played across the insides of her closed eyes. She could practically feel his presence, smell his hot male scent. Her eyes flicked open, almost expecting to see him in person, but no—it was her imagination working overtime.

Her fingers dipped and delved, running over slippery folds and now and then detouring to the hard nub of her clit. With an intense burst of heat, the sensations spiraled downward in a familiar low pressure signifying an impending climax.

"Jake," she whispered.

Her hips arched upward, pushing her fingertip into greater contact with her clit. The clawing tension rushed into a ball of heat, teetered on an almost painful pulse then exploded. Sorrel bit down on her bottom lip, to keep her cry of pleasure contained, continuing gently to stimulate the bundle of nerves until the spasms tailed off.

"Well," she whispered into the darkness. "Nothing wrong with that batch of cream."

A sound—out of place—made her stiffen. She groped for her clothes, tying the stuffing around her waist and yanking the robe over her head. She shoved the cream out of sight.

Someone forced the door, and the chair skidded across the floor with the anguished groan of wood meeting stone.

CHAPTER FIVE

"LET HIM GO."

The panicked words flooded his dream. Urgent, they made him hesitate instead of finishing off the enemy threatening his life. A second pair of hands gripped his shoulders painfully tight, digging into his muscles.

Jake cursed a blue streak and came awake swinging. His fist connected with someone's jaw. His gaze flitted left and right, assessing the danger, assessing the enemy. Greg stood over by the door, his ever-present grin lighting up his face. Joy suffused Jake at seeing his friend, then as he watched, Greg started to fade. All the fight went out of Jake as he woke fully. He slumped, his hands relaxing.

Another one of those fuckin' dreams.

"He tried to kill me." A masculine voice croaked with

fear.

The fog cleared from Jake's mind, the crispness of the real world overriding the dreamlike one. The light flicked on, illuminating the room. Jake straightened even as he realized he was bending over the bed of the brother who slept next to him.

Fuck.

"Sorry, man. I thought...I'm sorry." Jake backed away until the back of his knees struck his own bed, hands raised in a gesture of surrender. He dropped to the mattress hard enough to make the bed frame clunk in protest.

"He tried to choke me," the brother repeated.

"Where did you get all those scars?" another demanded.

Double fuck. Realizing he'd have to give some sort of explanation, he focused on his bare feet. "I was in an accident."

"Motor vehicle?"

Jake grabbed his robe, fighting to control the shudders attempting to take over his body. "A hit and run." A tame explanation, but one these men who knew nothing of the horrors of war would accept. God, he had to leave before he lost it totally.

"Need fresh air," he managed, pushing past the men loitering near his bed. He left them muttering between themselves, the man he'd almost choked complaining loudly about assault.

His eyes adjusted to the night gloom outside. Overhead stars twinkled in a determined fashion, not cowed by the scud of clouds across the sky.

Hell, he hadn't had the dream for over a week. He thought he'd done with the past, accepted it wasn't his fault Greg died, even though Greg's fiancée and Greg's brothers thought otherwise.

He walked to the boundary of the compound, even remembering to limp in case someone was spying on him. Behind him the light went out as everyone returned to bed now that the excitement was over. Jake continued walking through the dark, his mind in turmoil, his friend appearing to pace silently at his side. Finally, he ceased his restless motion, letting out a pained groan. "God, Greg." He covered his face with his hands. "Why do you have to hang around with me?"

A crash and a feminine scream jerked him from his pity party. He was running in the direction of Sorrel's workshop before the thought even registered. Another crash traveled to him plus the screech of a pissed female.

A figure burst from the workshop before Jake reached it. He or she—Jake couldn't tell—wore dark clothes rather than a white robe, and they disappeared into the night. Jake considered chasing them and disregarded the thought because of his cover.

"Sorrel. Sorrel? Where are you, damn it?" Jake scanned the workshop and headed over to the area where he knew she slept.

"Jake?" Sorrel's voice quivered from behind the door.

"It's me, sweetheart." He switched on the light, his gaze going straight to Sorrel. Her face was pale, apart from a red splotch on her left cheek. "What happened?"

"Someone wanted to get into my workshop. Thanks to your advice, I wedged a chair against the door. The sound woke me."

Jake eyed her cheek again. "They hit you."

"He started to mess up my supplies, sweeping my stock onto the floor. I tried to stop him, and he punched me."

"He?"

"I think it was a man. He'd concealed his face, but why would one of the women want to destroy my workshop? The women enjoy my products, and those who work at the store love getting away from the work grind here at the compound."

"Maybe one of the women is jealous because she wants to work at the store."

"No." Sorrel shook her head, remaining behind her workstation. "They take turns. Everyone who wants to work there ends up with a stint at the store."

"What's going on here?" Brother Rick stood at the door, glancing from Sorrel to Jake.

"Someone tried to vandalize Sorrel's workshop." Damn if he'd call her Bitter. She was the least bitter person he knew, which was amazing, considering the way the people here treated her.

"Where are they?" Brother Rick asked.

"They ran off," Sorrel said.

"Rubbish. You're exaggerating. No one here would do that. Clean up this mess, and I'll deal with you in the morning. The rest of you can go to bed." He glared at Sorrel before striding away toward his quarters.

"Did they damage the stock we made this afternoon?" Jake's gaze narrowed on Brother Rick's back. How had he arrived so quickly? And it was interesting the way he was wearing dark jeans and a T-shirt, rather than the robe he normally wore. He'd noticed Brother Rick and his favorites donned regular clothes sometimes when they left the compound. On their return, they usually changed back to their robes, so why not this time?

"He blames me. It could have been him. The intruder was a similar height."

"It could have been one of his friends," Jake said.

"It was too big to be Brother John, and the others aren't back from wherever they went."

Jake started to pick up the spilled herbs and raw ingredients. Sorrel kneeled beside him, righting the items that had survived the fall to the stone floor.

"I need Luke to discover where they go when they leave the compound." Jake fetched the broom and started to sweep up the bits of jars and the unusable stock. "How often does he leave the compound?"

"It used to be once a month, but lately he's absent more frequently."

"Someone will have to go and pick them up from wherever they are."

Sorrel shook her head. "There are bus services to Sloan. Or they could hitch a ride with someone. They won't stand out if they're dressed in jeans and a T-shirt."

A chuckle escaped Jake. "You admit the members of the cult are weird."

Sorrel snorted. "From what I hear there are loads of strange people in the world. Children of Nature members don't have exclusive rights."

She wasn't wrong. No doubt gossip about him trying to throttle someone would spread through the compound as rapidly as bullets spraying from a machine gun. By tomorrow morning everyone would give the weirdo a wide berth. One thing was sure. He needed to apologize to the poor brother he'd almost choked, and it would be better if he found somewhere else to sleep because he was positive Greg hadn't finished playing tricks on him yet. The haunting looked set to continue.

· ❤ · ❤ · ❤ · ❤ · ❤ ·

THE DAY OF THE gathering arrived, and Sorrel wasn't any closer to learning if Alice Bates wanted to market her product. A queasy sensation rested in the pit of her stomach, fighting her constant hunger for the position of honor. Horrid thoughts of Alice stealing her product darted into her mind, but no matter how she rethought her actions she couldn't have done it any other way—not when she was tied to the compound by a rigid schedule.

She half expected Brother Rick to stop her from making her deliveries, and she always made a point of dampening her face and hair and pinching her cheeks and chin to make herself appear sweaty before she wheeled her handcart through the gates on her return. Let him think the walk to and from the town was a punishment. She knew better.

"It's the gathering tonight." She glanced up from the pot she was stirring, knots of tension churning her belly.

Jake worked at her side, competently filling jars with a hand lotion she'd made from lemons and coconut oil.

"What are you going to do?"

She lifted her chin and met his gaze. "Brother Rick wants me to break. He wants to make me like the other women—the ones who make those disgusting goo-goo eyes at him."

Jake paused, a glint of humor lightening his eyes. "Goo-goo eyes?"

"You know." A trace of impatience filled her as she tapped the spoon sharply against the edge of the pot.

"I'm a guy. Any relation to a stink eye?"

She huffed out a sigh and turned to face him. His interested gaze made her want to squirm, and she sucked in a quick breath, her breasts straining against their binding. Angry with herself, because a future wasn't possible with this man, she squared her shoulders and blinked while pursing her lips into a sultry pout.

A wide smile broke, and she caught a flash of white teeth despite his bushy black beard.

"So that's a goo-goo eye," he said. "You look as if you have a smut stuck in there."

"I need practice. Not that I want goo-goo eyes in my repertoire. I'm not going to let Brother Rick force me into a life at the compound, which is why I'm attending the gathering with you." Shock that she'd told him made her freeze, and she held her breath while she waited for his reply. If he refused...

"Are you sure you want to attend? You're not twenty-five yet."

She made a scoffing sound at the back of her throat. "Most of the younger women attend. He's using the age requirement to taunt me. Brother Rick isn't expecting me to turn up, let alone take part. I can't wait to see the expression on his face when I walk into the communal hall."

Jake turned to her, his face serious. "Don't goad him, sweetheart. The man is dangerous. The last thing you want is your grand gesture to prod him into taking further action at your expense."

"What do you mean?"

"He could always force you to share his bed, and there isn't much you could do to stop him."

Some of the *oomph* seeped out of her confidence. Jake was right. Brother Rick held grudges. She'd already learned to her cost.

"He's tried before and failed. I presume it's part of the reason he hates me." She turned away to check the slow simmer of her pot. A quick stir of the creamy contents told her the mixture wasn't sticking. "I punctured his ego."

Jake grasped her forearm and tugged her to face him. "When?"

The single word was an order, a sharp bark of sound she

imagined worked well in the military world.

"Don't try to order me around. I get enough of that from Brother Rick and the other men."

He released her arm and lifted his hands in a gesture of surrender. "Sorry. Please tell me what happened between you and Brother Rick."

"Virginity is prized around here. Some of the girls choose to be honored and go through an initiation."

"Jesus. Why?"

"It's a sign of our acceptance of the Children of Nature philosophies and a rite of passage to adulthood." Each stiff word held shame. God, she hated living here. Maybe she should've left earlier, run away as a teenager, but she hadn't wanted to leave her mother.

"Who gets the honor?"

"The leader."

"But you didn't lose your virginity to the last leader. Brother Samuel?"

"No." Her gaze shot to her sandals and her shoulders rounded to make her appear smaller, weaker. Submissive.

"Sorrel, don't do that." She heard the scuff of his sandals on the stone floor as he neared her. His fingertips tilted up her chin until she watched him warily. "You're my equal. There is no need to act submissive around me. Is that why you gave yourself to one of the other brothers? Please tell me."

It was the please that did it. A wealth of emotion burst open inside her, much like a blooming flower. "I hated the thought of everyone knowing, everyone discussing my ceremony, and that was why I picked a younger brother once I felt ready. He was so excited it was over and done in seconds."

"I'll kill him," Jake muttered.

"Too late. He fell out of a tree and broke his neck."

Jake shot her a sharp look. "And that's the only time you've been with a man?"

"Yes."

"I see."

"What? What do you see?" He was judging her, making her feel stupid and embarrassed just as the other men did. At this rate she wouldn't need to turn on a burner to melt the wax for candles. She'd manage the job with the heat of her cheeks.

"You're still practically a virgin."

Sorrel frowned at him, not understanding.

"You can't go into the gathering. If anyone is watching, they'll notice." He gestured in the direction of her stomach, but she knew what he meant. She'd run the risk of attracting unwanted attention.

"What else can I do? I was hoping I'd hear from Alice.

Time is running out."

"I could get you out tonight. I have friends who'd help you."

She hesitated.

"What?"

"Brother Rick has the few books on herbs and natural beauty products my mother saved from her prior life," Sorrel said. "I want them before I leave."

"Hell. Why didn't you tell me this earlier?"

"You have your task, and I have mine. I'll have to take care while retrieving my stuff, but I need to be ready to leave the compound as soon as I hear from Alice."

"Do you know where he keeps them?"

"In his private quarters, I think. That's the last place I saw them, although they might have been shifted to the office."

"I see."

"Will you stop saying that? Are you going to help me or not?"

"I've already told you I'll help you."

"Good. You're right about the gathering. Maybe we should have a trial run this afternoon. From what I've seen and heard, everyone takes one partner or more. They have sex in the hall where everyone can witness. Then, I've heard through the gossip vine that this time, if they want, they can do it again with another partner or leave for more privacy."

"An old-fashioned orgy."

"We'll leave as soon as we can," she said in a prim voice.

"Hell, yeah," Jake agreed. "You could always say you have your period."

A flush suffused her face again. "That's a lie and not a good excuse."

Jake pulled a face but wisely didn't say anything.

"I thought we could take a break during the walk home. People are becoming used to seeing us together. If we arrive back at the compound looking mussed, no one will say much."

"You've got it planned, haven't you?"

"Yes."

"What happens if you get pregnant?"

"I'll have to risk it." She clenched and unclenched her hands. "And you'll have to promise if I get pregnant you'll help me."

"I can get someone to whisk you to safety today." He repeated his offer.

"I'm not going without my mother's books. My mother invented the cream. She taught me how to work with herbs. She was a genius. I'm good, but I need her books to guide me. I have one of her recipe books, but she had others."

"I could get you out and grab the books for you later."

"You don't know what you're looking for."

Jake stared at her—a battle of wills. Finally he sighed. If he were her, he'd want the mementos too.

"How come Brother Rick and the others have no knowledge of your mother's recipes?"

"My mother never discussed her recipes with anyone except me. None of the other young girls wanted to work here. They preferred to work with the children or at the shop. After her death, I took over."

The breakfast bell rang, a strident summons for everyone to break their fast.

"We'd better get going with the delivery. We're later than usual."

"I'll grab us something for breakfast." Jake limped from the workshop, making his way across the open ground in the center of the compound.

Sorrel watched him for a while, before jerking from her reverie. She loaded the final items into the handcarts, thankfully not too many short after the intruder, and grabbed the perishable face masks from refrigeration. While she toiled, her mind darted to Jake, and she wondered if he'd go ahead or balk at her request to make love.

They'd kissed a lot since his arrival, and he'd touched her through her robe. The thought of more... Something she recognized as anticipation throbbed through her veins. She pushed the handcarts from the lean-to and watched Jake as he limped toward her.

"Are you handsome without the beard?" She slapped her hand across her mouth. "Forget I spoke. It was inappropriate."

Jake chuckled. "Women seem to like me."

A flash of jealousy struck her at his words, and that was the instant she realized she was in trouble. "Bighead."

They pushed the handcarts through the compound gates and onto the dusty road. The center of the track was more even, and they walked single file in the middle. The sound of a vehicle and the impatient honk of a horn behind them made them hurriedly push their carts to the side of the road.

Brother Rick and Brother John sped past, dust billowing after them. Sorrel turned her head away, eyes squeezed shut until the cloud settled. "Arsehole," she muttered. "They must have managed to fix the truck after all."

"You okay?"

Sorrel shook the worst of the dust from her robe. "Yes."

"I wish I'd known he was intending to leave the

compound this morning," Jake said. "Did you know?"

"I would've told you."

He gave a clipped nod. "Maybe Luke can pick him up. He knows the registration of their truck."

"I wonder how long he'll be away. We might have time to search his quarters."

Jake shot her a long look. "We won't make it back in time. Not if we take care of this other business."

The squeak of the wheels of her handcart seemed extra loud. Sorrel concentrated on pushing it up the slight gradient, her breath starting to come in loud gasps. "Are you agreeing to my proposition?"

"At least I get to see you without your padding," he said in lieu of an answer. "I admit to curiosity."

Sorrel swallowed in an attempt to rid herself of the nerves threatening to close her throat. Honesty propelled her to admit she wanted this man, and better, she admired him. He treated her as a person. He *saw* her.

During the last few days she'd dreamed of him running his hands across her naked breasts, his mouth tugging at her nipple. She'd fantasized of his fingers skimming her body and touching her everywhere. And she'd looked at him, imagined her hands roaming his shoulders and chest, feeling more of the hard muscles. For the first time she wanted a man to look at her with lust in his eyes.

She wanted to stand proudly before him, her disguise discarded.

The butterfly ached to burst from the cocoon and flutter free to play in the sun, to taste freedom.

The rest of the trip to town passed in silence, which was normal for her. When they were almost at town, a vehicle stopped beside them.

"Wait here." Jake limped over to speak with the male driver. After a few minutes and a loud bark of laughter, the man drove away.

"Was that James Bates?"

"Yes." Jake set off again without appeasing her curiosity. Before they reached the rear of the shop, he said, "I'm going to let you unload as normal. I need to meet my contact and sort out a few things."

"All right." She watched him hobble from sight before knocking on the rear door.

"Oh, good." Sister Marigold's silver hair glinted under the bright morning sun. "You're here. We had a busy day yesterday. We're sold out again."

"I wanted to talk to you about pricing." Sorrel forced confidence into her voice and posture. "I think you're selling everything too cheaply. Can I see what prices you're charging?"

"But Sister Bitter, Brother Rick set the prices. I'm sure

he knows what he's doing."

"Let me look." She pushed past the woman, carrying a box of new stock. She scanned the shelves, her mouth dropping open in astonishment. "You're selling everything for one dollar?"

"On Wednesdays, we have a sale, and everything is fifty cents," one of the younger sisters added.

"But that doesn't cover the raw ingredients. You're selling everything at a loss."

"Sister Beth, Sister June, go and bring in the rest of the new stock." Sister Marigold turned back to Sorrel. "A man comes each day and buys most of the stock. I think he resells it at a profit somewhere else. We will fix this now. Sister Bitter, come and tell me how much you think we should charge for each product."

Sorrel walked down the newly stocked shelves, giving the prices they should charge. Brother Rick made her account for the cost of raw ingredients, so she knew to the cent how much it cost to produce every item.

"What are you going to do if Brother Rick questions the new prices?" Sorrel asked.

"I'm not sure," Sister Marigold said. "I'll think of something, but we can't keep going this way. I know you work late hours trying to make enough stock to keep the shelves stocked. I hate the way he treats you, Bit—Sorrel," she corrected. "Others share my opinion. We liked your mother, and you're a credit to her."

"Thank you." The words brought a rush of warmth and a sense of pride. Brother Rick was wrong. She *was* important—in her own quiet way.

· ❤ · ❤ · ❤ · ❤ · ❤ ·

JAKE SAT IN HIS usual spot by the river and waited for someone to join him. When the sound of footsteps told of an approach, he glanced up to see both Alice and Janaya. They carried coffee and a brown paper bag.

Janaya scrutinized the area, relaxing when she saw no one else strolled along the riverbank. "We brought you a coffee and a muffin." She handed over a coffee.

"Thanks. I don't have much time. Brother Rick has gone off somewhere in his truck. I presume it's to pick up the men who've been absent for a couple of days. Someone needs to watch for his truck."

Janaya settled beside him. "Do the cult people know where he is?"

"He runs the place on a need-to-know basis."

Janaya nodded. "Anything else?"

"We've had beef a couple of nights this week for dinner. The cooks were told Brother Rick swapped it for vegetables and wool. He also has some new farm equipment. Any complaints about theft of farm machinery?"

"I'll ask. We need to catch him red-handed," Janaya said in a hard voice.

"I'll keep looking around the compound, but they work everyone pretty hard. It's difficult to skulk when they expect you to work."

"It can't be all work if you're asking James for a packet of condoms." Alice flashed a triumphant grin at him.

Jake ignored the jibe. "Do you have a decision for Sorrel yet?"

"I thought Children of Nature residents disapproved of birth control," Janaya commented with an innocent air. "They're always waving their placards in front of the Fancy Free factory. You've read them, Alice. All the signs declaring condoms nasty and how children are the future."

Alice nodded. "They screamed slogans at me this morning."

Jake stood abruptly. "I need to meet Sorrel. Can I give her news?"

"Tell her the initial results look favorable, but we're still conducting tests."

Jake frowned. "Can I give her an estimate of when you'll

know?"

"Another two weeks."

"It really takes that long?" Jake frowned again. "To test a pot of cream."

"We have to make sure the person isn't stealing someone else's recipe or passing off an existing product as one of their own."

"When would she have time to steal someone else's product?" Jake was indignant on Sorrel's behalf. "She doesn't have any money and spends her days slaving away to make soap and bombs."

"Bombs?" Janaya's brows shot upward.

"He means bath bombs," Alice said. "One of those powdery balls you throw into your bath water."

"Well, that's a relief." Janaya's smile kicked up into sly. "I'm gonna have to try a bomb in my bath, but meantime, about those condoms."

"Do you have some for me?"

Alice smirked and produced a box from her handbag.

"Thanks. Ladies." After a brief nod, he limped away in the direction of the cult shop. He tapped on the rear door and waited until the door opened. "Is Sorrel ready?"

"Sister Bitter, it's time for you to go back to the compound," the young woman called.

Sorrel finished speaking with Sister Marigold and came

to join him. "Are you ready to leave?"

"Yes, we'll need to hurry if we want to collect more leaves and twigs to decorate your candles."

"I thought I might gather pebbles from the river to make a change in the decorations." She lowered her gaze. "Could we do that?"

Jake wanted to tell her he'd go out of his way to help her with anything she wanted. But determined not to cause her any further trouble, he paused, as if considering the idea. "We can't do both."

"No, of course not," she agreed.

"Your idea of river stones has merit," he decided out loud. They'd also have more scope for finding a private spot where no one would discover them.

He hustled Sorrel away, pushing his handcart at pace. The wheels let out a pained squeak, and Sorrel laughed. Startled by the sound, he cocked his head in her direction, and he found his lips curling in response. Sorrel didn't laugh much, but when she did, she was damn cute.

CHAPTER SIX

SORREL SCRAPED A HAND over her hair, fussing with the wisps around her face. Nerves. Her hands couldn't seem to stay still and jerked to a new position on her cart each time she thought of what she was about to do. In contrast, she was thrilled the first man to touch her with tenderness would be Jake.

"What *do* you look like without a beard?" She eyed the edges of his whiskers, ragged and unkempt. If it weren't for the deep black color, he'd give Santa Claus a good contest.

A flash of white showed against the black, and she found her lips twitching in response. She loved his smiles, big, full-on expressions of joy that made his cheekbones more pronounced and echoed in his eyes.

"I'm a very handsome dude," he said. "All my friends say

so."

"What? You have friends?"

Instead of snarling, he chuckled, and she was charmed all over again.

"My friends won't leave me alone with their wives." Amusement colored his words, and his brown eyes glinted with mischief.

The humor left her. "You'd cheat on your friends?" She couldn't hide her appalled reaction and stopped abruptly, the squeaky music from her handcart falling silent. She refused to give herself to a liar and a cheat.

"Of course not." He halted. "I met Nikolai and Louie at the Special Air Services training camp. They know I'd never make a move on their women. I flirt, and Summer and Mac flirt back. That makes my friends grumble." He stared into the distance, a memory bringing pleasure because he grinned. "We mightn't have blood ties, but they're my brothers. You'll like them. I'll introduce you once we get out."

Sorrel gave her handcart an extra hard shove to get it moving again. Jake fell into step beside her, the noisy chorus of squeaks startling the birds from a manuka tree.

"I'll shave off my beard once I leave. You can tell me what you think then."

He was talking as if they were a couple. "Are you going

back to the army?"

"If I can pass the tests the medical staff throw at me."

"But your friends aren't active soldiers now?"

"No, Nikolai has a new baby, and last I heard, Louie and Mac are expecting a kid too." He shook his head. "Times have changed."

And he was left behind, Sorrel thought. "There is a swimming hole up ahead and a nice grassy clearing. It's sort of private."

He shot her a questioning look, and she shrugged, recalling crashing James and Alice's picnic.

"Not my finest moment," she confessed. "I was desperate to talk to Alice Bates, but I couldn't ring her for an appointment. I followed her and her husband here one day. Before I could pluck up the courage to show myself and ask her about my cream, they started ripping off their clothes."

He let out a bark of laughter, and she watched, mesmerized as small crinkles appeared at the corners of his deep brown eyes. "What did you do?"

"I got caught because I panicked and stood on a stick. It's not something I prefer to remember."

"You'd like Nikolai's wife, Summer. Louie and I met her not long after Nikolai. Someone broke into her house, so she climbed out the window in her nightie and went to her neighbor's for help. Nikolai was her neighbor, and he thought she'd crawled into his bedroom window for a quickie."

"What happened?"

"Summer refused to stay put and followed us while we chased off the bad guys."

"That's not embarrassing."

"It is if your nightie is transparent."

"Oh." She paused, dragged her sandal through the pile of river sand to make patterns on the edge of the track. "I've never owned anything so frivolous." Even she heard the wistful sound in her voice. Maybe one day. "It would be nice to have a pair of jeans. They seem practical."

"I'll buy you some when we get out of here." His voice was rough with emotion as he pulled her to him and squeezed her. He made her feel safe. Secure. And best of all, he made her feel like an individual with rights and a voice.

"Will this spot work?"

"If it's good enough for Alice and James Bates, it'll work for us." He opened his handcart and pulled out a blanket. "Last chance to change your mind." His gaze was steady, although without pressure as he waited for her reply.

"No, I'm very sure. I-I like you," she ended on a rush.

He held out his hand. "Let's do this then."

141

The way he spoke made awkwardness jump to the fore. She stumbled, his grip on her hand keeping her upright. Panic flared, squeezing her chest, yet his touch kept her grounded, made her suck deep for courage. While this situation mightn't be ideal and the need for them to hurry added pressure, she wouldn't stop. In the short time she'd known Jake he'd impressed her with his behavior and his determination to complete his assignment at the compound.

"Do you think Brother Rick is stealing cattle?"

"I'm not sure," Jake said, "but he acts in the manner of a man with a secret."

"If he's arrested, it will split Children of Nature apart."

"Maybe. Maybe not."

"What do you mean?"

Jake scrutinized the clearing before choosing a sun-dappled spot near the riverbank. She realized they'd see or hear any intruders unless they were of the sneaky kind.

"I've met most of the people. Some of the women are strong and more than capable of running the place. I think they'd do a better job of it too. It would be more peaceful. A good leader is what they're lacking most."

"Did you know Brother Rick instructed the women in the shop to price every item at a dollar?"

His dark brows shot toward his hairline. "You're kidding. Even I know the products you make are worth more than a dollar."

She made a scoffing sound deep in her throat. It emerged as a frustrated growl. "They have sales on Wednesdays and sell everything for fifty cents."

"Hell. What did you do?"

"I told Sister Allison Marigold they weren't covering the costs of my raw ingredients and suggested prices more in line with reality."

"Good for you."

"I can't believe it never occurred to me to check before. Normally, I unload and head back to the compound without entering the front of the shop. Brother Rick will hear and punish me."

"You mean making you work every hour of the day and night and restricting your meals isn't enough."

She drew patterns on the ground with her sandal.

"I'm a soldier. I notice everything."

He spoke the truth. No one else noticed she wasn't making the most of her looks. "Has anyone ever told you you're a smartass?"

"Nikolai and Louie, usually when I'm flirting with their wives." The corners of his eyes crinkled again. "Come here."

She allowed him to draw her closer, and that was when nerves ran roughshod through her. Every sound around her amplified—the bubble of the water, the singing of a thrush over in a tree to their right, the harshness of her breaths.

"It's okay to feel apprehensive. We don't have to do this."

Sorrel sent him a sharp look. He meant it. He'd stop if she wanted him to go no further. It was this knowledge that settled her apprehension, made her realize she wanted this with both her head and her heart. "It's true I'm a bit nervous, but I want this. You make me feel safe."

"Would it help if I undressed first? We could even have a swim. It's warm enough today."

"A swim?"

"Yeah, you know. You get in the water and splash around."

"I can't swim."

"Do you want me to give you a lesson?"

She found herself nodding, intrigued by the idea. Brother Rick had left the compound. He wouldn't notice if she was late back. Besides, with the two of them working on making products, she had extra stuff ready to load into the handcarts.

"Strip. Last one in is a rotten egg." He kicked off his

sandals and flung off his robe and removed a knife from around his thigh in a frenzy of movement. In the sunlight, his chest was broad and tanned, the hair on his chest sparse but masculine. He peeled off tight white boxer-briefs. She caught a quick glance of a partial erection before he whirled away, running for the swimming hole. He plunged into the water, laughing in the manner of a gleeful child.

"But he doesn't look like a child," she whispered, unable to tear her gaze off him. A few days of good food made him appear healthier, and he was tanned all over. He bore scars on his back, although they didn't make him less in her eyes.

"Rotten egg," he taunted.

"I-you're beautiful."

"Do you realize I have a front row seat now? I can watch you disrobe at my leisure." There was a distinct dare in his voice.

"I'm not scared."

"You haven't seen my best leer yet."

Sorrel removed her sandals and set them together in a precise manner. She angled her back to him and felt the weight of his attention in the middle of her shoulder blades. Self-protection tempted her to flee, but that was the old Sorrel, the one everyone called Bitter. She was better than that, more than the colorless woman everyone taunted.

With her back remaining to him, she lifted the robe over her head. She folded it to give herself longer to gather courage. Shedding her layers of protection was much harder than she'd thought it would be. She sucked in a hoarse breath and unwound the binding that kept her breasts flat against her chest. Then went the padding she used to fill out her robe and make her appear plump.

Her breasts prickled at both the cooler air and the lack of restraint. Her next breath came more easily and was a sugar rush to her head. She expected freedom tasted much the same—unfettered joy.

Clad in her panties, she hesitated before whisking them down to leave her naked in more ways than one. Swallowing twice, she turned to gauge Jake's reaction. He stood, wading to the edge of the river to meet her. His gaze skimmed her from head to foot and back again.

"God, Sorrel. You're gorgeous. You have a body made for a bikini."

"I don't have one of those either." Some of her uncertainty faded.

"You will," he promised. "Come on in. The water's fine." He extended his hand, and she took it.

His inner strength helped to bolster her bravery. She stepped into the water and froze, the water lapping against her thighs. "It's cold."

"Only at first. The best way is to jump in. I'll give you a kiss as a reward," he added, his gaze tracking across her again.

If it was any other man looking at her, she would've faltered, but not with Jake. He made her feel good about herself. Steeling herself, she plunged deeper, the chill a wake-up tonic to her skin. She tingled from head to foot, her nakedness feeling natural instead of something she needed to hide in order to stay safe.

"The water is freezing."

"Come here," he said roughly. He wrapped his arms around her, drawing her against his chest. His lips came down on hers. Hard. Consuming, leaving her in little doubt of his mindset.

She kissed him back, releasing the last of her reserve. His beard tickled her chin and cheeks while his lips were soft and warm. He pulled back a fraction, resting his forehead against hers.

"How long have you been wearing your disguise?" His fingers trailed across her cheek and down her neck. His hand came to rest on her shoulder, leaving a fiery trail of sensation everywhere he touched. "Sorrel?"

"Since my early teens. My mother told me I was too young to deal with male attention."

"Their loss, my gain. What about the guy who took your

virginity?"

She snorted. "He was so excited he never noticed my padding. We lifted our robes, and a few seconds later, it was over."

Jake cursed softly and brushed a flyaway hair from her cheek.

"Do I look all right?" She bit down on her bottom lip, wanting to recall the words as soon as she spoke them. "Don't answer that."

"I'll show you how much I like you."

A trace of shyness crept into her. "Okay."

Instead of taking her into his arms again, he took two steps back. A mischievous expression darted onto his face as he scooped up a handful of water and splashed her.

The cool water hit her in the chest, startling a scream of surprise from her. His rumble of laughter jolted her from her shock. Right.

"This is war." She splashed him in return, throwing herself at him at the same time. A chuckle burst from her, foreign yet it warmed her inside. She splashed and kicked, limbs wet and slippery. Laughter spilled from both of them as Jake flicked handfuls of water in return, grabbing her arms and legs and holding her captive. Each touch sent longing through her. Need.

"Enough," he growled, yanking her against him. His

erection was full and hard and dug into her belly. He pressed a quick kiss on her lips, grasped one hand and led her from the water.

"We're wet. How are we going to dry ourselves?"

"We'll air dry," he said, as if it was unimportant. "Lie on the blanket for me. Let me look at you properly."

She basked in the attention even though shyness struck her too. He seemed so big, looming over her.

"God, you're sexy. All smooth skin and curves." His face was serious, yet she could see the banked emotion in him. He sprawled beside her, so close she could feel his body heat.

Sorrel couldn't take her eyes off him. Without his robe, he was more masculine, more everything, and the expression in his eyes... He was looking at her as if he found her beautiful.

She reached out, wanting to touch him, to test his flesh beneath her fingers. She inhaled his scent, the green tang of the grasses and trees around them. The fresh, almost crisp scent of the river water and the underlying herbal fragrance of the soap she'd made for him.

The skin of his biceps was smooth, a little chilled from their dip in the river. He had a tattoo, one she hadn't noticed before because his robe covered it. She traced it now with her fingers, following the curls and straight lines of the Māori pattern.

"Do you like it?" His gaze followed the track of her finger. When the path of her finger came to a halt, she lifted her gaze. A heated message winged between them, hot and heady and full of promise. Oh yes. This was what she wanted and the man she needed.

"Yes." The whisper expressed much more, and judging by the flare of his eyes, he knew it too.

He rolled over her, his move so quick that a squeak of alarm escaped her.

"Easy," he soothed. "I grow impatient, and unfortunately, we're short of time. I'm sorry for that, sweetheart. I'll make it up to you. I promise."

She nodded, even as she wondered how. If everything went according to plan, soon she'd leave the compound. Once he completed his investigation he'd depart too. They had no future together if he intended to return to his soldiering and she... Well, her life wasn't exactly predictable either. She just knew her future would be away from here.

That exciting flash of emotion shot across his face again, stealing her breath and making tension tighten in her belly.

He kissed her lips, a fleeting touch before he trailed small kisses down her neck. His warm hand settled over one breast, shaping the mound and testing the weight. Her nipple brushed his palm, the delicate friction better than she'd ever imagined.

He paused. "I understand the padding, but why do you bind your breasts?"

"My mother told me it was best if I diverted attention from myself."

"Why would she say that? Didn't she come to Children of Nature of her free will?"

"Yes, but I think she came to regret it. Before she died, she mentioned leaving, but I think Brother Samuel changed her mind. She loved him."

"Did she say why she wanted to leave?"

"She wouldn't tell me. I asked her several times, but she kept saying it was better if I remained ignorant of the facts."

"We'll talk later. On the way back to the compound."

His hands wandered to caress her breasts before he added a completely different sensation with his mouth. She drew a sharp breath as his tongue teased her nipple, then tugged and sucked on it. Every draw reverberated between her legs, bringing longing and restlessness. Her hand ran up and down his back, her fingers pressing into hard muscles, silently urging him on. She'd never guessed, never imagined touching a man could feel so good.

Her entire body sang a joyous tune of celebration and

distinct moisture pooled between her legs.

She grew more daring with her touches, kissing his throat, his shoulder and even licking along the whorls of his tribal tattoo. He tilted his head, catching her lips. He wasted no time in deepening the contact, pressing his tongue against the seam of her mouth, silently requesting she allow him entrance. The instant she did, his tongue pushed deep. In and out. An ache nipped her breasts, and she stirred, her entire being craving closeness.

She pulled away from him, breathing hard. "Jake."

"Do you want me to stop?" His voice was sharp. His body shifted, and his erection dug against her leg.

"No." She gripped his shoulders in panic, fearing he'd halt when it was the last thing she wanted.

"I'm not intending to leave you hanging." He moved, one of his hands coming to rest on her upper thigh. "Part your legs for me."

She followed his instruction, mentally pushing away the spurt of vulnerability. He wouldn't hurt her. The instinct to trust him was strong and unwavering.

"Perfect," he said.

His lips moved against hers, an unhurried kiss, before he moved his attentions farther down her body. Her neck, her collarbone, the upper curves of her breasts. He licked a rapid path around one nipple, his warm breath as he blew on it a surprising contrast.

Shyness threatened to overwhelm her, the exposure so new, yet his physical contact and the way he looked at her with such longing brought a blip of excitement. Her heart raced, thumping against the wall of her chest in anxious beats.

"Don't be afraid."

"I'm not. It's...I mean I know the mechanics, but it's different if I'm the one experiencing the act."

"I haven't had sex with a woman for a long time." His voice was hoarse, and she noticed the faint tremor of his hand as he stroked her belly.

"Why?"

"Circumstances," he said. "I'm going to put my mouth on you, and make sure you come before I enter you."

"Oh. Okay." What else could she say? She wasn't the one with experience.

A burst of laughter came from him. "I'm going to start now."

Before she could answer, his fingers stroked over the hair at her groin and lower.

"You're blonde. I bet your hair is pretty."

"I can hardly remember the color," she confessed with a frown. Then the thought faded because he was running his fingers down her folds. Streaks of sensation, sharp jolts of pleasure ran down her legs and up her torso. Her breath caught, an ache gathering inside her. It resembled a spring, a compressed one ready to explode and fly apart.

His finger ran back and forth, stirring the desire inside her into something bigger and superior. One finger moved lower and pushed inside her. Even as she was cataloging the feelings, he lowered his head and licked her. She froze, the warm lap of his tongue different from the caress of his fingers.

He stroked his finger in and out of her while his lips and tongue tasted and cajoled. The pleasure grew and grew, taking on a hard, almost painful edge. It swelled, and she squeezed her eyes shut to concentrate on the shining ball of sensations. Suddenly, it was too much. It felt as if she were flying from her body, the explosion of enjoyment sweeping her up like a rogue wave then smacking her down. She fell apart in a violent shudder, a moan escaping her tightly held mouth.

So this was sex with a man, she thought hazily. Wow, and double wow. No wonder people enjoyed the act.

When she came back to her senses she realized Jake had moved, and he no longer touched her. She missed the physical contact immediately. "Where are you going?"

"Condom," he said.

Her eyes widened. Children of Nature abhorred birth

control. They thought of children as a gift and considered contraception a weapon designed to kill a possible life.

"Do you have a problem with birth control?"

She thought for a few seconds longer and gave a curt shake of her head. But it was difficult shaking off an idea that had been reinforced since she was old enough to understand. But she had to admit to curiosity, and she wondered what this terrible device looked like because she'd never seen one. They were never mentioned unless the compound organized a demonstration in front of Fancy Free.

She watched the way he ripped open the foil wrapping and pulled out the contents. It was a pale violet color and much prettier than she'd imagined. Of course it could have a devil face painted on it for all she knew.

"It looks like a balloon."

Humor lurked in his gaze when he glanced at her. "It does."

"I haven't touched you." Regret shadowed her words because she wanted to explore his body with much attention to detail.

"Plenty of time for that. Tonight you can touch as much as you want. I like the idea of your hands on my cock. Your mouth."

Color flooded her cheeks at his suggestion, but she

nodded, wanting to experience everything with him. She watched the casual way he rolled the condom up his shaft. He pulled a face.

"What's wrong?"

"I think Alice Bates is laughing her arse off at me. She's given me a variety pack. My dick looks as if it has measles."

Sorrel grinned. "Not my problem."

He turned back to her with a glint in his eyes. "Probably not." He lowered his head to kiss her again, an unhurried meeting of lips and tangle of tongues. Her pulse rate did a jump before settling into a quick-step of excitement. The jolt of exhilaration soared down her body, stirring pleasure in her pussy. She swallowed.

"Ready?" His brows rose.

"Yes." Not a scrap of hesitation.

He ran his cock up and down her folds, teasing them both before lining up at her entrance. "This might hurt because it's been so long."

He pushed inside and she felt growing pressure. A quick nip of pain entered the equation, and she attempted to move away.

Jake kissed her again, splitting her concentration, all the while pushing deeper. She groaned, but the pressure gave way to mere discomfort. He growled, withdrew a fraction before surging inside her. Once he was embedded, he paused.

"I'm sorry, sweetheart. I don't enjoy hurting you."

She realized the sting was fleeting, and it wasn't unbearable.

He pulled back, and the sense of fullness faded. "Wrap your arms around my neck."

She did as he requested, trying not to wince as he surged into her again. She bit her bottom lip, hot tears stinging her eyes. This was it? It was nice being held, and she'd enjoyed it when he'd used his mouth and tongue on her, but this part she could take or leave.

"God," he muttered. "I'm sorry I'm hurrying things. It will get better. I promise."

She nodded. At least it wasn't hurting anymore.

He kept thrusting and retreating, his breath harsh against her ear. For some reason, he changed the angle of his strokes. Her breath caught halfway up her throat. That was better. Much better.

"That's it." The tendons in his neck strained. He went faster, his mouth sucking at the base of her neck. The faint play of his teeth should have brought pain. It didn't. Instead pleasure flared to life again, an ember catching a draft. She clutched his shoulders, hanging on, instinctively matching his movements with her own. Like a dance, she decided before the thought waltzed away and she concentrated on the good feelings.

He groaned, did three hard strokes into her body and stilled.

"Holy shit," he muttered.

After a while, he shifted, withdrawing from her. Unaccountably, she felt a flash of disappointment, the brightness of the sensations rippling through her, fading now that he'd ceased moving inside her.

He removed the condom, placing it inside a plastic bag. "Alice said they'd duplicated your cream and to try this on you." He pulled out a plain bottle and tipped some of the contents on his palm. He stroked the cream along her folds, around her clitoris.

Familiar sensations tore through her, rich and full, pleasure magnified, but the scent wasn't right. Not that the lack of scent made a difference to the reaction of her body. She gasped, her hips jerking. She arched upward, desperate for a firmer stroke of his fingers. "More," she demanded. "Harder."

He did as she instructed and seconds later she swore she saw stars behind her tightly squeezed eyes. Tendrils of pleasure were still rippling through her as she opened them again to stare up at Jake.

"Wow." His eyes sparkled with indulgence. "Your cream works."

Chapter Seven

Excitement bubbled through Sorrel for the rest of the day, even though she tried to restrain her feel-good mood. Her cream had always brought her pleasure during her testing, but she'd never felt as if she were flying out of her skin. She pondered the difference for an instant, her brow furrowing in a frown. She'd never tested the cream with a man. Yes, that must be it. Her gaze slid to Jake, who was pressing bath bomb mix into round molds.

In contrast, he'd become downright surly, making her worry. Hadn't he enjoyed the sex between them? He glanced up to capture her gaze, his brown eyes stormy with his emotions. "Brother Rick will watch if you attend the gathering tonight. What if he decides he wants to fuck you?"

"No, that's one thing I'm not worried about. One of the tenets of Children of Nature, a fundamental one, is that sex must be freely offered. If I say no, he has to accept my decision."

"And what if he pushes the point? He makes his own rules."

"Won't you fight for my honor?" She shot for humor, the attempt falling pancake-flat. Jake's glower didn't shift.

"Promise me if I'm not around, you'll make sure you're with one of the other women. Don't let Brother Rick get you alone."

"I promise." She set her wooden spoon down and went to him, lifting her hand to cup his cheek. "Maybe you could give me some lessons in self-defense. Just in case."

"Kick him in the balls, and if you can't do that, stomp on his feet. Gouge his eyes and use your elbows. Scream. Never stop struggling." His expression was fierce and almost brutal. "And if they overpower you, concentrate on surviving. I'll come for you."

Sorrel chuckled even as she shivered in reaction to his insistent manner. "I think our bigger problem is me getting pregnant. You can't use a purple condom in the communal hall. Someone will notice."

"We'll keep our robes on, pretend we're impatient to get to the deed and fake it. You can't get naked and let anyone see your breasts anyway. Or I'll play sick, which is the logical thing to do, even if we draw more attention."

"I know." She was playing a dangerous game, and she'd been lucky to escape detection thus far.

$\cdot\heartsuit\cdot\heartsuit\cdot\heartsuit\cdot\heartsuit\cdot\heartsuit\cdot$

THERE WAS AN AIR of celebration at dinner. Beef again, Jake noted. Brother Rick and his cronies had arrived back at the compound ten minutes before dinner in high spirits. They'd unloaded boxes from the back of the truck and stored them in Brother Rick's accommodation before strutting into the dining hall.

Jake intended to check out the mystery boxes. He waited until they'd settled at a table with their dinners, before leaving the line.

"Call of nature," he said to Sorrel. "Will you get me a plate?"

She nodded, and he limped outside.

Brother Rick's quarters were away from the main buildings, and the door was locked—a flimsy one, but still a deterrent. Jake slipped a knife from the strap around his thigh and made quick work of the lock. With a glance over his shoulder, he slipped inside, pulling the door shut after him.

He found the boxes stacked in the smaller of the two bedrooms. They were sealed, but he didn't hesitate, cutting the tape to find bags of colored pills. His breath emerged in a soundless whistle as he picked up a packet to study. Shit, party pills. After several deaths, the New Zealand government had recently outlawed the pills, popular for their natural high.

A sense of satisfaction filled him as he slipped a packet into his pocket and repacked the box, restacking them so the box he'd opened was at the bottom of the pile. At the door, he paused to make sure the way was clear. He relocked the door and after replacing his knife, sprinted across the open ground of the compound to the ablutions block, slowing as he neared his destination.

He wished he had time to contact Luke, but it'd have to wait. He'd been gone for too long already.

When he neared the communal dining room, the roar of a male voice had him breaking into a run again. He burst through the doors, lungs burning with the abrupt physical exertion.

Half a step inside the door, he remembered his limp and lurched, the sudden uneven gait throwing off his balance. He crashed into an empty chair and sent it flying. Everyone looked in his direction, some sniggering at his clumsiness. He had no trouble pretending embarrassment as he straightened.

Frantically, he sought Sorrel. He located her on the other side of the dining hall, two plates of food at her feet. Brother Rick stood in front of her, a sneer twisting his face. He ignored Jake's entrance, his gaze fixed on Sorrel.

"You're a pig, Sister Bitter. It's no wonder you're getting fatter all the time. Did you break your fast this morning?"

Anger filled Jake as he made a show of limping over to join them.

"Yes, I broke my fast." Sorrel had reverted to her subservient behavior, her gaze on her sandals, her voice barely audible.

"Then why are you eating a meal tonight? I believe I instructed you to eat once a day. Can you count?"

"Yes," she said, her voice so low Jake barely heard her.

"Then why do you have two plates of food?"

"I asked Sister Sorrel to get my meal for me." Jake's fists bunched and released. Seconds later, he bunched them again because the urge to hit Brother Rick was a bomb ticking inside him. "I had to go to the ablution block."

"Her name is Sister Bitter, and she still shouldn't have had two plates of food."

"Maybe I have a big appetite," Jake said.

"I'm not stupid."

As much as Jake wanted to snap a smartass reply, he

didn't. Instead he sucked in a hasty breath, ordering his thoughts. He focused on Sorrel. "Clean up the mess and get me another plate of food." She flinched at his tone, and Jake felt like a monster.

Hell, Brother Rick wasn't fit to lick her shoes. While he understood she lacked money and the means to leave, he was at a loss to explain her acceptance of this constant abuse. He turned away before he gave into the impulse to flatten Brother Rick's pointy nose and limped over to a table with four free chairs.

The men and women sitting around the table stared at him in reproach, making him feel as if he'd kicked a puppy. His gut churned while he waited for Sorrel to join him. God, he wanted to go and help her, but instead, he sat there—the dominant male.

Ten minutes later, she set a plate of roast beef in front of him. She pulled out the seat beside him and sat, her head bowed. The noise in the dining hall increased, and the occupants started to talk again. Tonight they were louder than normal, excited about the coming gathering.

Jake was no longer hungry. He took a bite of roast beef, but it tasted like dirt in his mouth. A loud grumble sounded, and his mouth firmed to a scowl. He tossed his knife and fork down and shoved his plate away.

Sorrel flinched at the abrupt sound, and the chatter

at their table faded. Jake stood. "Come," he barked and he limped from the dining hall without glancing over his shoulder to see if she followed him.

"Wait," Brother Rick's voice boomed across the room. Silence descended, and the prickle of gazes skimmed his back.

Slowly Jake turned. "I am not feeling well. I am going to the restroom and to my quarters."

"Sister Bitter can stay here."

Arsehole. "I require someone to look after me," Jake said. "If I am coming down with something, it is better for her to tend me to limit the spread of sickness."

Luckily the man saw the benefit of Jake's words. "Of course. Good thinking. You may go and you have leave to be absent from the gathering tonight."

"Thank you." Jake fought the urge to sprint across the room and thump the man into next week. Instead, he hobbled from the hall, out into the fresh air with Sorrel shuffling two steps behind him.

The days were becoming shorter, and the sun had already dropped below the skyline. He trudged across the compound toward the ablution block.

"Jake? Are you all right?"

"Wait for me at your workshop," he said, somehow managing to keep his voice even. "I won't be long."

Maybe this would work better. With everyone attending the gathering, he could sneak out of the compound and go to see Luke with the evidence. A phone would have come in handy right now, but they'd decided not to risk him taking one onto the compound. As it was he suspected someone had rifled through his duffle bag.

Jake made himself stay in the ablution block for ten minutes. He flushed the toilet and after washing his hands and face, he headed for Sorrel's workshop.

He gave a brief tap on the door. "It's Jake."

The door opened, and Sorrel stood there, her eyes red as if she'd been crying.

"Aw, sweetheart." He tugged her into his arms, holding her quivering body.

"I try not to let him get to me, but sometimes it's hard."

"If you want, I can get you out tonight." He shut the door before turning his attention on her again. "What do you think?"

"I'm not going until I get my mother's books."

"So we get the books, and we leave," he said. "Damn, I should've searched for them earlier when I was in Brother Rick's quarters."

"The books were with Brother Samuel's things since my mother spent most of her time with him. Brother Rick ordered the women to clean out Brother Samuel's quarters before he moved in. The books are either in his quarters or perhaps in his office. Or they might have packed them away in boxes."

"Damn, it will take a while to find your books. Are you sure they weren't destroyed?"

"I doubt it. Books are luxuries. He's probably shoved them on a shelf somewhere. Jake, tonight isn't a good time for searching. Although the gathering takes place in the communal hall, remember this time, the brothers and sisters will move outside and find other places for privacy once the formalities are completed."

His brows shot up. "Formalities?"

"Um, I don't know what else to call them."

"Then we'll have to search another night—the next time Brother Rick leaves the compound."

"There is never a right time," she said with a trace of frustration. "He's either in his quarters or I'm busy with work."

Jake pulled her into his arms again and held her. He felt protective as he slid his hand over her back. He couldn't feel the push of her breasts now. Instead, her stomach nudged him, getting in the way. Damn it. He couldn't wait to have her slender body pressed next to his again. "I'm staying here tonight."

"What if they ask questions?"

A whoop of sound carried across the compound.

"I'll tell them it was too noisy up there. Everyone is much louder than normal."

"Yes." Sorrel frowned. "They were during the last gathering too. I suspect Brother Rick added something extra stimulating to the celebratory punch everyone was drinking."

Sorrel's stomach let out a rumble, and Jake's arms tightened on her shoulders.

"I'll ask Alice if she can get us some food next time I see her. You shouldn't lose any more weight."

"Thank you."

Her gratitude made him want to snarl. *Not her fault.* "At least we won't need to worry about birth control." He nuzzled her neck and nibbled on her earlobe. "We won't attract any attention here."

"It's not very late yet," Sorrel said. "I might as well make a batch of bath bombs. I'm going to try a new scent combination. I thought of it while Brother Rick was shouting at me."

"Good for you."

"Make up the pallet. In case Brother Rick sends someone to check on you."

Jake nodded, seeing the sense in her suggestion.

They worked together, measuring and chopping herbs

to add to the bath bombs. Lavender, thyme and mint. The scents swirled in the air, both soothing and familiar to him now.

Voices outside made them both freeze.

"Sister Bitter might know where he is," a man said.

A knock sounded on the door, but Jake was already on the pallet and pulling a blanket over him.

Sorrel glanced at him before opening the door.

"Have you seen Brother Jake? Brother Rick was worried and wanted us to check on him."

"He's resting here." Sorrel indicated the pallet they'd set up on the far side of her workshop. "The noise was bothering him, and I thought it would be a little quieter in my workshop."

Two men—he thought it was Brother John and Brother Tyrone—stepped inside the workshop and peered at him.

"How are you feeling?" Brother John asked.

"A bit better," Jake said. "I vomited up the little food I ate at dinner, but my stomach is still churning."

They both backed up and exchanged glances.

Brother Tyrone gaped. "You really are sick?"

"Of course he's ill. Can't you tell by his face? It's flushed, and he seems to be sweating a lot." Sorrel nibbled her bottom lip, uncertainty in her expression. "I think it's one of these quick-acting things. I could be wrong, of course."

"Maybe we should take him to the infirmary," Brother Tyrone said.

"I hate to upset everyone's night." Sorrel kept her gaze downcast. "It's a celebration. I'm happy to look after him tonight. If he hasn't improved by the morning, I'll get someone to help me take him to the infirmary and Sister Agnes's care."

Brother John nodded. "That's a good idea. I'm sure Brother Rick will approve."

The two men backed from the workshop, and Sorrel shut the door. They both waited until they could no longer hear the brothers' voices.

"Do you think they'll come again?" Jake asked.

"I'm not sure. Maybe you should stay there."

"I—"

The workshop door flew open, and Brother Rick stood in the doorway with his two friends standing behind him. Brother Rick surveyed the room, the suspicion fading from his face when he saw Jake lying on the pallet.

"Do you think his illness is contagious?" he asked Sorrel.

Sorrel avoided Brother Rick's gaze. It made anger curl through Jake. His entire body stiffened, muscles coiling, ready to spring if Brother Rick made a wrong move.

"I don't feel sick," Sorrel said.

Brother Rick gave a curt nod. "If he gets worse, call

Sister Agnes."

"I will." Once again, Sorrel spoke to her feet.

Brother Rick strode away without bothering to close the door. From his position on the pallet, Jake couldn't see where they went, so he remained in place.

"They've gone back to the communal hall." Sorrel stepped around the counter to close the door. With the door safely shut, Jake clambered to his feet and joined her.

"I'll wait a while and let everyone get settled, then I'll do some skulking around the compound. I need to talk to Luke, but I hate to leave you here alone."

"You're not responsible for my safety. Give it another hour, and you'll be safe enough. I'll stay here and keep working."

Jake opened his mouth to argue. He wanted to be responsible for her safety. Hell, he wanted to give her the stars. The thought crashed through his mind, alien and unusual. Women were a commodity for him. He fucked them and moved on, normally remaining friends. It was different with Sorrel. He wanted to protect her, to cherish her, damn it. And he sure as hell wanted to get in her pants again.

He'd enjoy a slow loving in a big, soft bed. Maybe a flash hotel room with a spa bath and one of those showers with multiple showerheads. Big, thick cotton towels. Room service. Hell, yeah. As soon as this was over, he promised himself, already imagining Sorrel's eyes and her shy smile as she enjoyed the sensual treat.

Jake peeked out the window and slid from her workshop, returning an hour later, frustration simmering through him.

"There were people everywhere. I saw Sister Marigold's bare butt." He shuddered. "Not something I want to repeat. And I didn't learn anything useful to report to Luke."

"Did you search Brother Rick's quarters?"

Jake pulled off his robe and joined Sorrel on the pallet. "You were right. He took three women back to his room."

"Three?"

"Yeah—three of the younger, prettier ones."

"No doubt the women will be subtly bragging tomorrow. Not many people get to visit Brother Rick in his private space."

"I don't want to discuss Brother Rick." Jake switched off the light she'd left burning for him and discarded his sandals, clothes and concealed weapon. He slipped under the blankets and reached for her.

"Why are you still dressed?"

"I wasn't sure if one of the men would check on you again. I didn't want to risk it."

"Take off your robe," he said. "I'll run interference if anyone arrives unexpectedly."

He sensed her hesitation, even though he couldn't see her face clearly. It was a brief pause, and he held his breath, wanting her to trust him, to realize he'd protect her should the need arise.

A grin spread across his face when she sat up. He heard the rustle of her robe, the whisper of fabric as she removed her padding and lay back down beside him. A satisfied sigh whispered from him. He was right where he wanted to be—with Sorrel, her warm limbs sliding against his.

"Is it cold out there?"

"A little." He pulled her over him, so she stretched on top of his larger body. She wriggled a fraction before relaxing.

"Kiss me," Jake said. "Now is your chance to explore."

"Really?" She sounded thrilled at the idea.

"I'm all yours." He could imagine his friends' reaction if they'd heard that little snippet. Shock. Teasing. All the shit he'd given them while they fell for their women lobbed straight back at him. His elation deepened when the urge to flee remained absent. Not a hint of alarm surfaced.

Sorrel explored his face with her hands, mapping it in the darkness. His cheekbones, his eyelids. His lips. She tugged at his beard. "I don't like your beard. It hides too much of your face."

"I do look pretty without my beard."

"Are you sure your chin isn't weak?"

"Nope. You can't argue with the truth. I'm a catch."

Laughing, she wriggled down his body, and blood surged into his cock. She must've felt the prod of his dick, but she ignored it in favor of running her hands over his chest. Busy fingers searched out his nipples. She bent her head and explored his chest with her mouth. Teeth scraped the flat discs, and he flinched at the arc of sensation that roared straight to his groin.

"Damn, you're good at this."

"Think how good I'll be after more practice."

He laughed, the hoarse sound fading abruptly when her tongue circled his navel and dipped inside.

His scent, rich and masculine, with a hint of herbs filled the air, combined with her feminine one. She licked across his hipbone.

"Lower." He stirred impatiently, craving her mouth around his cock, her tongue licking and exploring his shaft. No sooner had the thought formed then her hand curled around his girth. A shudder went through him at the increase in friction. "That feels great, sweetheart."

Her hand moved up and down, stroking him and

learning texture, his size.

"Put your mouth on me," he gritted out. Damn, he hadn't meant to issue it as an order. "If you want," he added, hoping like hell she'd just do it already.

"Like this?"

Wet, hot heat surrounded his tip. "Fuck, yes." His fingers speared through her hair, fighting the urge to direct her with his hands. "Take me deeper. Lick me and suck."

She followed his instructions, her untutored mouth more erotic than anything he'd felt before. A tremor racked him. Her hair tickled his thighs and his belly, and he realized she'd freed it from her normal braid. He wished he had a visual. Imagination and the feel of her hair in his hands would have to do.

Her tongue flicked over his slit, lingered, and her mouth tightened around the head of his cock. A strangled curse tore from his throat, and his whole body hummed from the pleasure of her mouth. She licked along his shaft, down one side and up the other before closing her lips around him again. His hips jerked, driving him deeper. Raw need pulsed through him, yet he tamped it down, not wanting to rush her. This was her time to explore, and she deserved to move at her own pace.

She sucked, dragging a groan from him. "That's it. Your mouth feels good. Use your tongue a little more on the head."

Seconds later, he was in heaven, his balls so tight he thought he might explode. She added the suction of her mouth again, and he bucked, driving his cock farther past her lips. She made a coughing sound and jerked back.

"Sorry," she said.

"I'm the one who's sorry. Let me grab a condom." He lifted her off him and rolled onto his side, rifling through his pile of clothes for the box of condoms. He couldn't find it in the dark, but he found what was left of the strip of condoms they'd used earlier in the day. He ripped one open and rolled on the rubber.

"Uh, what color is that one?"

He glanced down at his shaft and groaned. Even though there was no light, the condom glowed like a peppermint stick in red and white stripes. "You mean you can't see my candy cane dick?"

She giggled, a surprising sound he hadn't heard before. It made his lips twitch and his heart lighten.

"It reminds me of an old-fashioned barber's pole."

Jake snorted and reached for her. "Should we try a different position?"

"Yes?"

He laughed at her doubt and lifted her over him. She automatically parted her legs and settled astride his thighs.

"I wish I could see your hair. I can feel it tickling my legs."

"Sorry."

"No, don't apologize. How long is it?"

"I've never cut it, not apart from snipping off the brittle ends. It reaches my backside."

"And a very pretty backside you have, sweetheart."

She giggled again, making him grin.

"Are you wet?"

"Yes."

"I want you to finger yourself and stroke your clit. Make yourself even wetter for me." He could feel her hesitation, yet damn if he'd force her to do anything that brought discomfort. "Only if you want to," he added.

There was a long pause. Jake strained to hear in the darkness. Her thighs flexed as she rose. He could almost hear her hesitation, a living breathing thing between them. Then he heard a liquid sound. He almost laughed, but he bit his lip, not wanting to embarrass her.

"Does it feel good?"

"I think sin usually feels good," she said in a dry tone. "At least that's what Brother Samuel told us all."

"Sex isn't a sin. Touching yourself isn't a sin either." He imagined anything that delayed the production of babies was a sin to the founder of Children of Nature.

"Do you touch yourself?"

"Yeah."

"Will you show me?"

"I'll show you if you show me." He was certain she'd chicken out.

"Okay," she said with a trace of eagerness.

This time his laugh barked out before he could slam on the brakes—a rich chuckle dredged from deep in his chest. Liberating. Relaxing. Joyful.

"Why are you laughing?"

"I thought you'd say no," he confessed. "Does it feel good?"

"Yes. Very good."

He heard the distinct rub of her fingers against her flesh. He imagined her folds would be swollen and flushed with blood, her clit a hard knot of arousal. "Once you think you've done that enough, I want you to give me your hand so I can lick it clean."

She inhaled sharply, the muscles of her inner thighs flexing against his. Then, as he wondered if he'd shocked her too much, she moved, wriggling her way up his body. Wet heat pushed against his stomach, the scent of her heady and enticing. She found his lips on the second try and dragged the tip of her finger around the outline of his mouth.

"You have soft lips."

"Is that surprise I hear?"

"You're hard everywhere else."

"And you like it."

"I do." She ran her finger across the seam of his mouth, and he helpfully parted his lips. He drew her finger inside, sucking on it, much as she'd sucked on his cock.

"Oh," she said, her tone startled.

He released her finger to speak. "I have a magic touch." Before she could reply he directed another of her fingers into his mouth and gave it the same treatment.

"Most people would accuse you of boasting."

He withdrew her finger, ready to move on to the next one. "I don't boast. Not much."

"I'm glad you qualified your words."

"Use your free hand to stroke your breast. Twist and pull your nipple. Pinch it until it's a little tender to the touch." Once she followed his instructions, he licked another finger clean. "Swap hands."

Silently, she presented her other hand to him, and he repeated the process, enjoying the hell out of the musky taste of her.

"What next?"

"Guide my cock to your entrance and sink down until you're impaled. Take your time."

"What are you going to do?"

"I'm going to lean over and kiss your breasts until you're ready to move." Suiting action to words, he roughly sucked a nipple into his mouth, drawing hard enough to send a spike of sensation to her pussy.

"Jake," she whispered in a broken voice.

"Take me inside you, sweetheart." He remembered the clinging warmth of her channel and could hardly wait to repeat the process. Tight, wet heat. There was nothing better.

She fumbled with his cock, unsure of her movements, but he thought the darkness helped because it masked her reactions, helped her feel bolder. She hesitated a fraction before pushing down. Unable to help himself, he surged upward, driving himself deeper into her body. A gasp escaped her, and he froze, his heart trying to hammer its way from his chest.

"Am I hurting you?" He'd injured her enough today with his harsh words, and he'd rip off his left arm rather than do it again.

"It—you feel strange. A good strange," she added before he could ask the question. She kept pushing down until he was embedded in her. "Now what?"

"Now I don't resemble a candy cane." He gritted his teeth, steeling himself against the impulse to take control.

No, she needed this. He needed to earn her trust. Once he could breathe without his eyes crossing, he said. "Now you rise and fall, like someone riding a horse. Experiment with the angle until you find one that feels good."

She trailed her fingertips across his stomach, making his skin twitch and sing with the contact. "What about you?"

"Don't worry. This is to help you learn what you enjoy."

"Okay." The happiness in her voice helped to tamp down his urge to manhandle her onto her back and power into her until he was sated.

"If it helps, you can touch yourself at the same time."

"Okay." This time her clear interest came through. She started moving, experimenting, making him crazy. A quick learner. Pride filled him at the thought, along with a rampaging fire, searing every inch of his body. He caught her hips, subtly guiding her into a rhythm to satisfy them both.

A sharp groan came from her, and her pussy rippled around him, gripping him in a sensual massage.

She leaned back and rose above him, sank back down. She quickened her pace, gasped. He felt her finger as it slid along the base of his shaft. Quick, hard strokes as she rubbed herself. She groaned, and seconds later, she was coming, squeezing his cock in tight pulses.

Jake gripped her hips and slammed her up and down,

pushing himself past the sweet pain and falling into orgasm. When the pulses ceased, he arranged her against his chest. A small part of his brain was telling him to pull out of her and deal with the condom, but she felt so good. He wrapped his arms around her and held her, breathing in the sweet scent of herbs and flowers, the underlying pungent aroma of her hair and the musky smell of sex. Yeah. He smiled against her hair. There was nowhere else he'd rather be right now.

CHAPTER EIGHT

THE COMPOUND CAME TO life more slowly than the previous day. As Sorrel wheeled her handcart to the entrance gates with Jake behind her, the breakfast bell hadn't rung yet. Jake had raided the kitchens and talked the only person he could find into giving him food.

"Is it always like this after a gathering?"

Sorrel nodded. "The noise went late."

"I would have expected the children to be up at least," Jake said.

"They probably are, but their minders would have warned them against waking Brother Rick. None of the children will risk punishment."

As they approached the exit, one of the men jerked awake. His hair stuck up, making him resemble an old toilet brush. The other man continued his snoring, his white robe smeared with grass stains. Sorrel averted her gaze to her feet.

"Good morning," Jake said.

Toilet brush man moaned. "What's good about it?"

Jake's brows rose. "It's not raining."

"Huh! You off to town?"

"Yes."

The gates creaked as they opened, and the snoring man grunted, his eyes flickering open. They were unfocused and confused.

Sorrel pushed her cart through, glad to leave the compound. The place had lost its serenity for her. Only Jake's company relaxed her and halted the rapid glances over her shoulder to scrutinize everyone in the vicinity.

The path widened, and Jake pushed his cart beside hers. "I'm going to risk meeting with Luke Morgan this morning. I'll leave you at the store. Wait for me at the bench by the river, and I'll come and get you as soon as I can."

"What if the ladies get suspicious?"

"I doubt they'll be feeling very bright after last night. From what I heard in the ablution block not many of the women abstained last night."

They arrived at the shop to find it closed, and a knock

on the door didn't bring anyone to answer their summons.

"Do you have a key?"

"I think they leave one with the neighboring shop owner, but they haven't arrived either. Why don't I sit and wait? Even if someone comes soon it will take me a while to unload, and you'll be able to spend longer with your friend."

Jake nodded. He brushed a kiss across her lips, holding her tight for a few seconds longer. "Take care."

· ♥ · ♥ · ♥ · ♥ · ♥ ·

JAKE WENT TO THE police station first, loitering behind the trunk of a pine tree and watched to see who was on duty. Some of the tension seeped out of him on recognizing Luke's father, Richard Morgan, who was also a police officer, arrive in his SUV. Jake darted around the rear of the police station in order to intercept him.

"I need to see Luke," Jake said. "Is he handy?"

"He's at home. I can take you to see him."

Jake considered and nodded. "I'll ride in the back and keep out of sight. I don't want anyone to see me." He slipped into the rear of the vehicle, ducked down and yanked the door shut behind him.

"Here's my phone." Richard handed it over. "You'd

better ring to let him know we're coming. Luke is speed dial two."

A short drive later they arrived at an isolated property on the outskirts of the town.

"You're safe to come out." Richard scanned their surroundings. "Go straight up the stairs and through the front door. It will be open."

Jake popped up his head, scrutinized the area to ensure he couldn't see anything out of the ordinary, and burst into action. He'd just stepped into the house when the growl of a dog froze him in his tracks.

"Damn it, Killer," Richard snapped. "He's come to see Luke. Let him in."

The dog growled again, this time with none of the hair-raising tone to its snarl. The bristle of hair along the dog's spine smoothed out.

"If you stand aside and let him pass, we'll all find out what he wants," Richard said.

Jake's eyes narrowed as the dog turned and trotted off.

"Follow Killer. They'll be in the kitchen."

Jake stared in bemusement for long seconds, before shrugging and following the dog. He found himself in a large, sunny kitchen. Luke sat at a table with his wife, Janaya. They both had mugs of coffee sitting in front of them, their attention on the growling dog. It was as if they were having a conversation.

"Your dog wanted to eat me," Jake said.

"I've no idea why." Luke's eyes twinkled. "You resemble an unappetizing hobo."

Jake took possession of a chair. "The hobo look is itchy. I can't wait to get rid of this damn beard."

Richard helped himself to a coffee and leaned against the central island.

"Do you have something for me?" Luke asked.

"We had beef for dinner again last night," Jake said. "We seem to have beef whenever Brother Rick leaves the compound in his truck."

"I don't have the manpower to watch for the vehicle."

"Hinekiri and I could help out," Janaya suggested.

Luke frowned. "You need to find a way to contact us."

"Coffee?" Janaya raised a takeout cup.

Jake nodded. "Please. I guess I could take a phone. As long as I can keep it hidden I should be all right."

Richard straightened. "I'll go and buy a phone for you now."

Jake pulled out the plastic bag of pills. "I found these in Brother Rick's quarters. I think they're party pills. He had boxes of the stuff."

Luke's frown deepened. "We haven't had any problems with party pills, at least not since they were made illegal.

Some of the regions are seeing the legal alternatives, but I haven't heard about any in Sloan. I'll get them tested. I can't go in without solid proof and let the weasel slither out of my grip."

Jake heaved a sigh. "I have to admit I'm tired of cult life and can't wait to get out. Brother Rick is an arsehole. His attitude to the women is disgusting. From what I can see the women do most of the work and keep the place going while the men sit on their butts and don't do much of anything."

"You're looking better," Janaya said. "So living at the cult hasn't been all bad."

Jake snorted. "I'm having trouble keeping my temper. Every time I see Brother Rick I want to smack the bastard." He glanced at the clock on one of the pale cream walls, noted the passing time. "I need to get back before Brother Rick starts to ask questions."

· ❤ · ❤ · ❤ · ❤ · ❤ ·

SORREL SAT OUTSIDE THE shop for almost an hour before the first of the workers arrived.

Sister Allison gasped and covered her mouth with her hand, consternation glinting in her dull eyes. "I'm so sorry. Have you been waiting long?"

Sorrel shook her head. It hadn't been so bad sitting still for once, listening to the waking town, the chirp of the birds in the trees and turning her face to the morning sun.

"I have such a headache." A scent of citrus and thyme wafted to Sorrel as the sister brushed past, a key in hand to unlock the door. "Do you know where the spare key is kept?"

"Yes, but Brother Rick instructed me not to enter the shop." Mostly she ignored the order, but today she'd obeyed since it suited her.

The sister appeared discomfited at the reminder. Most of the residents at the compound had heard that particular rant. "I'm sorry." Her hand fluttered at her temple, and she pulled a face. "I have such a headache."

"Try a drop of lavender oil on your temples," Sorrel suggested. "I'll start unloading the stock. Has anyone commented on the increased prices?"

The sister held the door open for her. "The man who comes twice a week to buy our stock was put out."

Sorrel repressed the instinct to grin. She'd bet he was irked at the price rises. "Brother Rick hasn't mentioned anything?"

"No. We haven't sold as much, but we made more money than we normally do. I think we'll keep the prices as is. Most of the women agree. It doesn't make sense to sell your products at a loss."

Sorrel's thoughts exactly, and she didn't understand why the women hadn't worked this out earlier. "Everyone is late today."

"A lot of the brothers and sisters aren't feeling well this morning."

Sorrel placed a box of bath salts on the counter. "Something you ate?"

"No, I think it was the celebration punch," Sister Allison said. "It made me feel as if I could do anything. I remember laughing and enjoying myself, but I woke up with a dry mouth and this wretched headache."

"Who made the punch?"

"Brother Rick ordered the ingredients from the kitchen and mixed it in front of us." She rubbed her temple again. "Some of the others are feeling under the weather."

Sorrel dawdled over the unloading and helped the sister price and shelve the items, even though she was forbidden to enter the front of the shop.

"I'll wait outside for Brother Jake."

"I was surprised he wasn't here with you."

Sorrel used the excuse they'd come up with at the start, repeating it for the sister's benefit. "His leg still pains him. He enjoys sitting by the river while he's resting for the walk back to the compound. I'll go and meet him there."

"But what about the second handcart?"

"It's not far. I'll wheel mine there and come back for the other."

The sister nodded and winced. "Will I see you tomorrow?"

"Let me know tonight how you're going with stock. I might not need to deliver more tomorrow, not with the higher prices."

"Will do." The sister held her head and moaned.

As Sorrel wheeled her handcart down the road, she came face-to-face with Alice Bates. The smooth purr of a vehicle and the flash of blue in her peripheral vision had Sorrel acting on instinct. "Down with condoms," she shouted, waving her fist in Alice's direction. "Bad, bad condoms!"

Sorrel caught Alice's startled expression, saw the way the other woman took half a step back as Sorrel balled her hand to a fist. The truck slowed, and she saw she'd been right. It was Brother Rick. "Down with condoms," she hollered.

"I wanted to see you," Alice murmured. "Maybe another time."

"Down with condoms," Sorrel shouted, her face flushing as she drew the attention of passersby. "Please," she lowered her voice. "I'll explain in private. Please, I'd never hurt you. Meet me by the bench near the river. I'll wait for as long as I can." The blue truck was doing a U-turn. "Bad, bad condoms. Give children life."

Sorrel's heart sank as Alice scuttled away and everyone else gave her a wide berth. If Alice changed her mind or decided Fancy Free couldn't market her invention, she didn't know what she'd do.

Brother Rick pulled up beside her, and the window whirred down. He had his friends with him. "Good job, Sister Bitter. You sure scared her off."

"Go, Sister Bitter," one of the men called from the rear seat.

For once Brother Rick radiated approval, and yet his encouraging nod filled her with distaste because she and Jake had used dreaded condoms yesterday and the sky hadn't fallen. People should have the power to choose when or if to have children. A radical idea, to be sure, but one that'd grown in her mind since Brother Rick had taken over running the cult.

"Where is Brother Jake? Is he well this morning?"

"His leg was hurting him, but he seems over the worst of his stomach upset. I left him sitting in the sun and resting." She bit the inside of her lip, battling the impulse to fill the silence with more words. *Less was better.*

To her relief, Brother Rick nodded and drove away. She relaxed a fraction, but conscious he'd still see her through his rear-vision mirror she shouted, "Down with condoms."

"Who is that lady?" a child piped up in a squeaky voice.

"A weird cult lady." The mother hustled her kid past, treating Sorrel like a virulent tropical disease. "You keep away from anyone wearing robes."

Sorrel winced at the verbal strike. She wasn't accepted by the other members of Children of Nature and people on the outside thought she was weird—a curiosity to poke fun at. She glanced left and right to check the traffic and pushed her handcart across the road. Jake wasn't waiting on the usual bench. She left the handcart, tucked out of sight behind a bush and went to retrieve the second one.

On her return she found Jake sitting on the bench, waiting for her. She'd hoped Alice would be there too. She wasn't.

"I thought you'd be pleased to see me," he said.

"I saw Alice Bates as I was coming out of the shop. I shouted anti-condom slogans at her."

Jake let out a bark of laughter. "Why?"

"Because Brother Rick was driving past at the time."

"Brother Rick is in town?"

"Yes, or at least he was. I didn't ask him his destination." She pulled a face. "He wouldn't tell me anyway."

"Which direction did he go? How long ago?"

"He drove out of town, so I presume he's going to Auckland. Not long ago, maybe half an hour."

Jake pulled out a phone and pressed a button. "He's left the compound and is heading out of town. Half an hour ago. Yeah. Okay." Jake tucked the phone away out of sight. "Come on. I need to get back so I can nosy around."

They set a fast pace on the return journey to the compound, traveling in single file. Sorrel studied Jake's back. He seemed all business today, impersonal with his mind on other things.

Her mood took a downturn as her mind shifted to Alice. Her stunned expression on hearing the anti-condom shrieks had branded Sorrel's guilty mind. Alice probably considered her a nutcase, and who wanted to work with a mentally unbalanced woman?

"I'm going to try to find my mother's books today," she announced.

Jake came to an abrupt halt, and she almost ran her handcart into his backside. "Stay away from Brother Rick's private rooms and office."

"But—"

"You told me the women cleaned everything out for him. They've probably been moved." Jake started moving again, and she hurried to catch up. "It's not safe. He has spies everywhere. What happens if you get caught? What are you going to tell him when he starts asking questions?"

"I'm not leaving without my mother's stuff."

Jake merely increased his pace, not limping until they were within sight of the compound gates. He slowed a fraction, his gait becoming heavy and uneven.

Puffing from the rapid ascent of the slope leading to the compound, she pushed her handcart a little harder to reach his side. The two men on the gates shuffled to push them open. Their pale faces and shambling gaits put Sorrel in mind of the zombies in the movie posters she'd seen in town. "Have you noticed a lot of the people who took part in the gathering aren't feeling well today? The sister who opened up the store blamed the celebration punch."

"It was spiked."

"But Brother Rick mixed it in front of everyone. It's become part of the ritual. They would've noticed if he'd put something weird into the punch."

"Maybe." Jake didn't sound convinced.

The compound appeared deserted, apart from a group of children playing a game of tag across the other side, nearer to the children's quarters.

Jake stowed the handcarts while Sorrel entered her workshop. She came to an abrupt halt, gaze darting left and right. The faint scent of freshly mown grass and manure made her nostrils flare. The hairs at the back of her neck stood to attention. Nothing seemed disturbed. She let her breath ease out and cautiously sniffed again, trying to distinguish the alien scents. Frowning, she took two steps and inhaled again. The odor was weak, but the clump of mud and sprigs of cut grass on her normally clean floor confirmed her fears. Someone had entered her workshop while they'd been away.

Jake padded up behind her. "What is it?"

"I think someone has searched my workshop."

Jake scanned the shelves and work surfaces. He checked the area where they placed their pallet at night. "Nothing appears disturbed."

She pointed at the pieces of grass on the floor. "I wonder what they wanted. There's nothing here to alarm the most fervent Children of Nature follower."

"Maybe someone was checking sleeping arrangements."

"I pack away my pallet every morning."

"I know. Will you be okay on your own?"

"Of course I will." She waved him away, fixing a wide smile on her lips, even though the fit felt downright uncomfortable.

"I'll be back in time to take you to lunch."

She managed to widen her smile and nod, but the second he left, her grin dropped away. She ambled through her workshop, picking up jars and bottles that sat off-center. A foreign whiff of smoke snagged her attention, but it was fleeting, and she lost it once she neared her washing-up area.

The visitor had done more than sneak through her domain. They'd touched her things.

The morning passed, and Sorrel attempted to ignore the sense of violation and mixed a batch of fresh face packs along with a skin scrub. These products would provide an excuse for her to walk down to the shop tomorrow morning.

This thought brought a twinge of despondency. In the short time Jake had been here she'd grown to admire him and enjoy his company. Even if she hadn't scared Alice Bates away with her antics this morning, she'd still need to find her mother's books.

She had to face the truth. If Alice turned down her product, she'd still have to act. Brother Rick was making things increasingly uncomfortable for her at the compound. She'd turn twenty-five soon. The idea of being forced to accept one or more of the men...

Sorrel dried the last bowl and stowed it away. She removed her apron, hanging it on the peg behind the door. The time for action was now.

Chapter Nine

Jake arrived back at Sorrel's workshop half an hour before the lunch bell. She wasn't there. The counters were scrubbed clean and the usual aroma of flowers and herbs filled the room.

Childish laughter carried across the compound, drawing a grin. Jake backed out of the workshop and pulled the door shut.

A purple balloon drifted into the air and the children cheered. Another one flew after it, this one a bright green.

"Look at the balloon," one of the boys shouted.

Jake froze, dread balling in his chest as he watched an inflated condom sail through the air. It floated toward the dining room where everyone was congregating for lunch, dipping abruptly and dive-bombing a group of sisters. A second condom soared on the same trajectory, striking a brother on the back.

"Fuck," Jake said in vast understatement. Hell, he must've dropped the rest of the box the previous evening while he was running across the compound.

Pandemonium broke out, hands flashing in distress, the shriek of voices filling the air, and when a third condom sailed over the roof of the dining room, the brothers in the group burst into action, sprinting around the corner of the building to discover the source of the balloons. He was too far away to hear the exact words, but this had all the makings of a cluster fuck.

The group of children sprang apart at the men's shouts. A boy held another inflated condom, releasing it at the man's shout. This one sported red and white stripes, and the condom sped through the air in a manic arc as the air in it bled free.

At the men's shouts, the children formed a straight line. As Jake neared he could hear the men demanding answers.

"We found them," one of the bigger boys said. His right foot drew a line across the grass.

"Where?"

"Over there on the grass." The boy indicated the direction. "We're sorry."

Jake joined the group of men, wincing at each

haranguing comment they unleashed on the children.

"Are there more?" another brother demanded.

The children handed over what was left of the box.

"Go to lunch," the brother snapped. "In an orderly fashion. We'll deal with you later."

Once the children were out of earshot, the men burst into speech.

"Where did they come from?"

"Condoms! Sacrilege."

"We will get to the bottom of this. Someone brought them onto the compound."

Yep, a real cluster fuck.

Jake looked around for Sorrel and couldn't see her. He wandered after the rest of the adults and joined the end of the line waiting for food. Sorrel arrived almost ten minutes later, and he'd already started eating his meal.

"Where have you been?"

On hearing his snarl, the excited conversation at the table faded. Everyone turned to stare at Sorrel.

Her chin shot up, and she glared back at him. "I have been collecting some cuttings from my herb garden."

"Get some food." He bit off the words, the curt tone rattling his conscience free. Damn, his behavior made him no better than Brother Rick.

She turned and stomped away, joining the end of the

line.

"I don't know why you bother with her," one of the brothers commented.

Another nodded. "She's peculiar. Brother Rick lets her stay because she makes so much money for us. It helps pay for the items we can't grow or produce ourselves."

Like party pills.

"Her mother was the same. Had strange ideas. She wanted to change the ways things were done."

"What sort of ideas?" Jake asked.

The brother gestured with his fork. "She thought women should have a say in running the place." He speared his fork into a pile of salad leaves. "Women are the weaker sex. They have no experience in leadership."

Jake nodded in agreement. Let the man spout any dribble he wanted. The truth was the brother was wrong. His friends were both married to strong women. While Nikolai and Louie might posture and pretend they were protecting their wives, Jake knew better. Both men respected their wives and treated them as equal partners. Nah, this was crap—men wanting to subjugate their women and keep them barefoot and pregnant. Sandaled and pregnant in this case.

Sorrel returned with a meal and took the seat beside him. Once she was settled, Jake ran his hand across her thigh and squeezed it. He had some heavy duty apologizing in his future.

Sorrel understood why Jake had spoken to her so sternly. Her absence had worried him, and he'd reacted in a typical masculine manner, lashing out with words.

Her mother had explained it to her shortly before she'd died. It was the way of men. Their tongues waggled before their brains engaged.

She started on her meal, eating too fast, but wary of Brother Rick appearing without warning and enforcing the one meal a day edict. With half her mind on the conversation around her, she pondered her next action.

The faint tick of a clock—*tick, tick, tick*—reverberated through her mind. Yes, the next time Brother Rick left the compound she'd break into each of his rooms—his quarters and his office to search through his possessions.

She couldn't see any alternative.

"—three of them floated across the compound."

The disbelief in the words grabbed Sorrel's attention.

"Condoms. It's shocking. What is the world is coming to?" one of the sisters cried.

"Condoms?" Sorrel asked.

"The children found a box of condoms on the compound lawn." Jake's tone carried the perfect nuance of disapproval. "They thought they were balloons."

"Oh dear."

"I don't understand," one of the brothers said. "How did they get onto the compound?"

"Simple." Brother Rick spoke from behind them. "Sister Bitter, I wish to speak with you in my office."

The hall burst into a babble of speculation, white noise that didn't come close to drowning the spurt of unease rippling through Sorrel.

"Me?" She hesitated, half standing.

Jake stood. "I'll come with you."

"Just Sister Bitter," Brother Rick snapped before he strode from the dining hall.

Her hand jerked as she set down her glass of water. She hadn't done anything wrong. Despite popular opinion, condoms were not the invention of the devil.

She followed Brother Rick from the dining hall and dawdled to the room he used as an office. At the door, she paused to suck in a huge draft of air to steady her nerves. She took another breath for good luck and lifted her hand to knock. Jake appeared and pointed to indicate he'd be around the corner should she need him.

"Come in."

She entered the office to find Brother Rick plus his three closest friends. The three sat behind the large oak desk with Brother Rick. There was no chair for her. Obviously she was meant to stand in front of them like a naughty child.

"No loitering." Brother Felix jerked his bald head in an indication to hasten. "We don't have all day."

Sorrel moved closer to the desk, her quick gaze taking in the pictures on the wall, the three bottles of alcohol on a small shelf and the crystal tumblers sitting beside them.

To her right was a bookcase. It was full of books, and her breath caught as she scanned the titles. She tripped, barely catching herself before she head butted the desk.

Brother Rick's lips curved into a sneer. "You're so inept."

Sorrel focused on her sandals, all the while wishing she could flatten his pointy nose. She wasn't clumsy in the normal scheme of things.

"You wanted to see me?" She kept her voice even, proud of her steadiness when her emotions roiled like one of her potions simmering on a high heat.

"You've been delivering stock to the shop every morning this week."

She stared at him. Was that a question?

"Answer." Malicious glee fired deep in Brother Felix's blue eyes.

"Yes." Sorrel's gaze shot automatically downward, but

something stopped her from concentrating on her feet as she usually did. Slowly her gaze rose. Her eyes felt heavy as she forced them upward, awkward almost, yet pride filled her when she finally stared at Brother Rick's chin.

"Do you visit other shops while you're in town?"

"No. Why would I? I don't have—"

"Yes or no answers," Brother Felix snapped.

"Have you visited the shops this week?"

"No."

Brother Rick steepled his hands in front of him and rested his nose on top, as if he needed to consider his next question. "Tell me what you did today."

"I walked down to the town with Brother Jake this morning. I had to wait because they were late arriving. The first sister was on her own, so I helped her unpack the new stock and price it."

"Then?" Brother Felix prompted after a long pause.

"Brother Jake and I came back to the compound. I made some face packs and scrubs and spent half an hour before the lunch bell picking fresh herbs from the garden." She pressed her lips together, waiting for one of the men to speak again. The silence lengthened until she wanted to fidget. Another habit, she intended to break.

Brother Rick and his cohorts were bullies. They'd been the same way growing up, but Brother Samuel had kept them in line. With him gone, they seemed to think they could do anything. Someone needed to stand up to them, but it wouldn't be her because she had too much at stake.

Two seconds later, her conscience called bullshit on that, and she took pleasure in thinking the crude word. It was wrong to let them behave without checks, to run Children of Nature without the say-so of the rest of the residents.

She stood a fraction taller, seeking out Brother Rick's gaze and holding it. "What is this about?"

"You had an opportunity to purchase the condoms. No one else. You brought them onto the compound."

"Where would I get money?" She stated the obvious because none of the men seemed to grasp the reality. One required money to purchase goods.

"You were seen meeting one of the owners of Fancy Free. You spoke to her. No lies, Sister Bitter. I saw you myself."

"I don't have money." This time, she punctuated the words with a glare since the idea hadn't seeped through their thick heads. "Anyway, I wasn't talking to her. You know that. You heard me."

"It would be easy enough to barter some of your products," Brother Felix said.

Disbelief bloomed in Sorrel, reality slapping her across the face. Suddenly she got it. No matter what she said, they intended to stick to their version of events. A jury who'd tried and hung her, despite the fact commonsense indicated she hadn't committed the crime.

There was no point arguing.

"Do you have anything further to say in your defense?" Brother Rick was attempting a solemn judge demeanor. It wasn't working.

"Other brothers and sisters leave the compound." Including the real culprit, but she wasn't going to inform on Jake. No point in both of them getting into trouble.

Brother Rick shot her a look as dark as a nightmare and just as scary. "But none of them behave in a suspicious manner."

"How do you know?" She pretended she was speaking with Jake, a man who expected her to express her thoughts, her doubts.

Brother Rick blinked, taking a few seconds before he recovered his normal aplomb. "I have eyes everywhere."

"I see." She doubted it. If he'd seen her flout his rules, he would've confronted her sooner. He hadn't learned of her meeting with Alice and James.

Another silence fell, but Sorrel could've sworn she felt the pulse of Brother Rick's glee, his pleasure in what was going to come next. Yes, she could see the sparkle of a secret about to burst from him.

"Sister Bitter you will leave the compound."

"But I went to the store this morning. They have enough stock to last the rest of the week."

"You misunderstand, Sister Bitter. Let me be blunt. You're no longer welcome to live in the compound."

"But—"

He held up his hand in a demand for silence. "Don't try to contact anyone here because, as far as we're concerned, you're no one. Nothing. You are officially shunned. You may leave now."

CHAPTER TEN

JAKE CURSED IN QUIET frustration. He couldn't hear a bloody thing—except footsteps approaching him. He retreated, noiseless in his sandaled feet. Anxiety churned his gut because Sorrel had been in the office for a while now. She knew he was waiting for her. Surely she'd shout if she required aid.

"Brother Jake, we require help with a task." Brother Felix called from the doorway of the building Jake had hastily exited. Brother John and Brother Tyrone followed Brother Felix outside.

Jake hesitated. Maybe he'd take the opportunity to subtly grill Brother Felix for information. But he hated leaving Sorrel with Brother Rick.

You weren't there for Greg. Jake shook himself, although

he heard Greg's confident voice ripple through his memories. *No prob. It'll be a breeze.*

This was a different situation. They were in New Zealand, not in a war zone. Sorrel would be fine.

"Damn, I forgot the keys." Brother Felix's round face creased in a scowl.

His ears pricked at the mention of keys, but his unease lingered. "I wanted to see Sister Sorrel."

"She's still with Brother Rick, discussing extra help during the afternoon. Meet me at the truck, and I'll grab the keys. You can *talk* once you return."

Jake's hands fisted at Brother Felix's smartass attitude, but he forced back his instinctive reaction, aware this might be the breakthrough he needed.

"Come on." Brother Tyrone jerked his bald head in the direction of the truck.

Jake nodded agreeably and set off with them. Sorrel would be here on his return.

A few minutes later Brother Felix came jogging out of the office. Sorrel and Brother Rick exited seconds after him, and some of Jake's apprehension faded. She was okay. He'd speak to her later.

They drove from the compound with curiosity sitting like a fidgety child on Jake's shoulders. He concentrated on the passing scenery, picking out landmarks to remember to help Luke identify their route through Sloan. Brother Felix turned the truck and drove along the main street of the town.

It was pretty, as towns went, with baskets of red, white and purple flowers hanging from poles. No litter clogged the gutters, and there was a noticeable lack of graffiti on the fences and buildings. The locals stared as Brother Felix drove down the street.

"Where are we going?" Jake asked.

"We have some business that needs taking care of," Brother Felix said.

"I hope it's not too physical." Jake frowned. "I'm still not as fit as I was before I was sick. The doctors told me it would take a while to return to full fitness."

"We'll manage between the four of us," Brother Felix said.

He seemed to do most of the talking while Brothers John and Tyrone stared at the passing scenery.

They drove past the police station, but Jake didn't see Luke. Another thought occurred, one that brought a scowl. He glanced at Brother Felix's broad back beneath his robe. Brother Felix was big but on the chubby side. Jake was confident he could take him in a fight. The other two men were smaller than Jake. On their own, he could deal with them, but if they jumped him together, he might have problems.

The shops and office buildings gave way to houses and countryside. Jake was no wiser as to their destination. They pulled off the main road onto a gravel one. The road wound around the base of a hill before entering a plantation of pine trees. Soon the road petered out, and Brother Felix halted the truck.

Jake climbed out of the vehicle with the others. A low, mournful *moo* carried on the wind.

Bingo.

· ❤ · ❤ · ❤ · ❤ · ❤ ·

SORREL WATCHED JAKE DRIVE away with Brother Rick's friends, her heart sinking to a level near her sandals.

Brother Rick remained at her side. When she turned toward her workshop, he grasped her elbow and directed her forcibly in the direction of the gates.

Heck, what did it matter?

She'd wanted to leave the compound.

But not like this, without her plans in place.

Not without her mother's books, and definitely not without the battered recipe book she'd left sitting on the counter in her workshop.

A warning prickle started behind her eyes. She bit on her

inner lip, the jolt of pain refocusing her. She wouldn't give Brother Rick the satisfaction.

She wrenched from his touch and marched away, head held high.

"Open the gates," Brother Rick called.

Two of the elderly brothers were on security, and it took them ages and much grunting and straining to unfasten the catch and push open the gates. Sorrel wanted to help them. A decent man would've helped, but Brother Rick remained silent at her side, judge, jury and now security guard seeing the accused off the premises.

Finally the gates opened.

Sorrel marched through and didn't look back.

She heard the gates creak shut behind her, heard the puzzled questions from men she'd known since she was a young child, but she kept walking.

Once she was out of sight of the compound, she sank to the ground, tears streaming down her face. What in the stars did she do now?

·♥·♥·♥·♥·♥·

"I DIDN'T REALIZE WE had stock up here." Jake turned to read their expressions.

Brother Felix lifted his shoulders in a careless shrug. "We

have several operations outside the main compound."

The rumble of another vehicle sounded. The brothers remained relaxed, which meant they'd been expecting an arrival.

"Right on time," Brother Felix said.

They wandered over to the paddock and studied the grazing cattle. Jake counted them. Four head. He couldn't see ear tags or brands from this distance. Not that it mattered. He had the location and that would help Luke put a stop to the rustling. A set of basic yards stood to their left.

"Which beast do you want slaughtered?" the new arrival queried.

Brother Felix shrugged. "Doesn't matter. Just pick one."

"Usual terms?" the man demanded.

"Usual terms," Brother Felix confirmed and pulled a wad of notes from his robe pocket and handed them over.

"What do you want me to do?" Jake couldn't figure out why they'd brought him with them. It seemed strange after the previous secrecy. His gut was shooting him warning messages, yet he forged ahead, playing things by ear.

This was an opportunity to get the evidence he needed to kick their robe-covered butts.

The chance to free Sorrel to leave the cult.

He'd take her with him. God, he couldn't believe he'd

known her for less than a week. He felt as if he'd known her his entire life, that she was the one he'd been waiting for all along.

"We need help with loading and the clean up afterward," Brother Felix said. "Actually, can you grab both the tarpaulins from the truck? We'll need one for the offal and one for the meat."

"Sure." Jake limped back to the truck. He considered texting Luke, but he wasn't sure how much time he'd have alone, and he wasn't one hundred percent sure the second arrival had come on his own. He glanced at the number plate and frowned on noticing the mud obscuring the numbers. On purpose? Jake wasn't sure. Perhaps the make and model would be enough. The color. Besides, he had a description of the man too. If he was a local, Luke would know him.

He retrieved the tarpaulins and returned to join the men. One of the animals—a black-and-white one—was in the yard now. A shot fired. The animal went down.

During the next hour, Jake helped the men dress the beast. They loaded the carcass onto the truck, secured a cover over it, and followed the SUV down the gravel road. Instead of driving back to Sloan, they turned toward Auckland, stopping on the outskirts of Papakura, the suburb on the very edge of the city boundaries, and where both Nikolai and Louie lived with their wives. Jake was familiar with the area since much of their army training had taken part in Papakura. It was home base for the SAS.

But he didn't comment, just stayed quiet in the back, taking careful note of their surroundings and where they were going.

They pulled into a driveway and drove past a white bungalow to a huge iron shed behind. Jake helped the other men carry the beast into the shed. The stranger opened another door, and a wave of cold sprang out at Jake. They lifted the beast, hanging it on a hook in the chiller.

A camera flashed in Jake's face. He frowned at Brother Felix. "What the hell?"

"Just to make sure you won't discuss today. Some insurance."

The other men laughed, the humor bearing a distinctly nasty edge. It raised Jake's hackles.

"Why the fuck would I tell anyone?" Jake demanded. "I've decided I want to live at Children of Nature."

Brother Felix smirked. "Good to know. Brother Rick will be pleased to hear you've decided to join us."

· ♥ · ♥ · ♥ · ♥ · ♥ ·

After ten minutes Sorrel forced herself to stand. She sniffed, wiped the back of her hand across her eyes, balancing on teetering legs. No time to dither. Already it was late afternoon, and she wasn't sure where to seek shelter for tonight.

Shunned.

Stars, what age did Brother Rick think this was?

Fury struck her then, strengthening her weak resolve and shoring up her wonky knees. Brother Rick wasn't going to get away with this. *Shunning her*. He might think he was the boss of her, the boss of all of them, but by the time she finished he'd learn otherwise. Yeah, he'd rue the day.

Sorrel started stomping toward town. The walk seemed much longer without Jake's company. Jake. Brother Rick had purposely distracted Jake with a chore so he could expel her from Children of Nature with minimal fuss.

The more she thought about Brother Rick's actions, the angrier she became, tension reverberating through her body with each furious stomp. Brother Rick was a terrible leader. He'd changed the group and not for the good of the members.

The town came into view. Sorrel marched past their shop. Several women inside were looking at and buying her products. Maybe she could set up her own business at a later date.

But right now, she had something else on her mind. She strode past the florist shop, past the cafe and the town hall. She stomped right to the police station, thumped up the front steps and pushed through the door.

"I want to speak to the policeman in charge please."

· ❤ · ❤ · ❤ · ❤ · ❤ ·

JAKE AND THE OTHER brothers arrived back as the ring of the dinner bell echoed through the compound.

"I'm gonna take a shower before I go for dinner," Jake said, after climbing from the rear of the truck. The camera flashed in his face, catching his bloody robe and disreputable appearance. He knew what he looked like—a man who'd helped butcher and dress a stolen beast. "Enough with the fuckin' camera," he snarled, turning away. Ten steps into his charge across the compound, he realized he wasn't limping, and that pissed him off even more.

Jake stopped by the men's quarters to grab a clean robe. In the ablution block, he stripped, taking special care not to drop his knife or phone. The water still ran cold as he stepped under the showerhead. Maybe it would help cool his temper before he gave in to his urge to throttle Brother

Rick.

He couldn't wait to tell Sorrel about Brother Rick's latest move. The man was a dictator, ruling over his small kingdom. Jake couldn't wait to take the bastard down.

Garbed in clean clothes, and firmly back in character, Jake hobbled into the dining hall. As he joined the line waiting for their food, he scanned the room for Sorrel and ignored the men who whispered of his nightmares and violent tendencies. He couldn't see her, but she'd been here at lunch, which meant she'd eaten her one meal of the day, the second actually, not that he'd tell. Jake snarled under his breath at the injustice, not quietly enough because the sisters in the line in front of him put a larger gap between them.

He slapped an extra two dinner rolls on his plate plus more roast beef and ham than he could eat. Scanning the room, he noted it was fuller than usual. He dropped into an empty seat and filled the two rolls with meat before eating his meal. Damn, it wasn't right enjoying a meal if Sorrel went hungry.

Brother Rick entered the dining hall, his three friends following him—a robed entourage.

"All he needs is a swirling cape."

His snide comment earned Jake a passel of glares from the brothers and sisters who shared the table with him. So shoot him. He didn't give a crap. Leaning back in his chair, he allowed a sardonic smile to curve his lips.

The dining hall fell silent as Brother Rick climbed onto the dais at the far end of the room. He stood there, presenting a calm front. "I'm sorry to interrupt your dinner, but something important has occurred. I felt I needed to tell you before our next weekly meeting." He paused for a long moment.

Jake snorted, earning himself a heap more censure in the form of sniffs and glares.

"I'm sad and disappointed to announce I've had to take an unusual step today." He paused again for dramatic effect. "I'm sure many of you witnessed the terrible episode before the lunch hour." The tone of his voice changed to one of distinct disapproval. "This…transgression goes against everything Children of Nature stands for. Everything. Of course, I investigated, and this afternoon, I officially expelled the culprit from the compound."

Foreboding filled Jake. He straightened abruptly, steeling himself for the rest of Brother Rick's announcement.

"Sister Bitter is no longer a member of Children of Nature."

A hum of chatter sprang up in the dining hall, echoing

the buzz in Jake's head. Brother Jake had forced Sorrel to leave the compound, like a damn chick pushed from the nest by a bigger and meaner cuckoo.

"Where has she gone?"

"Did she apologize?"

"Will she be back?"

"Who is going to supply the shop with products?"

The questions fired at Brother Rick in staccato beats, one after the other. *Bang. Bang. Bang.*

Brother Rick smiled and held up his hands in a gesture for quiet.

"Sister Bitter will not be back. She is shunned."

Silence greeted his announcement then everyone burst into more excited chatter.

"Shunning doesn't happen very often," a sister said.

"Condoms." A brother shuddered. "It's against God's will. We are put on this earth to beget children."

Jake scowled. The man would beget his fist if he didn't shut his mouth. Jake jumped to his feet, unwilling to listen to another word. Shunned? How the fuck could Brother Rick live with himself?

"Brother Jake, are you going somewhere?" Brother Rick called.

"Call of nature," Jake gritted out. God, he had to get out of here before he blew his cover. Now, more than ever, he needed to keep to character. He exaggerated his gait, listing from left to right like a drunken sailor.

"You should go to the clinic," Brother Rick called. "It sounds as if you have a bladder problem."

"I'll be back shortly." Jake burst through the dining room doors, the breeze outside flapping his robe around his bare legs. He needed to find somewhere private so he could ring Luke. He scratched at his chin. Damn beard itched all the time. The day he could shave it off would be a celebration.

He glanced over his shoulder and couldn't make anyone following him. In the ablution block, he checked the stalls and cursed under his breath. The last one was occupied.

After using the facilities, he headed back to the dining room. Sorrel was smart. She was resourceful. She'd find shelter, somewhere to stay until she managed to sort herself out.

"Ah, there you are," Brother Felix said when Jake entered the dining room. "Brother Rick wants to see you in his office."

Jake nodded and continued farther into the dining room.

"Now," Brother Felix said.

"I haven't finished my dinner."

"I'll get the sisters in the kitchen to box it up for you to have later."

Jake turned slowly, scanned the man. He had a hell of a poker face. Jake nodded. "Sure. I'll come now."

Outside the dining room, Brothers John and Tyrone fell into step with Jake, flanking him.

"You attending the meeting too?" Jake asked.

"We're witnesses," Brother Tyrone said.

"I see." It was shakedown time. Hell, maybe he could help Luke get the bastard for blackmail and extortion as well as cattle rustling. The thought made his mood perk right up.

Outside the closed office door, the trio paused, and Brother John knocked on the door.

A snort escaped Jake unbidden. "Why do I feel like I'm back at school, visiting the principal?"

"Quiet," Brother Felix barked, coming up behind them. "Have a little respect."

Respect had to be earned. Wisely Jake kept his mouth shut.

"Come in," Brother Rick called.

Jake stepped inside, hesitating at the lack of chairs. Better and better. Brother Rick intended to treat him as a lackey.

Yes, sir. No, sir.

A snort of derision pressured his chest, but he didn't

allow himself the luxury of releasing his emotions. Better men than Brother Rick had interrogated him and failed. Let him do his worst.

"Thank you for helping today," Brother Rick started. "I understand you've decided to stay with us."

"That's right."

"Then I won't need to use any...persuasion to ensure your loyalty."

"Of course not," Jake said. "I enjoy it here. I feel right at home, even though I haven't been here long."

"Good. Good." Brother Rick clasped his hands behind his head, leaning back in his chair. "Do you have any idea about what tasks you want to perform around here?"

"I don't mind. I'm happy to work in any area I'm required. I enjoy variety." Somehow he managed to get the words out without choking.

Brother Felix eyed his legs. "Is your limp still improving or is that as good as it will get?"

"The doctor I saw indicated it will never be a hundred percent again." The truth, even though it pained him to voice the fact.

"Pity," Brother Rick said. "That might make you a liability in some situations."

Jake shrugged. What the hell did they expect him to say? "Did you need me for anything else tonight?" He wanted to get Luke to find Sorrel, to make sure she was in a safe place.

"There is the contribution of your assets to Children of Nature."

"Of course," Jake said. "I'll need to go into town tomorrow morning to withdraw my funds. I can let you have them tomorrow. Is that all right?"

"You could transfer your funds via the Internet."

"You have Internet access here?" Jake didn't try to hide his surprise.

"I intend to take Children of Nature into the future."

"I see."

Brother Rick's gaze was piercing, but he couldn't hide the faint tinge of greediness in his expression. "Which bank are you with?"

"I'm sorry, but it will have to wait." Jake pulled out a suitable expression of regret. "I haven't registered for Internet banking. Computers give me headaches. I'll get you cash as soon as the bank opens tomorrow."

Brother Rick gave a curt nod. "Excellent. That's all for tonight. I'll see you in the morning."

Jake accepted his dismissal with good grace. He exited the office, and by habit, he limped over to Sorrel's workshop. It was as good a place for privacy as anywhere.

In the workshop, Jake switched on one lamp and

checked the place, making sure there was no one present to eavesdrop on him.

Once assured he was alone, Jake pulled out the cell phone Luke had given him. He pushed speed dial and waited anxiously for someone to pick up.

"Luke?"

"Yeah."

"Have you seen Sorrel? They kicked her out of the cult while I was away. Have you seen her?" The words wouldn't stop spouting out of his mouth. His hand trembled, and he clenched it harder around the phone. "Luke?"

"She's spending the night in our spare room."

Jake slumped against the wall, relief buckling his knees. "Is she okay?"

Luke chuckled, and Jake heard the rustle of paper. "Sorrel marched into the police station this afternoon and dropped a bombshell. Have you got anything for me?"

"What bombshell?"

"According to Sorrel, Brother Rick might be responsible for the death of the original cult leader."

"Does she have proof?" And more to the point, why the hell hadn't she told him when they'd discussed the matter earlier? Or was she merely making trouble for Brother Rick?

"Only her intuition. She wants us to search Brother

Rick's office."

"Maybe this is a way for her to regain her personal property." The realization sent a sliver of pain darting straight to his chest. She hadn't trusted him to keep his promise. "I've got info for you." Jake rattled off the details of his day and directions to where they'd left the beast in the chiller. "There's something else. They took photos of me, photos to make it look as if I was responsible for killing and butchering the animal. Tonight they were ready to blackmail me into joining the cult. When I informed them I'd decided to join the group, they wanted me to transfer my money to their account right away. I got the impression they're desperate for money."

"Good."

"What is Sorrel going to do? Can I talk to her?"

"She's taking a shower," Luke said. "Can you get into town tomorrow some time?"

"Yeah, they want me to get my money for them tomorrow. But they seemed so desperate. It wouldn't surprise me if they offered to drive me down and waited for the cash."

"Could you put them off for a day?"

"Why? What are you thinking?" Jake hated to stay on the compound for longer than necessary.

"If I could get a search warrant, we could serve it while

they're away in town. That way I could take Sorrel with me. She knows the place and would be helpful."

"I don't want Sorrel getting mixed up in this."

Luke sucked in a quick breath. "Holy hell."

"What?" Jake said. "What's wrong?"

"Sorrel just walked into the room. She...she..." Luke trailed off with a soft whistle.

"You're married," Jake snapped. "Keep your damn eyes off."

A long pause. "Ah, so that's the way of it. I wondered."

"Don't. Have you got the tests back on those pills?"

"Not yet," Luke said. "I should have them next week."

The creak of one of the steps outside made Jake mutter a curse. "Gotta go. I'll try to see you tomorrow." He clicked the phone shut and tucked it out of sight under his robe. He dropped to his knees and bowed his head, muttering random things out loud.

"Please I seek guidance on this matter," he murmured. Meantime every one of his senses scrambled to let him know how many people loitered outside the door.

At the last moment, instinct propelled him to remove the cell phone from his person and tuck it out of sight.

"I need to know how I should act, what I should do." Memories of Greg flooded him, the wounds of loss painful and tender.

The door behind him flew open without warning. Brother Felix and Brother Tyrone stood in the doorway.

Jake gave an obvious start and hoped he hadn't overdone it. He cowered a fraction before straightening.

"What are you doing?" Brother Felix demanded. "Who were you talking to?"

"I was praying." Jake remained on his knees, despite the silent urge propelling him to stand to gain even footing with the two men towering over him.

"Why are you doing it here?" Brother Felix remained suspicious.

"Habit." Jake kept his voice low and timid. "I knew I'd be alone down here."

"Search the building," Brother Felix snapped.

Jake forced himself not to react. He climbed laboriously to his feet, grunting for effect. "I may have overdone things today."

"You were talking to someone," Brother Felix said. "Who?"

"I was talking to God." As much as it galled Jake to buckle under anyone's gaze, he forced himself to do it this time. He stared at his sandals in the same manner Sorrel employed.

"Put your hands in the air."

"Why?" Jake kept his focus on Brother Felix, sensing

he was the more dangerous of the two. Brother Tyrone was busy searching the workshop, but not in a systematic manner. Jake was pretty confident he wouldn't find the phone.

"I want to search your person."

Damn, he'd find the knife. Too bad. While he preferred a weapon of some sort, there was more than one way to kill a man. "W-why?" Fuck, he hated acting the ninny. Luke was gonna buy him a beer or two after this stint. At least Sorrel was safe, out of their clutches. Just a bit longer, he told himself as he raised his hands in the air.

Brother Felix patted him down. His eyes narrowed on discovering Jake's knife. "What's this?"

"A knife," Jake said.

"Why do you have a knife?"

"Habit. It comes in handy for all sorts of things."

Brother Tyrone concluded his half-hearted search and rejoined them. He laughed now in disbelief. "What sort of things?"

"Well." Jake paused, flicking through his mind for suitable reasons. "While I've been helping Sister Bitter I've used it to cut sprigs of herbs and leaves. I've cut rope, strips of cloth to bind wounds. I've used it to quarter apples and cut meat." Surely that was enough bullshit to bury them?

"We don't condone weapons on this compound,"

Brother Felix snapped.

"But it's not a weapon." Jake's gaze shot to his sandals again. They were dusty and still bore dirt from this afternoon. Maybe he should clean them tomorrow.

"Give it to me," Brother Felix said.

"I...okay." Jake slipped his hand under his robe and removed both knife and sheath. That sucker was sharp and he wouldn't want anyone to hurt themselves.

"I will be informing Brother Rick of this."

"Of course. I'm sorry. I didn't realize I was breaking the rules. The last thing I want to do is upset anyone."

"You should leave the workshop. This place is out of bounds until Brother Rick decides what is to be done with it."

Surprise hit Jake at the decision. "I thought the shop earned Children of Nature a tidy income."

"You thought wrong. The place doesn't break even."

Because for some reason Brother Rick had told the shop staff to practically give away Sorrel's products.

"Of course. I'm a newcomer here. I believed what I was told."

Brother Felix snorted. "Sister Bitter lives in a fantasy world. I hate to say it, but she's as crazy as her mother."

It was the first Jake had heard this particular accusation. Brother Rick and his cohorts went out of their way to belittle Sorrel at every opportunity, and he still had no idea why. If he added murder into the mix, perhaps he could make better sense of matters.

"She did say a few weird things," he allowed.

"Like what?"

"I hate to repeat gossip."

"Right," Brother Felix said. "You're coming with me. You can tell Brother Rick what Sister Bitter told you."

Hell, he didn't want another interrogation tonight. "Nothing that I believed. Could it wait until morning? I'm very tired. Sometimes my leg pains me, and I have trouble sleeping."

"Very well," Brother Felix said. "We'll speak with you in the morning. Brother Tyrone will escort you to the men's quarters."

Well hell. That put paid to his explorations tonight. He needed to get into Brother Rick's office to get a look at their financial records, and now he should look for proof to implicate Brother Rick in a murder as well.

"Of course. I would welcome the company."

"Don't come here again," Brother Felix said. "If you wish to pray, you can use the spiritual room."

"Oh? Where is that?" He turned to Brother Tyrone. "Is it near the men's quarters?"

"It's near the office. If you're up to walking that far, I

can show you tonight."

"My leg is tired," Jake said. "But I do need to pray. I find my faith very comforting."

Brother Felix turned for the door, and Jake hobbled after him, exaggerating his limp. He lurched to one side, fell to the floor, snatched up his phone and thrust it into his pocket in one smooth move. "Oh dear. Perhaps I should retire for the evening. Yes, I fear I have overdone things today."

He needed to get into the office, and preferably tonight. Something was up, and he intended to get to the bottom of the conspiracy.

CHAPTER ELEVEN

FOR THE FIRST TIME in her life, Sorrel slept in a bed in a bedroom by herself. A soft snore interrupted her thoughts. Okay, she had a small spotted dog for company. The creature seemed to have taken a liking to her and had followed her around all evening. Another first in a multitude of others.

Luke and Janaya had been kind to her, instantly offering her a room for as long as she needed. The loss of her few possessions—well, they could be replaced eventually. All she wanted was her mother's recipe book from the workshop and her mother's other books, and she now knew where to find them.

"Stupid," she muttered.

The dog stirred, its eyes flickering open. It gave a soft

whine.

"It's all right." Sorrel smoothed her hand over the dog's silky head.

She set down the novel Janaya had given her to read and switched off the bedside lamp, plunging the room into darkness. She closed her eyes, physically tired, although her mind darted in a hundred directions at once.

The compound. Brother Rick. Jake.

Ah, yes. The big one.

Jake.

Worry gnawed her, contributing to her wakeful state. Was Jake all right? She didn't trust Brother Rick. He'd been a sneaky child and hadn't changed during the intervening years. She'd told Luke her suspicions regarding Rick murdering Brother Samuel, and Luke had told her since the coroner had already ruled an accidental death it was unlikely they'd manage to charge Brother Rick with the crime.

But evidently Brother Rick was up to his ears in bad things. Luke hadn't given her full details, but Sorrel knew enough from Jake to make educated guesses.

Restless, she turned over, wriggling to get comfortable. She missed Jake's body warmth, his arm around her waist as they cuddled. How was that possible? She hadn't known him for long.

She must've fallen asleep because the next thing she knew there was a light tap, and Janaya popped her head around the bedroom door.

"Are you awake?"

The dog made a grumpy growl, and Janaya laughed.

"I never sleep this late."

"Breakfast is almost ready. I rang Alice, and she asked if I could drop you at the factory later this morning. I thought we'd meet my aunt for coffee and do some quick clothes shopping before I leave you at Fancy Free. What do you say?"

"I don't have any money."

"I can give you some," Janaya said. "Enough to buy clothes. You can't walk around in my old sweat pants all the time."

"A loan," Sorrel said in a firm voice. "I would appreciate a loan."

Two hours later, she walked out of Kellie Anne's Ladies Wear, dressed in a pair of skinny black jeans and a body-hugging red shirt that showcased her assets. Beneath the outer layer, she'd donned lacy black underwear. On her feet, she wore a pair of black leather boots with a bit of a heel.

"I feel sexy," she blurted, tilting her head a fraction so her loose blonde hair fell forward to cover her chagrined expression.

"You look sexy too," Janaya assured her.

Janaya's aunt, Hinekiri, laughed and clapped her hands together in a delighted manner. "I doubt any of those robe people will recognize you." She was an older version of Janaya, blonde with violet eyes and a vivacious manner.

"We're about to find out," Janaya said, her tone grim. "Jake didn't think they'd let him come into town on his own."

Sorrel froze when she saw the blue truck driving toward them.

Janaya gave her a sharp nudge in the middle of the back. "Keep walking. They're not expecting to see you dressed in street clothes. They won't give you a second thought, except to notice how sexy you look."

Jake noticed her. She felt his gaze, a sensual stroke over her entire body as Brother Rick drove past. Heat suffused her but not shame.

"Ah," Janaya said in an undertone. "I should've known Jake would be the exception. He's a soldier, and they're trained to observe."

"We need to stop at the bakery." Hinekiri gestured across the street. "There's a board meeting today. Alice told me to make sure I arrived with a cake."

Janaya snorted, an inelegant sound coming from the

pretty blonde. "The board at Fancy Free consists of retirees. They spend their days making a nuisance of themselves and eating cake."

"Do you think Alice will give me a tour?"

"Aren't you against condoms?" Janaya's brows lifted in a teasing manner. "I've seen you picketing the factory."

"I can't speak out against condoms if I've used them." Sorrel clapped her hand over her mouth in an effort to hide her embarrassment.

Hinekiri chuckled, a fan of fine lines radiating from the corners of her violet eyes. "You should try some of their other products. They're lots of fun."

"I'm sure Alice will show you around," Janaya said.

Sorrel nodded and followed the two women in a bit of a daze. It was the first time people sought her opinion and listened to her reply. In the clothes shop, they'd offered honest advice when she had no clue.

A glance over her shoulder told her the truck had pulled up outside the bank. Jake climbed out, sending a quick look in her direction before entering the bank behind Brother Rick. She could have sworn he smiled.

After visiting the bakery and purchasing a gigantic carrot cake, Janaya and Hinekiri ushered her back to their car, and they drove to Fancy Free.

This morning a group of men and women picketed the

entrance, waving their signs about the perils of condoms. Sorrel stared back with interest. Not one of the brothers or sisters recognized her.

"I feel invisible," she said while they waited for the gates to swing open to admit their vehicle.

"You might have been before." Janaya smiled. "But people will notice you now. Normal people that is."

"Especially men," Hinekiri piped up from the passenger seat.

"I don't want men to notice me."

Janaya cocked her head. "What do you want?"

Sorrel didn't hesitate. "I want to be my own person. I want to make my decisions. If some of my decisions are bad ones, it's okay, as long as I make them myself."

"You want independence." Hinekiri nodded. "I understand, but it isn't necessary to close yourself off to get the freedom you desire. Some men like their women to stand at their sides as partners."

"But not all," Sorrel said. "I've had my share of bossy men telling me what to do. I'm not going to put up with that again."

"Nor should you have to." Janaya pulled up in a parking space reserved for visitors. "This is us. Let's go."

"We're here," Hinekiri trilled, leading the way into a room full of people. They sat around a large oval table, chattering to rival a flock of noisy sparrows. The scent of freshly brewed coffee wafted in the air.

"Oh, good. You're here. Sorrel? Is that you?" Alice advanced with a smile of astonishment coloring her expression. "It is. You look fantastic. Everyone, this is Sorrel Thyme. She invented the cream we're discussing today."

"I brought a cake as requested." Hinekiri set it in front of her husband, Richard, who Sorrel had met earlier at breakfast. "You can guard it. Janaya and I are off to Auckland to do some shopping."

Richard's brows rose. "Should I worry about my wallet?"

"Of course." Janaya grinned and waggled her fingers. "We'll see you later this evening, Sorrel. Luke or Richard will give you a lift back to the house after you've finished here."

Sorrel hovered inside the doorway, unsure of what she should do.

"Come and sit by me," an elderly Māori lady ordered. She was busy knitting a sock in an eye-popping lime green and purple. "My name is Harriet. Would you like a cup of coffee?"

Sorrel nodded. "Yes, please."

Alice performed quick introductions. "Harriet." She

pointed at the knitting lady. "This is Sam Glengarry, Katarina Wilson, Ben Kumar and Joseph Craig. You've met Richard already, and James will be here soon. He got held up by a phone call from one of our distributors."

Sam had a full head of grizzled hair. Katarina possessed startling pale blue eyes, Ben hailed from India, and Joseph reminded her of a pixie with his bald head and pointy ears.

Harriet finished a row and turned her knitting around. "Go and help yourself to coffee and come back. I can't wait to hear about your invention. It'll be so exciting to have another product to test."

"Did you want some more coffee?" Sorrel asked.

"Bless you, dear. That would be lovely."

It was so nice not being ordered around. Sorrel fetched the coffee and sat beside Harriet.

James arrived and slipped into an empty seat.

"Are we ready?" Alice glanced around the table.

"We will be as soon as Richard hands out slices of cake," Joseph declared.

Alice rolled her eyes. "By all means. Let's distribute the cake so we can concentrate."

Five minutes later, silence fell, and Alice started the meeting. "I've already introduced you to Sorrel. She approached us recently with a concept for a new product. We've conducted initial tests and compared it to other products on the market. Sorrel's cream is new and creative." She beamed at Sorrel, excitement dancing in her eyes. "And it works beautifully."

"What does this cream do?" one of the elderly gents asked.

Alice grinned. "It seems to stimulate nerve endings, and it brings on very intense orgasms, especially if combined with good foreplay."

"Do we have to discuss your sex secrets?" Ben sounded crabby, his brows almost meeting between his eyes, but Sorrel could see suppressed humor lurking in him.

"Ben, you know about foreplay." Harriet clicked her knitting needles. "You're not clueless. I discussed it with your wife when we were comparing our impressions of the new vibrator design. She told me—"

"Don't start," James warned. "We have a lot to get through during this meeting."

"Do you have samples?" Katerina's pale blue eyes glinted with interest. "I can't wait to try this wonder cream. Where is it applied? On and around the clitoris or somewhere else?"

"Sorrel? Would you answer this one?" Alice prompted.

Sorrel willed the rush of blood to keep from her face. It didn't work. "You can apply the cream anywhere on the body. Nipples, private parts. It's good if you use the cream in a massage." When no one made fun of her, she added, "The cream is very versatile. My mother and I created the cream to help sore and aching joints and went from there."

Alice nodded encouragement, and Sorrel's confidence took a leap. She might not have a home, but she'd found a temporary place to stay and possessed skills to support herself given time. No matter what Brother Rick thought, she wasn't useless.

"How does it work?" Harriet stirred in her seat with a flourish of her knitting needles.

"Basically, we used a combination of herbs to stimulate blood flow," Sorrel said.

The man with a full head of grizzled hair frowned. "Is the cream safe? We don't want people dropping off from over excitement."

"Our tests show there's nothing harmful in the product," Alice said. "Of course we will do further tests should we decide to go ahead with production."

"All the ingredients in the cream are natural."

"Would it be possible for you to make another batch for us?" Alice asked.

"I could, but I need my herbal supplies." She paused, catching her bottom lip between her teeth as reality struck her in the middle of her chest. The tightness made it hard to draw breath for a second. "Everything I need to make a new batch is at the compound, but they've forbidden me to return. It'll take me a while to collect more herbs and dry them."

"Richard," James said in a crisp voice. "What rights does she have to obtain her supplies? Can they legally stop her from retrieving them?"

"Who collected the herbs?"

"I did everything on my own. Brother Rick took pleasure in making things difficult for me. I made all the products by myself, at least until Jake arrived at the compound."

"I'll see what I can do," Richard said.

"How long have you been with the cult, dear?" Katarina's eyes were full of curiosity.

"All my life. I was born there."

Richard rubbed his jaw, his manner thoughtful. "Does anyone else know how to make your products?"

"Yeah, how will they stock their store?" Alice asked.

Sorrel shrugged away her pain. "It's not my problem."

"You could always set up your own shop in opposition," Ben suggested.

"I'll need to find a job and earn some money before I decide what to do with my future."

"Oh," Alice said. "I assumed you'd work for Fancy Free. Don't you want to?"

"I—" Sudden tears welled at her eyes, the wash of emotion tightening her chest again. "I'd love to work here, but what would I do? I'm not qualified to...all I know is herbs."

"We'll need your help with the cream." Harriet's knitting needles sparkled silver in a ray of sun.

"It's time to think about our Valentine's Day promotion and also our Christmas promotion for next year," Alice said. "I wondered if we could do small gift boxes featuring some of your soaps, bath bombs and other products along with some of our products."

"Good idea." Katarina nodded approval.

"Maybe you could do a play on words with bombs and orgasms," Joseph said. "Seems to me that might be a good marketing angle."

"I think that's a great idea." Ben dusted cake crumbs off his hands. "We've become known for our clever holiday advertising. This would work."

"Can you make the bath bombs into rude shapes?" Sam demanded.

Alice tapped her pen on a memo pad. "What sort of rude shapes?"

"A penis shape might work packed with our condoms," James said what they were all thinking.

Everyone turned to stare at Sorrel. "I can make almost

any shape as long as I have a mold. I mean the design can't be too fiddly, but I remember my mother telling me about the carrot-shaped bombs she made one time for Easter."

Richard barked out a sudden laugh. "You could do egg-shaped bombs and package them with condoms. I like the irony of it all since condoms are designed to prevent eggs and sperm meeting."

Sorrel closed her gaping mouth. She couldn't believe the discussions and the banter flying around the boardroom table. These were men and women who were confident and comfortable in their skins.

Alice smiled. "So are you willing to join this madhouse?"

"Yes, please."

"Pooh." Joseph waved his hand. "Ask them what they're paying you first. And discuss your hours."

"We can discuss that at our meeting," James said. "No need to make a decision now. We'll give you the contract to take away and think about for a few days."

Sorrel nodded, but she'd already decided she wanted to work here with people who weren't afraid to offer their opinions or listen to others.

Alice interrupted the chatter to hand out tiny pots of her cream and instructions on what she wanted them to try.

The rest of the day passed in a blink. Alice and James spoke with her about her cream and gave her an agreement to sign, since she'd already decided to take a job with them. The amount of her remuneration brought tears to her eyes, and all she could do was nod dumbly. It was either that or cry.

"Ready for a tour around the den of iniquity?" Alice asked.

"I'm looking forward to it."

"I hear the children discovered Jake's box of condoms." Alice chuckled, a rich, infectious sound that had Sorrel's lips twitching. "I would have loved to have seen that."

"I missed it, even though I was the one who got the blame."

"The event will go down in the history of Children of Nature. You'll be famous."

"You should probably make that infamous," Sorrel said drily.

"Don't worry. By the time I finish with you today, you'll be beyond redemption. You can't work for us as an inventor without knowing about our existing products. Have you tried a vibrator before?"

Sorrel shook her head. "I'd never seen a condom before the other night."

"I'll give you clear instructions with everything," Alice

told her. "If you have any questions, all you need to do is ask."

· ♥ · ♥ · ♥ · ♥ · ♥ ·

"WHAT DO YOU MEAN he can't get his money out today?" Brother Rick demanded with an edge to his voice.

The teller explained again in a calm voice that the particular investment relating to Jake's account required ten days' notice before the money could be accessed.

"But we need the money today."

Curiosity roused in Jake. Brother Rick seemed on the verge of panic, and Jake had no idea why. "That's okay," he told the teller. "Please do whatever is necessary to give notice, and I'll come back in ten days."

"Do you have another account?"

"I do, but there's only a hundred and five dollars in it."

"Withdraw a hundred," Brother Rick ordered.

Jake shrugged. "Sure."

The male teller handed him a withdrawal slip, and Jake filled it out, signing it with a flourish. The teller handed over the money—five twenty-dollar notes—and Brother Rick snatched it before Jake could pass the cash to him.

Jake's brows rose. If he wasn't mistaken Brother Rick was scared of something or someone.

Outside the bank, Brother Rick said, "We need to go to Auckland. We'll drop you at the store. The women aren't there today. I want you to sell the rest of the stock. Get rid of it. Discount prices if you have to. The lease is due for renewal. Since Sister Bitter has left there's no one available to make stock. I've decided to let the lease drop."

"What about the key?"

"There's a spare one in the bookshop next door. They won't ask any questions because you're wearing a Children of Nature robe."

"No problem. Should I wait there for your return or should I walk back to the compound?"

Brother Rick hesitated and exchanged a glance with Brother Felix. "We'll be gone overnight. You'll need to walk back."

"All right," Jake said. "I'm sorry about the money. I'd forgotten the notice period."

Brother Rick grunted and pushed past him. Jake hesitated a few seconds before leaving the bank to go to the store. The blue truck sped past and disappeared around the corner. Jake pulled out his phone and dialed Luke.

"Something is up. Brother Rick is behaving weirdly. I thought he was gonna hit me when the teller informed us I couldn't have the money for ten days. He's heading for Auckland and will be gone overnight."

Jake paused to listen. "Nah, he's just left. I'll do some snooping around later this afternoon and tonight. Yeah, okay." He hung up and returned the phone to his pocket.

He had a lot to do, but he might have a quick solution for the stock. Aware there might be spies lurking, and he'd already pushed his luck, he strode to the shop. He stopped at the bookshop to ask for the key. Once inside the cult shop, he pulled out his phone again and checked the internet for the number to Fancy Free.

He glanced around the shop while he waited for someone to pick up the phone. The shelves were full of stock, but if he discounted everything to a dollar again, he should make two or three hundred-dollars. It would be enough stock to start Sorrel up in business for herself, if that was what she wanted.

Someone answered, and he asked for Alice. He explained his proposal, and Alice let out a girlie shriek that almost deafened him.

"We'll be there in a few minutes." The phone clicked in his ear.

Jake found the boxes Sorrel used for packing stock out the back and started stripping the shelves. A tap on the rear door announced Alice's arrival.

Jake cracked the door open a fraction, saw it was Alice and opened it wider.

"Sorrel." Without taking his eyes off her, he stood aside for Alice to enter the dim store. When Sorrel went to pass him, he wrapped his arms around her to steal a kiss. They were both breathing hard at the conclusion of the kiss.

"Ahem," said Alice. "This is a time-sensitive issue. We need to move fast before stupid Brother Rick finds his brain again."

Jake released Sorrel but couldn't make himself drop her hand. "Brother Rick told me to sell the lot, discounting if necessary to clear the shelves. The lease is up and he doesn't want to renew."

"Silly man," Alice said. "Don't you see, Sorrel? We buy your stock, at a discount, and approach the owners of this building. You already have customers, and we can start experimenting with our gift boxes to work out what sells best. This is perfect."

"Will I still work in developing the cream for sale?"

"Of course. We'll hire some staff. Maybe Katarina and Harriet would take over the shop. At the very least it would get them out from under my feet."

"Brother Rick will be furious."

"Let him have his tantrum," Jake said. "There's nothing he can do, as long as you move on the lease now."

"What do you think?" Alice bubbled with excitement. "Once we get ourselves sorted we can set up a lab for you and work out how to mass produce everything. Would you be all right with that?"

Jake watched the wonder on Sorrel's face, her building excitement and realized there was no damn way he was leaving Sloan. He'd have to put his mind to a new career, one that would keep him close. As his friends would say, he was toast.

"I'd like that very much." Sorrel appeared stunned at her good fortune.

"Good. I'll leave you to help Jake since you'll know best how to pack up everything. I think it's best if we store the stock at Fancy Free. We don't want anyone from the cult coming in and destroying everything. I'll go and get my car so you can pack everything inside."

She hurried off, leaving him alone with Sorrel.

"You look beautiful. Most people wouldn't recognize you." He studied the snug black jeans and red shirt. "Sexy."

"You recognized me."

"Ah, but you forget. I've seen you naked." He watched in fascination as a wave of red crawled up her neck and into her face. "I missed you last night. I sleep better if I'm with you." The truth. Greg stayed out of his head if Sorrel was with him. He reached for her, pulling her to him. Her soft breasts flattened against his chest, and if he looked down, he could see the swell of her curves.

"You had another nightmare?"

"Yes." He didn't want to discuss it, so he used distraction. For both of them. His lips covered hers, holding back further questions. Then he was drowning in her touch, her scent. Her taste. What had started as a diversion backfired on him, dragging him into a world of sensations. He took the kiss deeper, stroking his tongue along hers, molding her body to his. She felt right, perfect in his arms. He wanted to go on kissing her, to strip off every single item of clothing and take her, thrusting deep.

"God." He shuddered. "This isn't the right time." He pressed his forehead to hers, resting it there for long moments. "Soon, okay? We'd better start packing. I want to get back to the compound and do a search as soon as I can. Brother Rick told me he intended to stay away overnight, but I can't trust anything he says." Jake picked up a box and started to stack soaps into it. "He seemed panicked this morning. You have no idea what he does when he leaves the compound and goes to Auckland?"

"No." Her smile held an edge of mockery. "We mere women weren't informed of the day-to-day running of Children of Nature. No need to worry our little brains."

"I know better. This book you mentioned to Luke—can you describe it for me? I'll look for it during my search of the office."

"It's a book with a red cover. I'm positive I saw it on the bottom row of the bookshelf in Brother Rick's office along with my mother's other herbal books." She made a scoffing sound in the back of her throat. "He wouldn't know a book if it bit him on the butt. I need my recipe book too—the one I use most days. It's on the counter in my workshop. You could go back to the compound now and leave this to me."

"No." He was definite in his refusal. "I don't want to leave you alone, just in case Brother Rick turns up unexpectedly."

"You haven't taught me the self-defense moves yet."

"Tonight."

Something about the way he uttered *tonight* suggested he had a lot more in mind than self-defense. She placed some violet-colored bath bombs into a box and surrounded them with wads of newspaper to lessen the chances of breakage.

With both of them packing products it didn't take long.

"How much money are you giving to Brother Rick, and where is it coming from?" she asked.

"I'll withdraw some money from my account. Do you have proof against Brother Rick?"

She laughed. "Just suspicions. I know I can't prove his duplicity, but I can cause him discomfort. You have

254

another account Brother Rick doesn't know about?"

"Of course. And it has more money in it than the one I intended to sign over to Children of Nature."

Alice knocked on the rear door and stuck her head inside. "Sorry. That took me longer than I wanted. I had to take a couple of calls."

"We're done with the packing. I'll help you load the car."

"We'll do it. You go," Sorrel said.

"Yes," Alice agreed. "I'll help Sorrel with the stock."

Jake strode the three steps separating them and seized her for a quick kiss. Sorrel didn't struggle. She melted against him and enjoyed the physical contact. Unfortunately it was over too quick, and soon Jake left.

"Well, that was quick work on your part."

Sorrel frowned.

"I wasn't being snarky. From the little I've seen of him he seems a nice guy."

"He is, although nice isn't the word I'd use to describe him."

A laugh burst from Alice. "I know what you mean. He sort of prowls and slinks despite his limp. He doesn't smile much either."

"He smiles at me."

"Well, that's all that matters," Alice said. "Is that everything?"

"Apart from the dust. I suppose I should sweep up."

"Why? The cult is responsible for the lease. They can clean up."

"Oh." Chagrined by her first instinct, she bit her lip. "I forgot. I've lived at the compound for so long I—"

Alice touched her arm in silent sympathy. "There is no need to apologize for thoughtfulness. There aren't enough people in the world who think the way you do." She squeezed Sorrel's arm and released it. "Do you know who owns the building?"

"A Mr. Montgomery," Sorrel said. "I know because he came to buy a gift for his wife, and he mentioned he liked the scents in the shop. The previous tenants sold exotic goods and burned incense. He told me the incense made him sneeze."

"Jason Montgomery?"

"I don't know."

"Oh, I do hope so. Jason is Gaby's father. Remember Gaby from our tour?"

"Of course. The woman who designs condoms and sex toys for Fancy Free."

"That's the one. I'll ring Jason as soon as we get back. If we manage to get the lease, would you set things out differently?"

"The interior walls need painting—maybe cream with

stenciled borders around the top and bottom of the walls."

"Something classy," Alice mused. "Yes, I can see your products displayed in that way. We could even do mail order."

The rest of the day passed before Sorrel knew it. For the first time in months, she felt excited about making her products and the challenge of taking her cream and turning it into a mass-marketed product. Alice gave her a lift back to Luke and Janaya's house, just after five thirty. It was strange entering a building with no other people present, no chatter or laughter. No whispers or insults.

Woof.

Sorrel jumped and spun around. Her right hand slapped over her leaping heart, as she attempted to still the racing. The small dog barked again and trotted away, its tail wagging.

Shaking her head, Sorrel wandered into the kitchen. Her stomach grumbled. She rubbed her belly, wishing she had something to eat.

The dog walked around the corner of the kitchen counter, stopped by the fridge and barked again. It looked at Sorrel expectantly then at the fridge door.

"I guess we're both hungry," she told the dog. She pulled the fridge door open, the novelty of helping herself both foreign and wonderful. She decided on a chicken and salad sandwich and hunted out a plate, knife and a chopping board. The entire process of assembling her sandwich was a novelty and immensely satisfying.

A few pieces of chicken found their way down to the dog.

Finally, she cut her sandwich in half and sat at the breakfast counter. From the first bite, the flavors and scents rolled across her senses. Delicious. She swallowed and sighed happily.

"So this is freedom," she murmured to the dog. "I think I like it."

Janaya arrived home from her shopping trip and handed several bags to Sorrel. "These are for you."

"But I don't have any money."

"I'm not worried. From what I hear you're gonna be rolling in cash soon. Pay me back then."

The evening passed in a pleasant fashion with Luke and Janaya making her feel at home. Sorrel helped make dinner and enjoyed every moment of the changes in her routine.

"I'm going to take cooking lessons," Sorrel announced.

"You can't cook?" Janaya asked in surprise. "I thought you'd know how to do all that sort of stuff."

"There's a clear division of labor at the compound. As youngsters we either go into child care and teaching or food prep and cleaning. Once we're in a category, we're stuck."

"Huh." Janaya fished a pot out of the cupboard. "Who made the rules?"

"Brother Samuel. The founder of Children of Nature."

"What about you? How did you end up working with herbs?"

"My mother. She needed a helper, and I showed both aptitude and an interest."

Conversation drifted onto other topics, and then dinner was ready. It was a change not to wonder if she'd get a meal. And she absolutely didn't miss having to act subservient to every male present.

Luke rose at a tap on the window. "That'll be Jake." Seconds later he was back with Jake at his heels.

Jake's gaze went straight to her on his entrance.

"Did you find my mother's books?"

"I couldn't search the office today. Two of the brothers set up shop there this afternoon. They were still working on something when I left. It looked like a set of accounts. They had a laptop and several of the old-fashioned ledger books open." Jake glanced at Luke. "I have no idea what's going on. Brother Rick was frightened today, and they needed money. I've got your recipe book though." He pulled it from inside his robe and set it on the counter.

"Thank you."

"No problem."

Luke glanced at her before turning his attention to Jake. "My constable followed them to the casino. They stayed there for most of the day but didn't gamble. He thought they might be waiting for someone."

"Gambling?" Sorrel frowned. "That doesn't make sense."

"What about blackmail?" Janaya asked.

"The constable is still tailing them," Luke said. "I'm hoping he'll discover something to help our investigation."

"Are the tests on those pills back yet?"

"What pills?" Sorrel demanded.

"Brother Rick drugged the punch on the night of the gathering," Jake said. "I found pills in Brother Rick's quarters."

"Everyone complained of headaches the next day." Sorrel frowned. "It was out of character."

"Did you check out the place where we delivered the beast?"

Luke nodded, a gleam of satisfaction filling his eyes. "Mystery solved on that one. We recovered the cattle at the location and arrested the man we found at the farm."

"What about Brother Rick?" Sorrel asked.

"I've organized a search warrant for tomorrow. But I've decided to wait to execute it until Brother Rick is back. I want all the players in place first."

"Can I stay the night?" Jake demanded abruptly.

Luke glanced at his wife. "Will you be requiring a guest bedroom?"

Jake caught Sorrel's gaze. "No."

"Sorrel?" Janaya sought her opinion.

Sorrel wasn't sure where to look, but she forced herself not to revert to habit and stare at her bare feet. "I..."

"Which way?" Jake asked her.

"I was going to make coffee," Janaya said.

"Not for us." Jake spoke for both of them.

Janaya cocked her head, her lips twitching. "You don't have to follow his orders."

"Maybe I'll have a cup of—" Sorrel broke off abruptly as Jake hauled her to her feet. The next minute she was dangling over his shoulder, her gaze on the floor.

"Which way?" Jake demanded.

"Down the hall, second on the left," Luke said with a grin.

Janaya winked at Luke. "Will you be here for breakfast?"

"No, I want to be back at the compound before the bell goes for breakfast. I'll keep looking to see if I can find something useful for you."

Sorrel eyed Jake's arse as he strode from the kitchen. "That was very embarrassing." The blood was rushing to her head from dangling upside down.

"I don't care."

"I have to sit with them for breakfast. It's bad manners not to have coffee."

Jake shouldered his way through a door and set her on the bed. "Do you want to spend time with me?"

All the starch went out of her. "Of course I do. Alice gave me lots of free samples today."

Jake sat on the edge of the bed and yanked off his sandals. "I hate wearing this fuckin' robe. Give me jeans any day. Hell, even the army uniform is better than this."

"I bet you look good in jeans."

His eyes narrowed. "You're flirting with me."

A gurgle of laughter escaped her. "Is it working?"

He nodded. "What sort of samples?"

"Condoms. Lube. Two different vibrators." Her cheeks glowed with heat as she listed the taboo items. Brother Rick would have a lot to say about her evil ways. "There's even a vibrating condom. We should try that one."

"Whatever you want, sweetheart. Did I tell you how sexy you look?"

"I'm still the same person."

"I know." He reached over to tug a lock of her hair. "I like your hair better this color."

"What?" Her brows shot up in disbelief. "You dislike

the color of muddy mouse?"

"Your hair smells better too." He used brutal honesty. "Please don't ever put the goop on it again."

"Yes, sir." She gave him a snappy salute, part of her amazed at the ease with which she flirted with him. It seemed easy to smile now.

"Stand up and take off your shirt and your jeans. Show me what you're wearing underneath. You are wearing something sexy, right?"

"You make me feel shy."

"But you're going to do it for me." Jake's eyes glowed. Under his gaze, she felt beautiful, feminine. Not even his honesty scared her or the hidden secrets simmering in him if he thought no one was paying attention. No, she'd rather have Jake's rough and ready ways than Brother Rick's charming subterfuge.

"Why yes I am." Sorrel stood, her hands going to the buttons of her new red shirt. The fabric was soft against her skin instead of abrasive like her robe. The sensual drape delighted her, made her feel sexy and womanly. Aware of his close attention, she slid the next button out of its hole. The silky material gaped to reveal her new black bra.

"You must be more comfortable without the binding."

"Much," she said with feeling. Another button slipped from its hole and another until she was able to shrug out of her shirt. The garment slithered to the floor. Her jeans were next. She gave a wriggle of her hips, a tug, and the denim gave way and peeled down her legs. She stood before Jake in her matching bra and panties. Pleasure and awareness streaked through her and heat pooled low in her belly.

He stood and went to her, his callused hands sliding over her shoulders and down her upper arms. Appreciation glowed in his dark eyes, his gaze tracing the lines of her body.

"Lose the robe," she whispered against his neck. "It's ugly, and it brings back memories I'd rather forget."

Jake pulled away and ripped off the robe, tossing it aside without ceremony.

"I'm sure your underwear isn't regulation Children of Nature." Sorrel eyed him, fascinated by the way the tight white boxer-briefs cupped him, covering yet displaying his masculine assets in a totally sexy way.

Jake grunted. "I wasn't about to show Brother Rick my underwear. I'm not that guy."

A giggle burst from her, the merriment unusual yet enjoyable as it spilled into the bedroom.

His hand snaked behind her back, and her bra sagged. "I still have it." His fingers slipped beneath her bra to cup her warm breasts.

She sighed her pleasure, leaning into him and savoring his strength. "I never realized how much I needed someone to touch me. Before you my life..." She shook her head. "It was barren. Thank you." Even if this was all the time she had with Jake, she'd always remember him, remember this.

He drew her bra down her arms, the cool air making her nipples pucker and pull to hard nubs. She sucked in a quick breath as he dragged his thumb over one nipple. The tug, the friction on her flesh reverberated through her body. His caress was still so new, yet it was familiar too. He did it again, this time harder, and she gasped. She arched into him and offered her mouth, desperate to step into the sensual snare he cast. He bent his head, took her lips with his, demanding a response from her.

She didn't even have to think. His touch fueled her actions, left her wanting more. She shivered at the petal-soft caress of his lips traveling across her jaw and down the side of her neck. The scrape of his teeth brought another tremor. His touch blanked her mind, straining her ability to think. All she could do was wonder at the sensations he drew forth and how much she wanted him.

His hands tightened around her, and she felt the sensation of weightlessness.

"You enjoy toting me around like a box of bath bombs."

"It makes me feel manly."

She bounced on the mattress, and he loomed over her.

"Take off your underwear. Let me see you in the light."

"You want to ogle me."

"Guilty. You're so pretty. I love ogling your muscles." She stared at him while he pulled his underwear down his long legs. She admired his muscular thighs, and the hair she knew would feel a little tickly against her own limbs but in a good way.

He tugged his beard, a rueful gesture. "I keep telling you I'd be even prettier without this scruff on my face."

"Are you fishing for more compliments?"

"I can't wait to shave off the bloody thing. I'd much rather talk about something other than undercover operations."

"I thought it might rain today. From what I hear the local farmers are hoping for the same thing." Sorrel tried but failed to restrain her grin.

"People have had their bottoms smacked for less."

Her grin widened, an impish mischievousness springing to the fore. "They were discussing spanking at the lab this afternoon. I think I'll learn a lot of interesting things there." This could backfire. Already embarrassment crept into her face, making her skin prickly and hot.

"We'll explore them," he promised.

"All of them?"

"If that's what you want."

"Yes," she said slowly, liking him so much in that moment she struggled to take her next breath. Freedom was a heady thing. She stretched out her arms, silently asking him to join her on the bed.

He was at her side in an instant, his naked body covering hers. Their lips met and the laughter and teasing faded away. His lips were soft, and a hungry little sound escaped her. She wrapped her arms around his neck and let the passion sweep her under.

She'd half expected him to hurry the process because she knew he'd have to leave soon, but he didn't. He gentled the kiss, the lazy stroke of his tongue teasing. A row of kisses down her neck shouldn't feel so decadent, nor should the skim of his hands as he touched and caressed her shoulders. His fingers dipped close to her breasts, then darted away. She let out a cry of frustration, desperately wanting him to tug her nipples again, to taunt and tease her to a point shy of pain.

"Tell me what you want."

"You know what I want."

"Tell me," he prompted again, his husky voice sending a shiver through her.

She chewed her bottom lip, her earlier bravery deserting her. The last thing she wanted was to sound silly.

"Sorrel." He lifted his head to study her. "I like your new confidence. I enjoy the way you're smiling more. The sound of your laughter—it makes me happy. Tell me what you want me to do next."

Sorrel sucked in a quick breath for bravery. She knew what she wanted. All she needed to do was get out the words. Another breath inflated her lungs. She exhaled, ordering her thoughts then started. "I want you to touch my breasts. Suck them into your mouth. Bite my nipples and soothe them with your tongue."

"I can do that. Anything else?"

"I want you to kiss and tongue my private parts. Then I want to try out the vibrating condom."

Jake barked out a laugh, but she sensed he was surprised and pleased by her requests. "Sounds like a perfect plan to me. Let's get started."

The pulse at her throat beat a tattoo, an indication of the exhilaration flying through her. His warm lips charted a path down her throat, alternatively nibbling and soothing. She was never sure whether she'd feel the nip of his teeth or the delicate stroke of his warm tongue. The sensations bled into each other, her pussy clenching, as if hungry for the act to come.

"Jake." Soft, needy sounds spilled from her mouth, her body arching as his lips encircled one nipple. She felt the sharp tug bungee downward, springing back, reverberating. Each of his touches was an erotic assault, and she quivered, desperate for more.

When he lifted his head, satisfaction curved his sensual mouth. "I'm doing a good job."

"Yes, you are."

Through her heavy fog of desire, she watched him kiss his way down her body, dipping his tongue into the indent of her navel. His lips skimmed the jut of her hipbones. His teeth scraped the tender skin of her inner thighs. Automatically, she parted her legs, allowing him free access to her body. Approval flashed across his face, a captivating smile blooming, followed by a wink. Then he lowered his head again, sliding his hands beneath her butt, lifting her.

The first stroke of his tongue took her by surprise, the wet warmth of it. The delicate lap down her folds. She caught her breath, desperately wanting him to repeat the move. How else would she know what she liked best? The thought made her smile, but the second stroke brought a frisson of pleasure. One long finger pushed inside her, filling her before she'd even realized that was exactly what she'd craved. He feasted, each added intimacy turning her breathing shallow.

"Jake." It was a request for him to move faster, and thankfully he seemed to understand. He focused on her clitoris, circling the hard nub with his tongue, sucking with his mouth. She moaned, sparks of light exploding behind her closed eyelids. His finger plunged deep, caressing a tender spot, and hot, sensual flames licked across her skin. His lips teased, tongue delicately massaging while the pressure within her grew hotter. *More.* And then she was exploding, taking flight from her body while he maintained constant contact.

Gradually she returned to herself, the tension fading from her limbs. She sighed.

"Good?" He removed his finger from her, licking away the juices that made it glisten, watching her all the while.

"Better than good."

"Where are the condoms?" He lowered his hand, his dark eyes gleaming. All over again, she felt the heat of desire strike at her, her pulse race for what she knew would come next.

"In the red-and-white-striped bag, the one sitting on the floor in the corner of the room. The vibrating condoms are the ones in the red packaging."

He retrieved the condom, scanned the instructions and rolled it onto his cock. Moisture pooled between her legs, the scent of her desire and his, heavy on the air. Joining her again on the bed, he took the time to brush his fingers across her cheek, his expression soft before his lashes shielded his thoughts.

"Jake, please." She wanted to feel him plundering her body.

"Patience, sweetheart." Jake moved between her parted legs, guided his cock to her and pushed inside.

She sighed at the welcome pressure, the closeness she felt to Jake in this moment. Fully embedded, he paused, letting her body adjust to his size. He bathed the puckered tip of one breast with his tongue before he withdrew and glided inside her again. He paused for a second, reaching down to push on the power switch on the condom. The vibrations lined up with her clit, dragging a startled moan free.

A muttered curse escaped him, a grunt that was half laughter. "That's different."

"A good different," she said.

And it was. His hard, almost forceful strokes filled her, and each time he plunged inside her, the vibrations connected with the base of her clitoris, rekindling her excitement.

Jake increased his speed, his large body trembling as she wrapped her arms around him. This felt so right, so perfect, and there was nowhere, no one she'd rather be with.

Her climax broke over her on his next stroke—long, languorous pulses that seemed to go on forever.

Jake's breathing was loud in her ear, a rough growl vibrated in his chest and he stilled. She glanced up at him, seeing the tautness of his face, the closed eyes. They opened without warning, and she was trapped in his gaze, the fierce joy and satisfaction. Still the vibrations of the condom continued, almost painful against her tender clit.

"What say I get rid of this thing?" An edge of humor lurked in his raspy voice.

He withdrew to remove the condom and returned to her side. Their skin stuck together, clammy and uncomfortable, yet she cuddled closer. Languid and lazy, after her orgasm, already sleep pulled at her. Her last thought as she drifted into sleep was that she'd miss Jake when he returned to his soldiering.

Yeah, she'd miss him a lot.

CHAPTER TWELVE

BROTHER RICK SAT AT a cafe table near the window and glared at the woman crossing the road. Brother Tyrone was right. He *had* seen Bitter in town the other day.

His eyes narrowed as she entered Kellie Anne's Ladies Wear, hate writhing through him like a parasitic worm. It was all her fault. She'd driven him to take this path.

If only—

He broke off the thought. Wishing things were different would yield nothing. No, it was a self-destructive direction, and he knew better. He was cleverer than that, which was why he was the leader of Children of Nature.

The stupid bitch had no idea Brother Samuel had wanted her to take over the leadership role. And she hadn't even offered an argument when, on Brother Samuel's death, he'd seized control. The takeover had been simple and getting rid of his father even easier.

Now, everything was falling apart. He needed money, damn it. Despite the ideals of Children of Nature, it was ludicrous thinking one could get through life without cash.

Money was everything.

Money was king.

He'd made a serious error. Now, he needed to get Sister Bitter back to the compound and under his control. His mouth pulled tight over his teeth, and the small child at the table next door started wailing on seeing his expression. If he'd known she held the key to him getting the Children of Nature money, he wouldn't have expelled her from the compound.

Fuck, he hated making mistakes.

No, he had to get her back and by the end of the week.

Sister Bitter left the shop with a shopping bag in her left hand and a happy smile on her face.

Brother Rick stood and left the cafe. He strode across the street, waiting impatiently for a car to pass before he could get close enough to speak with Sister Bitter.

"Bitter."

Her steps faltered before she recovered. Her shoulders stiffened, but she kept walking.

Brother Rick started running to catch up. He grabbed her arm and yanked her to a stop. "I'm talking to you, Bitter."

She was shorter, but she still managed to look down her nose at him. Her snooty glare jerked his temper.

"My name is Sorrel. You've mistaken me for someone else."

Brother Rick took note of the changes in her then. Her hair—it was a different color—and the new clothes. His gaze dropped to her breasts and the deep cleavage between. "You have breasts." He snapped his mouth shut, appalled at the comment. Fuck, he sounded like an imbecile.

Sorrel tugged her arm free and stalked away. Once again, the differences in her assailed him. She was thinner, bustier. How the hell had she managed the transformation from plain to outright sexy?

"Wait." He grabbed her again and forced her to face him. "You have to come back to the compound."

"No."

A car pulled up alongside them. An elderly woman wound down the window. "Sorrel, I'm going to the factory. Want a lift?"

"Harriet, thank you."

Sorrel pulled from his grasp and darted away. She jumped into the passenger seat of the vehicle before Rick could protest. He cursed under his breath and swore again as the car pulled away from the curb.

He'd done a good job of alienating Bitter from Children of Nature. Too good. She hated him, and it was obvious he'd have to find another way to get her under his control. She'd sign the bloody document the bank required to let him withdraw the deposit if it was the last thing he did.

He'd worked hard, and by damn, he was going to take the money as a reward. Bitter wasn't going to muck up his life any longer.

· ♥ · ♥ · ♥ · ♥ · ♥ ·

Children of Nature Compound

The roar of motorbikes split the air, drowning out the dinner bell. Birds roosting in the nearby trees took flight with squawks of indignation.

Inside the compound, Brother Rick stilled, a sliver of fear sliding down his spine. Shit, this wasn't good. He had to get Bitter soon.

Failing wasn't an option.

And meantime, he'd just have to bluff it out.

"They're here," Brother Felix said.

"Remember, I told you I thought they'd send someone. That's what I'd do in their position. We'll have to stall them until we regather Bitter."

Brother Felix frowned. "I thought she refused to return."

"She did, but there's a reason I've been following her around and getting to know her routine. Tomorrow we'll grab her. I'll force the bitch to sign the document then get rid of her."

"Murder?" The color fled from Brother Felix's face. "You can't...I can't... No."

Rick made a sound of disgust, deep in his throat. "Not murder, you idiot. I thought I'd give her to the leader of the Rebel Brothers. He has a weakness for women. He'll take her off our hands with no questions."

"But I've seen their women...the drugs..." Brother Felix trailed off.

"Don't go weak on me now, Felix. We need to stick together and sweat this out or we'll lose everything."

Felix sighed and gave a curt nod, acting more his normal self. "You're right."

"Excellent. Let's go and greet our visitors and show them how good our hospitality is out here in the country."

Rick strode from the office he and Felix had holed up in to discuss what should be done. Of course, there was little doubt in Rick's mind as to the solution to their problem, but it didn't hurt to maneuver Felix onside. He couldn't do this alone, needed Felix's help. He aimed for confident as he stalked to the compound entrance.

Outside, the sound of motorbikes faded, replaced by chatter.

"Open the gates," an imperious voice shouted.

The two elderly men on security looked to Rick.

He nodded. "Please open the gates and let our guests enter."

The gates groaned as the men unlocked them.

"About time." The man at the head of the bikers revved his machine.

Brother Rick curved his stiff lips into a welcoming smile. Despite his words to Felix, worry churned his gut. He wanted to tell them to leave, but he wasn't stupid. He held his hands behind his back in an effort to hide his tremors.

"Welcome to Children of Nature, Elijah," Rick said. "Good timing. Dinner is ready." The last of his words were drowned out by the roar of motorbikes. They sped past him, ten in all. Not good.

Pulling confidence around him like a cloak, Rick glanced at Felix and walked in the direction of the gang members. Ten Rebel Brothers. The rest of his day promised excitement if he lived to tell the tale.

· ❤ · ❤ · ❤ · ❤ · ❤ ·

"Luke, something is going on here at the compound." Jake scanned his surroundings. "Ten members of the Rebel Brothers have turned up. I've no idea why they're here, but Brother Felix is green around the gills. Brother Rick is harder to read, but even he is uneasy."

"Interesting. The Rebel Brothers were into drugs and weapons when I worked in the city. I need to chat with my contacts. Can you keep me posted? Keep a low profile. I've heard rumors of people disappearing after involvement with this gang."

"I'll try." Jake hung up and tucked his phone away, double-checking it wouldn't fall from his pocket at an inopportune moment. The condom fiasco had taught him a valuable lesson.

Jake hobbled into the dining room, keeping his head low and his shoulders slumped. He joined the line of people waiting to collect food, sneaking a peek at the visitors in his peripheral vision.

They were loud, their guffaws ringing out in the large room. By contrast the cult members remained quiet, and Jake could smell the stench of fear and uncertainty wafting on the air. Frankly, he thought them smart to worry. The arrival of gang members didn't bode well.

With his meal in hand, Jake scanned the tables and limped over to one near the visitors in the hope of eavesdropping. Hopefully, he'd learn something of interest to help Luke discover why they were here and what it meant.

"I'm waiting for one of the signatories to arrive back from holiday." Brother Rick spoke calmly, but Jake saw the underlying tension in the man. "I told you on the phone."

"And I'm fine with waiting," the man sitting next to Brother Rick declared with a jovial smile.

Jake knew the type. Big and rough in appearance, he relied on fear to keep challengers at bay.

"We wanted to see the setup. No point in a partnership if the compound is crap."

"Partnership," the woman sitting next to Jake muttered, horror coating her tone. "What partnership?"

Jake got it. "Shush," he murmured in warning. He didn't want anyone to get hurt. "We can discuss this later."

Cattle rustling was the least of Luke's problems.

"How long are you intending to stay?" Brother Felix asked. "We'll need to organize accommodation and food for you."

"And drinks," one of the men called. "I deserve something stronger than lemonade to wash down my meal."

"Lemonade is for pussies," another snarled.

"There is a pub in town," Brother Rick said.

"Good. Organize some rum and a few beers," the man who seemed to be the leader ordered.

"Of course." Brother Rick never missed a beat. "You're our guests. We want you to feel welcome."

"I wouldn't mind a woman." The man scanned the room.

Jake tensed, his gut twisting with foreboding.

"That, too, can be arranged," Brother Rick said smoothly.

Fuck. Not good. He was one man and lacked weapons, apart from his brain. Jake shoveled mashed potatoes into his mouth, swallowing automatically while he tried to shape a way out for the residents of Children of Nature. They were innocent and didn't deserve the hell that'd just descended on them.

· ♥ · ♥ · ♥ · ♥ · ♥ ·

JAKE HADN'T VISITED LAST night. Sorrel pushed herself out of bed, worried because he hadn't arrived as he'd promised. She hurried through her shower, dressed in a new black miniskirt and a black-and-white top.

"Have you seen Jake?" she asked Janaya as she entered the kitchen. The scent of coffee filled the air, and she helped herself to a cup. "Do you want me to pour one for you?"

"Please," Janaya said. "There's been a development."

The tight note in Janaya's voice made Sorrel's stomach buck in alarm. "What sort of development?"

"Ten gang members turned up there last night."

"A gang? At the compound? Why? Children of Nature—stars, we, I mean they, don't have anything to do with gangs."

"Luke and Jake think Brother Rick has gang connections. They're there because of him."

"Are the brothers and sisters in danger? Can Luke do something to help them?"

Janaya shook her head. "The tests came back on the pills yesterday. They're party pills, but they're free of the banned substances. Luke can't do anything unless the law is broken."

"But Jake is still at the compound?"

Janaya nodded. "Do you want scrambled eggs?"

"I...no, thank you. I don't think I could eat right now. I can't believe Brother Rick would do this. It's inviting the devil to dine. Do you know if Jake has had a chance to search the office yet?"

"He told Luke the office has been occupied. They're using it most of the day, and he hasn't had access yet."

"I should march up there and demand my property

back."

Janaya caught her arm as she paced past. "No. Please tell me you won't go anywhere near the compound. It's dangerous." She frowned. "Luke told me not to tell you, but Jake heard Brother Rick offer to get the gang visitors alcohol and women. That's a recipe for disaster, and I'd hate you to get caught in the middle."

"But the young girls at the compound..." Sorrel gripped the edge of the counter. "He wouldn't. Please tell me..." She stared at Janaya. Every scrap of knowledge she possessed regarding Rick told her he'd dare anything, if it meant saving his own skin. "He would. Stars, Luke has to help."

"Luke can't do anything yet. Jake's there, and he's the best weapon the cops have to keep control over the situation. Luke's working on identifying the gang members. If they have records, he'll have a reason to enter the compound."

Sorrel nodded, the coffee she'd sipped swirling uneasily in her belly. She swallowed, setting down her mug.

"What are you doing today?" Janaya asked.

"Alice has discovered another building for lease that's right in the center of the town. She thinks it might be better because of the pedestrian traffic and it's available right now. I'm going to view it with her this morning." She glanced at the new watch she wore on her left wrist.

"Where are you meeting Alice? I can drop you off when I take Luke his breakfast."

"Thanks, we're meeting at Fancy Free. I'll go and grab my stuff."

After Janaya dropped her off, Sorrel couldn't stop thinking about the compound. Her new cell phone buzzed and Sorrel answered.

"It's Alice. I'm running late. Mr. Montgomery is attending a breakfast meeting at the cafe. Grab the key from him and go and look at the building. I'll be at Fancy Free this afternoon. Let me know what you think of it and if we should take a lease on this one or wait until the end of the month to take over the one nearer to Fancy Free."

Despite her distraction, Sorrel felt a surge of pride because Alice trusted her to undertake the task. "Okay. I'll see you this afternoon." Sorrel hung up and set off for the cafe.

She collected the key from Mr. Montgomery, and after grabbing a takeout coffee, she wandered across the street to the vacant building. She walked around the back and unlocked the door. Her boots echoed on the wooden floor as she entered the empty building.

The front of the shop, which overlooked the main street, was beautiful, with two large windows perfect for displays. A gorgeous stained glass window above the door reflected a rainbow of colors over the plain white walls. She retraced her steps, pausing to sip her coffee.

This was perfect, and they could move right in without worrying about redecorating. Out the back, there was plenty of storage room for stock. She set her coffee on a counter and pulled a notebook out of her handbag to scribble notes. She'd seen enough, could imagine the stock displays. With the airy spaciousness, this was much better for their purposes. She tucked the notebook away and picked up her coffee.

An out-of-place creak brought a frown. Was that a footstep? She stilled, gazing in the direction of the sound.

"Alice?"

When no one replied, she chalked it up to imagination. Humming under her breath, she headed for the rear door.

Rough hands grabbed her from behind. Her coffee went flying, landing with a liquid splat against the wall.

"What—"

A cloth was pressed over her nose before she could protest further, the acrid fumes making her eyes water. She gasped in a breath, her mind growing hazy, and that was the last thing she remembered.

· ♥ · ♥ · ♥ · ♥ · ♥ ·

"Got her." Felix dragged Sorrel's sagging body to the truck and thrust her into the rear. He checked she was still unconscious and slammed the door shut before joining Rick in the front.

"Good job." Rick grinned, dizzy with relief. They'd done it. Now that she was under their control, he'd get her to sign over the money. He could replay his debt to the Rebel Brothers and then the sky was the limit.

He nosed his truck from behind the vacant shop and headed for the compound.

·❤·❤·❤·❤·❤·

"Have you seen Sorrel?" Alice asked.

"Not since this morning," her office assistant replied. "She always pops her head around the corner and says good morning. Such a nice girl."

"She is. We're lucky she's willing to join us. I've checked the labs and the factory floor. No one has seen her since this morning."

Alice checked her electronic diary and picked up the phone. "Mr. Montgomery, did Sorrel pick up the key from you this morning? She did. Did she return the key? Okay. Thanks." She hung up the phone. "She didn't return the key."

"Have you checked the vacant shop? Maybe she's fallen and hurt herself."

"I'll go and check now."

Five minutes later, Alice parked behind the shop. From the driver's seat, she could see the rear door was ajar. She picked up her phone and rang the police station.

"Stay in your car," Richard said after she explained her fears. "Lock the doors and wait until I get there."

Richard arrived promptly. The police car pulled up beside her, and Alice exited her vehicle.

"Wait—"

"I'm not waiting here," Alice broke in. "I want to know what's going on. I don't know Sorrel well, but it isn't like her to disappear. She spends the afternoons in the lab."

"Keep behind me," Richard said. "Don't touch anything."

He pushed the door open. A black handbag lay on the floor. Farther inside a cardboard coffee cup sat upside down, its former contents splattered over the wall. The black plastic lid had rolled across the floor and settled across the room.

"Sorrel? Sorrel!"

The two of them searched the shop. Sorrel wasn't there.

· ♥ · ♥ · ♥ · ♥ · ♥ ·

AFTER A NIGHT OF alcohol and debauchery, the gang members were still asleep. Jake kept an eye on the situation without getting too close to attract attention. Brother Rick and Brother Felix had left the compound earlier.

Jake worked in the garden near the office, frustrated because Brother John and Brother Tyrone were still laboring over ledgers in there. He had no idea what the hell they were doing. They scarcely left the place, and on the rare occasions they did, the door was locked. He hadn't been game to break in because their absences were half an hour at most. Not enough time for him to enter and do a search without getting caught.

The sound of a vehicle dragged his attention to the gates. They swung open, and Brother Rick drove the truck onto the compound.

Instead of parking in the normal place, Brother Rick drove to his quarters. Both he and Brother Felix exited. They opened the rear door and pulled out something.

Jake squinted then stiffened.

That wasn't an object. That was a person.

He sauntered through the garden to the far boundary, catching a glimpse of blonde hair. It was enough to make the back of his neck prickle.

Brother Rick and Brother Felix entered Brother Rick's quarters, closing the door after them.

Jake frowned, checked over his shoulder, and found one of the elderly brothers watching him. Cursing under his breath, Jake limped back to the row he was responsible for weeding. His hands worked automatically while he kept an eye on Brother Rick's quarters.

"Watch out," the elderly brother warned, an edge to his brittle tone. "You're pulling out seedlings. I thought you knew what you were doing."

"Sorry." Damn, he was going to blow this and lose the perfect vantage point to spy on Brother Rick.

"Use more care."

"I will."

The man grumbled under his breath as he ambled along the row of radishes.

Jake went back to his weeding, taking more care. He finished, noting neither of the brothers had emerged from the quarters.

At least he knew Sorrel was safe. It couldn't be her, so who the hell was in there with them? Kidnapping? It seemed unlikely, yet he couldn't rid himself of his disquiet.

The lunch bell rang, calling everyone to dine. The brother supervising him set down his tools and lumbered off. "You coming?" he asked over his shoulder.

"I'll finish this row. There'll be a queue anyway."

The elderly man nodded and continued his rush toward

the dining hall. Jake moved a row closer to Brother Rick's quarters and scanned the compound. He approached cautiously, freezing when the door to Brother Rick's quarter flew open.

"I shouldn't have given her so much of the drug," Brother Felix said. "What if she doesn't come around?"

"Then we'll be guilty of murder as well as kidnapping," Brother Rick snapped. "I'm sure she'll regain consciousness soon. Go and have some lunch. We need to keep an eye on our visitors. Bring me back something to eat."

Brother Felix's unhappiness didn't clear from his expression. After swiping a hand over his bald head, he gave a curt nod and stomped away. Brother Rick re-entered his quarters, shutting the door after him.

Jake considered his options and decided to take the opportunity to call Luke before attempting to peek through the windows. He had Brother Rick's confession of kidnapping already. Surely that was enough for Luke to investigate.

He retreated to a private area where he could see anyone coming before they saw him. After a final scan of the vicinity, he pulled his phone from his pocket and hit speed dial. "Luke, it's Jake. Something's up here. I overheard Brother Rick discussing a kidnapping. I saw them haul someone from their truck."

"Hell. Sorrel's missing. She went to look at a vacant building on the main street. Dad and Alice found her handbag on the floor and the remains of her coffee splattered over the wall and floor."

Fury tore through him. "Bastard."

"Jake." Luke's voice was urgent in his ear. "Don't do anything rash. We need to make the charges stick. Are the Rebel Brothers still there?"

"Yeah." God, this was history repeating itself. What if he was too late to help Sorrel? He'd failed Greg.

"Seen anything that might give us reason to arrest them too?" Luke jerked him from his sudden fear.

Focus, dummy. "Caught a whiff of drugs last night. They took their choice of the women and hauled them off to bed for the evening. The women seemed willing enough."

"All right. Sit tight until we get there."

"How long?" Jake wasn't fuckin' leaving Sorrel alone with Rick. No telling what the sick fuck would do to her.

"An hour to arrange for extra cops from Papakura. I don't want to botch this."

"Too long."

"Jake."

Jake dealt with Luke by ending the call. His first instinct was to turn the thing off so Luke couldn't contact him, but he knew he'd need the cops. He shoved the phone into his pocket, taking extra seconds to make sure it wouldn't bounce out if he needed to move fast. After a quick scan of the compound, he ran across the open ground and slipped into the shadows cast by Brother Rick's quarters. At a window, he paused to listen. Not a sound came from within.

He rose on tiptoe to peek through the window. Brother Rick was still inside, pacing the open spaces, in ceaseless movement. Jake's gaze went to the bed. Sorrel lay there, silent and still. The warrior in him snarled, ready for action, and at his side, Greg shimmered into sight, his ghostly figure tense and battle ready.

· ❤ · ❤ · ❤ · ❤ · ❤ ·

SORREL LAY STILL, KEEPING her eyes closed. Anger pulsed through her, enticing her to jump to her feet and thump Brother Rick over the head. She reined in the impulse, needing a plan first.

The footsteps came close again. "Why aren't you waking up?"

She could feel his fixed stare, his strange agitation. It was like a writhing beast filling the room with its tentacles, stroking along her arms and bare legs and leaving a slithery trail of goose bumps. Her mind was full of questions, and one reasonable answer presented itself.

Brother Rick loathed her. He'd taken pleasure in expelling her from the compound, yet maybe the rest of the Children of Nature members had censored him for his actions. It was the only thing that made sense.

"Wake up, damn it." He grasped her shoulder and shook violently.

Enough! Sorrel bolted upright, flailing with her right arm and aiming for his face.

He let out a roar when she walloped his nose. "Sister Bitter."

Sorrel rolled away and bounded off the bed, her eyes trained on him. She calculated the distance to the door and knew she wouldn't make it. He was too close, and her head was swimming from whatever drug they'd used to subdue her.

"Dammit, Bitter, you've made my nose bleed."

Her brows squeezed together. "My name is Sorrel."

"What are you wearing? It's indecent."

"Not your problem." She reached for the wall to hold her steady. "Why have you brought me here?"

"Come and sit down. Help me stop my nose from bleeding."

She snorted. "What did your last slave die of? Oh, wait.

You shunned them."

"Watch your mouth." His face hardened. "You have something that belongs to me." He went to a drawer and pulled out a pristine white handkerchief. The moment he pressed it to his nose, the fabric turned blood-red.

As Brother Rick paced away from her, his words registered. Her brow knit. What the heck did he mean?

She watched him pace back and forth, back and forth, his head held at an awkward angle to stem the nosebleed. She edged to the closed door. No matter what nonsense he was spouting, she intended to leave. Her first steps were wobbly.

Brother Rick swiveled toward her, freezing her on the spot. "You're going to sign the money over to me."

"I have no idea what you're talking about."

"You're the signatory on the trust."

She stared at him. "What trust?"

"Don't play dumb." Brother Rick tossed the bloody handkerchief aside and advanced on her.

Sorrel's first instinct was to back up. She forced herself to stand her ground. "Give me details."

He cocked his head to the side. "You've changed."

"Thank you."

"Not for the better."

"I need details. You might jog my memory." Humor

struck her at his pronouncement. Brother Rick was a bully and belittled anyone who attempted to stand up to him. He hadn't seen anything yet.

"Brother Samuel and your mother concocted a plan to keep the bulk of Children of Nature's money in a trust for lean times. I didn't know about the account until last week when a bank statement arrived. For some reason, there was no paperwork in the office."

Sorrel eyed the door. "What's that got to do with me?"

"You're the signatory on the account."

Sorrel laughed. She couldn't help herself. She had no idea how—no wait. She'd witnessed Brother Samuel signing several papers. Was it possible? She frowned, trying to remember. Her mother had rushed into the workshop while she was trying to make a batch of soap, demanding she come immediately. Alarmed, she'd taken her pot off the heat and run after her mother. There had been nothing wrong with Brother Samuel. He'd been sitting at his desk, his normal smile wreathing his mouth.

"Ah, I'm glad you're here. I need you to witness my signature," he'd said in his booming voice.

"Couldn't Mother have done it?" she'd demanded in exasperation.

"I need her to sign as well."

Yes, she remembered sighing papers now, recalled

asking, "Do I need to read anything? I'm in the middle of making a batch of soap."

"No, my dear. All you need to do is watch me sign the papers and sign too. It will take a few minutes at most."

So she'd signed and rushed back to the workshop to save her soap, putting the entire incident to the back of her mind because it hadn't seemed important.

Despite Children of Nature's self-sufficiency, the outside world intruded with paperwork—things to do with home schooling and census returns, special licenses. She recalled Brother Samuel's words of never-ending paperwork.

"It's not funny," Brother Rick snarled. A dried bit of blood clung to one of his flared nostrils. "I need the money."

"You need the money?" Sorrel asked in a dangerous voice. "If it's a trust, the money belongs to everyone. It's not yours to spend."

"Brother Samuel had no right to give the power to a woman." Venom coated his voice as he pushed his face close to hers. "You will sign it over to me."

"No." She didn't hesitate. "I won't."

Brother Rick grabbed her arm and shook her.

Sorrel wrenched away. "Get your hands off me."

His eyes promised retribution, and before she could

heed the warning, he backhanded her. Her head snapped back, the crack of palm against skin almost as alarming as the jerk of pain. He grasped her shoulders again, shaking her for a second time, fury a dark slash on his face. "You will give me that money."

"No." She backed away, old fears gripping her for an instant.

The door to Brother Rick's quarters flew open, startling them both.

"Get out," Brother Rick snarled without looking over his shoulder.

Brother Felix hovered in the doorway.

But Brother Rick's concentration was divided, and Sorrel found her mettle. She shoved him hard, the brief self-defense tips from Jake coming back. She stomped on his foot, kicked his knee and headed for the door.

She managed to get past Brother Rick, but he grabbed her from behind, his fingers digging into her upper arms. Sorrel forced herself to relax, to sag against his chest. Then, she lifted her right leg and kicked back with her heel, striking his groin with every ounce of force she could muster.

He let out a pained howl and a whimper, dropping to a heap, cupping his groin.

"What's going on?" Jake's voice.

Sorrel pushed past Brother Felix and fell straight into Jake's arms.

"They kidnapped me. I want to press charges."

CHAPTER THIRTEEN

JAKE IGNORED BROTHER RICK writhing on the floor and the gaping Brother Felix. He wrapped an arm around Sorrel's waist and urged her toward her workshop, the one place he could think of where no one was likely to barge in on them. Sorrel would be safe until Luke came to take over.

"Did he hurt you?"

"Not really. There's something weird going on though. He's acting desperate. He needs money for something."

"Is that all he said?"

Sorrel stopped walking, her gaze on something across the other side of the compound. "What are those?"

Jake exerted enough pressure at her back to make her start walking again. "Brother Rick has visitors."

"With motorbikes?" She scrunched her nose. "Wait, Janaya mentioned something about gang members. Brain is foggy."

"Sorrel, not now. Please." He should've guessed she'd ask questions. She'd gained her independence and relished the lack of personal restraints. It was silly of him to expect her to stuff her newfound freedom back in a box and blindly obey his orders. "Brother Rick invited members of the Rebel Brothers to visit."

"Why?"

"No idea. They arrived last night." He'd watched those guys. They had an eye for women. Damn if he'd let them near his woman. He directed her around the outskirts of the open ground, relaxing once they reached the workshop. Opening the door, he urged her inside.

"Hoy. You."

"Fuck," Jake said.

"I'm talking to you," the hard male voice roared across the compound.

Jake fumbled in his pocket for his phone and shoved it at Sorrel. "Ring Luke. Speed dial one. Tell him we need him *now*."

Jake took a deep breath and consciously slumped. He turned to face the two gang members standing in the doorway of the dining room. Cursing under his breath, he started limping in their direction until he was a few feet from them. "Can I help you with something?"

"Who is the woman?"

Jake glanced over his shoulder. He relaxed a fraction when he saw Sorrel speaking on the phone.

"She's from the council," he explained with deference that almost choked him. "She's checking the facilities here at the compound to make sure they're up to standard."

The compound residents started drifting out, streaming around the two gang members.

"What is Bitter doing here?" one of the men asked. "Why is she dressed like that?"

"I thought she'd left the compound," one of the women said.

"You know the woman?" a third gang member asked.

Jake hated the way this was heading.

The first man focused on Jake. "Why did you lie?"

Not good at all.

"Could it be," the man continued, "you have an attachment to this woman?"

Jake didn't reply. Instead he prayed for reinforcements soon because this had the makings of another cluster fuck.

· ❤ · ❤ · ❤ · ❤ · ❤ ·

SORREL'S HAND TREMBLED AS she pushed speed dial.

"Morgan," Luke barked.

"It's Sorrel. I'm at the compound. Jake said get your butts here now."

"We're on our way already. Five minutes."

Sorrel shoved the phone into the waistband of her skirt.

"Girlie, over here," one of the gang members hollered.

More people spilled from the dining hall at his yell. More gang members. Their presence screamed something illegal.

"Don't make me come and get you."

The warning in his voice didn't go unnoticed. Bother, she should've hidden. She eyed the gates to the compound then the big, bald man in scruffy jeans and leather vest. Anger bristled off him in waves. Her gaze drifted to the gates again.

Maybe it wasn't too late to run. She was off, sprinting toward the entrance before the thought half-formed.

"Stop." An angry shout whipped her fear. She pushed herself harder. Her feet pounded the gravel path, her heart galloped, dread giving her an extra edge of speed.

"Open the gates," she screamed at the two elderly security guards. As usual, they moved at the pace of runny honey on a cold day. One of them exited the small shelter to the side and stood, staring at her.

Sorrel kept running, kept screeching at them.

The roar of a motorbike split the air. Sorrel gasped, saw the bike with the rider leaning low when she risked a glance over her shoulder. Even from this distance, anger emanated off him. She reached the gates and started climbing, fervently wishing she'd donned her new pair of comfortable jeans. The sound of the bike grew louder, meaner, until it vibrated inside her head.

Danger. Danger. *Danger.*

The bike screeched to a stop. A dust cloud clogged her throat. She coughed and kept moving. Rough hands grabbed her just as she swung her leg over the top rail. She struggled, kicked, but to no avail. The man grasped her by the waist and hoisted her down as if she weighed nothing more than a batch of bath bombs.

"What have we here?" he rasped in her ear.

His breath wafted over her, the blast of garlic telling her everyone had dined on lasagna during their recent meal.

"Girlie, where have you been hiding?" He hauled her toward his motorbike.

"If you think I'm getting on that, you've got rocks in your head," she snapped before she could think better of the remark. She closed her eyes, heart still trying to burrow from her chest. Maybe now wasn't the best time to channel Janaya and Alice.

When he reached his bike, he kept an iron grip on her wrist. He straddled the machine without releasing her. "You will get on my bike behind me. You will hold on to me because I'd hate you to fall off and graze this pretty skin." His finger traveled up one of her arms and skipped to her upper chest, impudently slipping downward into her cleavage.

Sorrel held still, instinctively knowing if she disobeyed the situation would worsen. She gave a clipped nod of acknowledgment.

"Girlie, I can tell we're going to get on well together."

Luke had told her five minutes. Where was he?

The man patted the seat behind him. Sorrel eyed it with disfavor. Yeah, those jeans were looking good right now. Taking a deep breath, she lifted her leg and swung it over the bike.

"Matching black panties," the man purred. "Sexy."

She hated the way he was eyeing her like a luscious treat. She'd much prefer the anger he'd displayed when he'd hollered at her.

The bike took off with a roar. Sorrel let out a shriek and clutched his waist. She heard his laughter as he raced across the compound.

Thankfully, it was a quick trip. She scrambled off the instant the bike stopped, attempting to wriggle free of his grip.

"You're coming with me." His eyes gleamed with heat. Sexual lust.

Sorrel gave another futile tug for freedom. "No. I won't."

Silence fell, scary in its nothingness.

Jake scowled at the man. "She said no. Let her go."

The man ignored her objections, ignored Jake and started towing her toward the men's sleeping quarters. "I'm going to fuck the feistiness out of you, girlie."

"No," Sorrel said.

"Get your hands off her," Jake snarled, advancing two steps.

Before he could reach the big man holding her captive, two of the other bikers grabbed him. Sorrel struggled, and Jake fought to help her, despite the two men impeding him.

Sister Andrea appeared from the kitchen entrance of the dining hall, a pot in hand. "Sorrel, what—" She broke off abruptly. "You let her go."

"What are you going to do about it?" The man holding Sorrel captive snickered.

Sister Andrea fired the heavy pot at his head. It hit with a resounding thump. Sorrel jerked free and turned to flee. The man let out a wounded-bull roar and charged Sister

Andrea.

Another pot flew through the air, fired by another one of the sisters who'd appeared behind Sister Andrea.

Suddenly the mood of the crowd changed. Instead of cowering, they flocked around the gang members, overwhelming them by sheer numbers and inventiveness when it came to weapons. Rolling pins, sandals and more pots lobbed through the air.

A siren became audible in the distance. Strong arms surrounded her, and she whipped around ready to fight.

"Steady, sweetheart." Blood trickled down Jake's cheek from a nick above his left eyebrow. He drew her to a clear space near the exterior dining hall wall. "Are you okay?"

"Maybe a bruise or two."

"I'm proud of you," he whispered against her ear.

"Why?" Despite her confusion, warmth built in her chest, a small spark of pleasure. No one, apart from her mother, had ever been proud of her before.

"You fought back."

Three police vehicles arrived, and the security men moved with alacrity to let them inside the compound. Luke and the other policemen soon had the gang members subdued.

Brother Rick appeared behind them. "What is going on here?" he asked, the strident voice of authority. He approached in a gingerly manner, his slight limp raising a smile. Go, her.

Luke approached him with confidence inherent in his every move. "You're under arrest for the kidnapping of Sorrel Thyme."

"I didn't kidnap her. Look, she's standing over there. Bitter. Bitter!"

Sorrel's eyes narrowed. "My name is Sorrel, and I want to press charges. He grabbed me in town, drugged me and brought me here without my consent. He tried to force me to sign a document so he could spend the funds Brother Samuel set aside for the benefit of the people who live in the compound." She paused to take a breath, anger a serpent slithering through her veins.

"She's lying."

"I am not. I also suspect him of poisoning Brother Samuel."

"That's a vicious lie."

"You've treated me like a slave. Why have you encouraged everyone else to treat me in the same manner?"

"She's lying," Brother Rick spat. "My father ate poisonous mushrooms by mistake. Others were sick too."

"I might not be able to prove what I'm saying, but I know the truth in my heart."

The members of Children of Nature had fallen silent,

listening to every word Sorrel uttered. Now they started low murmurs of discontent.

"I knew I didn't put poisonous mushrooms in my stew," Sister Andrea said with an emphatic nod.

A dull fan of red moved up Brother Rick's throat. "Surely you're not going to listen to her. She's lying. Look at her." He appealed to the brothers and sisters. "She's gone against every one of our beliefs. She's sold out."

"You forced her out." Sister Andrea advanced on him. "The chickens are treated better than Sorrel. You made sure she ate no more than once a day. You instructed us to call her Bitter, and you worked her hard to keep the store stocked with products."

"Aye, and you told us to sell everything at a dollar each so she had to work even more to keep up with demand," another sister called. "The stallholder in Papakura was furious because his supply of cheap stock ceased."

"Take him away," someone else called.

"We're better off without him."

"He brought those men here."

"He made me sleep with one of them," a young girl said.

Luke hauled Brother Rick away, still protesting his innocence. The crowd continued to throw complaints after him. The other officers dealt with the gang members.

"Where is Brother Felix?" Sorrel asked.

"I haven't seen him." Jake kept his arms loosely circled around her, giving Sorrel a sense of safety and support. "Don't worry. Luke will catch all the culprits. He's good at his job. Are you ready to leave?"

"I'll just grab my mother's books from the office," Sorrel said.

Jake took her hand and turned in the direction of the office.

"Are you going?" Sister Andrea asked.

"As soon as I get my mother's books."

"I thought you'd stay and help us regain our original form and intent," Sister Andrea said.

"No, I have a job now. I'm ready for change."

"But what will we do?" another sister asked. "We need a leader."

"You do. But it won't be me. You need a man or woman who treats everyone as equal, someone who is open and transparent in their dealings. Have a meeting. Everyone interested in the job should toss their names in a hat then hold an election."

"Yes." Sister Andrea's gaze strayed to the distant horizon, her brow puckered as if she were involved in heavy thinking. "Yes. I'm tired of following the orders of a man, tired of the way we've been treated. I think we should have a female leader for a change. We need to make money.

How will we do that?"

"Keep up the lease on the shop and sell the extra produce. Make jams and chutneys. Those who are skilled at needlework or woodwork could make other things to sell. You need to assess your skills and make a plan," Sorrel said.

Sister Andrea nodded, once again thoughtful. "Yes. Yes. We must call a meeting." She hurried off to join a cluster of women and started talking, hands flashing to punctuate her words.

When Sorrel and Jake reached the office, the door was locked, but the distinct sound of rustling and frantic whispers reached them.

Jake rapped sharply on the door. "Open up. Now." Authority rang out along with his words.

More frantic whispering.

"Problem?" Luke asked from behind them.

"Someone's in there." Jake took two steps back and kicked the door. Wood cracked but the door didn't give. He kicked again and it flew open.

Brother Felix stood in the office with Brothers John and Tyrone. When Jake and Luke prowled into the office they cowered against the walls.

"The rest of the culprits," Jake said.

"Who are you?" Brother John demanded in a quivering

voice.

"You're under arrest for cattle rustling and conspiring to kidnap." Luke produced his ID.

"Me?" Brother Tyrone drew himself up. "I had nothing to do with the cattle rustling." He pointed a trembling finger at Jake. "He was so proud of committing the crime he made us take photos."

"Why you snivel—"

The three men took a collective step back.

"Jake." Luke grabbed him by the shoulder, hauling him to a stop. "You're all under arrest. We can discuss the facts at the station."

They put up little fight as he ushered them from the office. A sea of shredded paper decorated the floor.

Sorrel stared at the paper, her lips twisting at the irony. They were still trying to cover their tracks.

"Can you see your mother's books?"

Alarm twisted her stomach tight. Her breath caught as her gaze went to the bookcase. Relief had her knees buckling, her breath exploding in a whoosh of pure relief. The red-bound notebook sat squeezed between two larger tombs on herbs and flowers, a layer of dust attesting to the length of time the books had remained unread. She reached forward to extract the notebook, blew off the dust and opened it.

Her mother's scrawled writing and drawings filled the pages. Some of the older recipes she'd developed with results of her failed experiments.

"Do you think Brother Rick murdered Brother Samuel?" Jake asked.

"It's a gut feeling. There's no doubt Brother Samuel was getting older, but until he ate the mushrooms he was healthy. Sister Andrea swears she didn't add mushrooms to her stew. Brother Rick had visited his father during dinner. They'd argued, and Brother Rick stormed out. I saw him."

"That doesn't make him guilty of murder."

"No, that's true. I—" She broke off abruptly. "Look at this. It's a diary entry by my mother." She read aloud. "I don't have any proof, but I think Brother Rick has been giving Brother Samuel something in the glass of juice he brings his father every morning. Samuel has complained of dizziness. I'm going to try a few mouthfuls of Brother Samuel's meals and the drinks he takes in his private quarters. If I start to become sick, I'll have proof Brother Rick is up to no good. I can't believe Sister Andrea is complicit in poisoning." Sorrel lifted her head. "That's not proof, but it's enough to cast doubt."

"Unless they find something concrete it won't be enough." Jake slid his hand across her shoulder in silent commiseration.

"I know the truth. That's what matters. Brother Rick knows the truth too."

"Luke is thorough. Brother Rick won't escape charges."

"Good."

"Are you ready to leave?"

"Yes." Not a shred of hesitation entered her at the thought of leaving the place she'd called home for most of her life. "Is your undercover job finished now?"

"Yes, and I can't wait to put on a pair of jeans instead of wearing this bloody robe."

·❤ · ❤ · ❤ · ❤ · ❤·

LATER THAT NIGHT, JAKE and Sorrel shared dinner with Luke and Janaya.

Janaya's violet eyes gleamed as she stared from Jake to Sorrel. "I take it you're staying the night, Jake?"

"Please."

Janaya's lips quivered, and Sorrel suspected whatever Janaya was thinking made her want to laugh. She managed to hold it back, restraining her humor to a twitch of lips. "I'll prepare a room for you."

"That's not necessary. I'll share with Sorrel."

"Told you." Janaya held out a hand to her husband. "You owe me twenty dollars."

Jake growled. "Yet bet on us sharing a room again."

"That's not exactly what she bet on, and she hasn't won yet."

"All's fair in betting land," Janaya quipped.

"On that note, we're retiring for the evening," Jake said. "I have an early start tomorrow."

Sorrel rose, removing the empty glasses from the table and stacking them in the dishwasher. Jake was returning to Papakura, returning to the army base for medical clearance and possibly reporting for duty. The knowledge left a hollow feeling inside her. It expanded until her entire chest ached. She hated him to go, but she couldn't ask him to stay either. Jake had a job, responsibilities.

Jake tugged on a lock of her hair to gain her attention. "Hey, don't think so hard. It might never happen."

Her throat closed up, and she had to force words to exit her mouth. "I'm going to miss you. What happens if you pass the medical? When you pass the medical?" she corrected herself.

"It won't be so bad. My contract will be over in three months. It won't be long until I'm back." He pressed a kiss to the tip of her nose. "You'll hardly have time to miss me."

Her head tilted back to meet his gaze. "You're coming back to Sloan?"

"For you. I've had enough of army life. It's not the same

now that my mates have left the team. I'm not sure what I'll do once I get out, but I'll give it some thought while I'm away."

"You're coming back to Sloan for me?" She felt like the proverbial parrot, but she needed to have things clear in her mind.

"Sorrel." Jake stopped in the doorway of the bedroom she was occupying. He cupped her cheeks and smiled down at her. "You're special. I want to see where the future will take us. Will you wait for me?"

"Yes. Yes!" She threw her arms around his neck and clung. Their lips met in a kiss, then he was lifting her into his arms, entering the bedroom and closing the door behind them.

"Good." His sigh held relief, and the realization made her tip her head up to search his features. He grinned, an open display of happiness that pushed her pulse rate into a gear change-up. He hadn't been certain of her, had harbored doubts. Probably some of the same worries she had about trusting herself enough to step forward into the future.

"Can I write to you while you're away? Um...doing soldier things?"

"We can do better than that, sweetheart. I'll buy you a laptop. I won't have time to show you how to use it, but

I'll ask Luke and Janaya to help you set it up. You'll be able to send me emails and talk to me online."

After spending months as an outsider, his kindness overwhelmed her, brought a touch of giddiness and even disbelief. "You'd do that for me?"

Jake laughed. "It's for my benefit too." He released her, letting her slide down his body and lowered his head, crushing his lips to hers. Gradually, he backed her up to the bed, and they toppled to the mattress together.

Somehow her clothes disappeared, and he was kissing her everywhere he could reach. He plundered her mouth, his fingers spearing into her hair, holding her captive.

"My turn. I enjoy exploring you."

"You mean you want to torture me? " He pulled away and lay on his back, his dark eyes gleaming. "I'm all yours."

So she trailed her hands over him, pleasing herself and cataloging his reactions to her caresses. The catch of his breath as she skated the tips of his fingers across his ribs. The way he trembled when she licked his nipple.

"More," he encouraged softly. "Explore my cock."

"What if it bites me?"

He barked out a laugh. "Pet it a bit and see what happens."

Fun and laughter had never entwined in her mind when she'd considered sex in the past. With a smile curving her lips, she ran her fingertips down the length of his shaft. Silky skin. Warmth. A masculine scent, musky, but not unpleasant. She curled her fingers around his cock, testing, stroking. Exploring in whichever direction her curiosity led her, she teased him and learned his body.

"Enough."

She froze, but a tiny smile curled her lips. "Did I do something wrong?"

"Never." He paused to grab a condom then lifted her by the hips and positioned her over him. "Guide me inside you."

She did as he requested, saw the way he watched where they were joined. Her inner muscles stretched as gravity impaled her on his cock. His hands at her hips guided her through the erotic dance until they both soared. They coasted back down together, and she stretched out on his hard chest, her last thought as she toppled into sleep was that Jake felt like the home she'd never had.

Chapter Fourteen

After Jake left the only time she had to herself were the evenings. It was during those quiet times she missed him—his solid presence that made her feel safe and protected. At least she'd felt that way until their separation stretched to six months and his calls and emails stopped coming. After a month of unanswered emails, she accepted the truth. They didn't have enough of a foundation for a lasting relationship.

Now, in the small hours of the night, she brooded, wondering if she should have done something different. She stifled a yawn. The lack was sleep was starting to tell.

"Hey, enough with the daydreaming," Alice said. "We have a lot to do. We need you at the board meeting. It starts in three minutes."

Sorrel set her pen aside with a rueful sigh. "I'm trying to think of an interesting scent combination for a new range of Star Sign bath bombs. Something different but not so radical it'll put off customers."

"I have faith in you. Come on. You need a break." Her gaze zeroed in on the shadows Sorrel knew she hadn't managed to cover with light makeup. "You look tired."

Sorrel bit her lip.

"Something wrong?"

"Jake has stopped contacting me. I haven't heard from him for weeks."

Alice wrinkled her nose. "I'm no expert on men, but are you sure there's something wrong?"

"A month of silence? That spells problem in my language."

"Maybe he's away from his base?"

"Or maybe he's seeing his old girlfriend. We were together for such a short time. We had a fling. I read about flings in one of Hinekiri's magazines."

"So email him, tell him how you feel and say you're moving on."

"No, that's similar to breaking up in a text. It's not cool, according to the magazines."

"Don't believe everything you read," Alice said in a crisp order. "They brainwash you into thinking there's something wrong if you're not coat-hanger thin with big lips and hair. We'll organize a girl's night out soon. That'll perk up your spirits." Her gaze flicked to the wall clock. "Time for the board meeting. Let's go."

The boardroom was bedlam, as usual. The oldies were already present, full cups of tea and coffee at their elbows, their eyes fixed on a container of homemade chocolate chip cookies.

"Ah, there you are." Harriet's needles clicked and clacked musically, black-and-white knitting spilling onto her lap in a long tail.

Alice disappeared and reappeared again with a gift-wrapped box. The lid of the box sported a pretty purple bow and trails of curling ribbon. In her other hand, she carried a plain brown bag. She set both on the table in front of her and slipped into a chair.

"Is everyone ready?" James studied each of them in turn.

Silence fell, faces bearing eagerness and filling the air with expectation. Nerves simmered in Sorrel, propelled by the anticipation and prompted by the worry of failure. So much depended on her product. What if it went wrong? Look at what had happened with Jake. The thought steadied her. As long as she tried her best. No one could demand more.

"Production started on our *Dream Cream* today. We've

made enough for our market testers, so we can get feedback on use and any potential problems." Alice pushed the gift-wrapped box across the board table toward Sorrel. "Open it."

Sorrel fumbled the box a little, her hands trembling in her excitement. This was the culmination of her tests and the lab perfecting the formula for mass production. She pulled out a plain black tub and lifted it for everyone to see. Someone had written on it with a gold pen in elegant script. *Dream Cream. Give your lover the gift of pleasure.*

"It's beautiful." Sorrel couldn't get another word out, the lump in her throat causing an emotional blockage. She turned the tub around so everyone could see the label.

"Perfect." Katarina bobbed her head. "Simple and classy. It's perfect. Is that the final packaging?"

"Yes, I think so," James said.

"Dreams should be wrapped in simplicity." Sam gave a decisive nod. "The plain packaging puts the spotlight on the product."

Alice handed out samples to everyone. "These are the reports we want you to fill out. I'd appreciate them back by Monday next week. Our time frame is short for this one because we need to get our promotion underway. Any objections to Monday?"

"Works for me." Richard glanced at his wristwatch.

"Was there anything else important to discuss today? I need to get back to the police station to relieve Luke."

"You go," James said. "We're going to discuss marketing ideas. If you have any suggestions, bring them with you to the meeting on Monday."

Richard left, and everyone settled back to a discussion on how they should market the *Dream Cream*.

"I still like our initial ideas of packaging products together," Alice said. "It worked well for our vibrating condoms and the vibrator. I think we should stick with the ideas we know will succeed."

"Other companies have copied our marketing strategy." Ben tapped his fingers on the tabletop. "I say we try to come up with something different."

"We need a loyalty card, something to market in combination with our social media pages," Harriet suggested.

"That might work for those who are computer savvy. We could still do the loyalty card. Good idea, but we need something more," Alice said.

Sorrel listened to the ideas flow back and forth, her mind racing to keep up. This group of people was amazing, and she felt honored to be part of the team. "You could offer discounts if customers purchased more than one product. Make it so the more products they buy the bigger discount they get. Buy one product and get a free gift."

"We wouldn't want to discount too much because that might backfire, but we could do an introductory discount." Alice's pen raced across the page as she jotted down the ideas.

A phone rang in the distance, and a tap sounded on the door. A secretary stuck her head through the door. "Phone call, Mr. Bates."

"Are we done yet? Ben and I need to get to bowls practice," Sam said.

"Off you go. I'll see you all on Monday afternoon." Alice made shooing actions with her left hand.

There was a mad scramble until only Alice and Sorrel remained in the boardroom. Alice glanced up from her notes. "Did you think of something else?"

"Yes. I love working here. Everyone has made me so welcome even though I have no formal qualifications. Thank you for giving me this chance."

Mere words couldn't convey the gratitude she experienced each day. Alice and her friends had gone out of their way to help Sorrel find her feet in Sloan. The name Sister Bitter no longer existed, and she held not a single regret about leaving the compound.

"You're welcome." Alice pulled a comical face. "One day I'll tell you the story of how I came to live in Sloan, perhaps over a glass of wine at The Thirsty Cricket. Maybe this weekend. I'll call around and see if everyone is free on Saturday night. Are you free?"

"Nothing on my social calendar." Which was a bit sad, according to the magazines. Sorrel stood and winced. Alice was right. Reading those magazines just depressed her. "Thanks again. I'd better get back to the lab. I want to brainstorm my star sign bath bombs before I leave today."

By the time she left Fancy Free, she'd come to tentative decisions regarding the scents to use for the new products she had in mind, and she had an entire Friday night stretching ahead of her. Some of the inventors in the lab had asked her to go for drinks at the pub, but she'd declined. Despite her bravado about giving up on Jake, carrying out the idea made her want to howl.

More fool her.

She had the house to herself, and after a half-hearted attempt at eating pasta for dinner, she shoved it aside. Unable to help herself she walked to her room and hit the receive button for her email. Three hard thumps of her heart later, she stared at the empty inbox. She retreated to the kitchen and filled her glass of wine.

Janaya's dog trailed after her, pausing at the fridge with a hopeful bark.

"Janaya told me not to feed you, no matter how pitiful

you look."

The dog grumbled a protest, almost as if it were talking to her. Sorrel carried her glass of wine out to the deck and sat watching the night push the day away, shrouding everything with darkness. Soon, the stars twinkled into prominence, and in a nearby stand of trees, a Morepork owl hooted its mournful cry. *More pork. More pork.*

Sighing, Sorrel rinsed her empty glass, stacked it in the dishwasher and retreated to bed. A glossy magazine sat on the nightstand. *Cure loneliness*, one of the subtitles on the cover practically screamed.

"Rub it in," Sorrel muttered.

The tub of *Dream Cream* sat nearby, and Sorrel decided to do some work. She'd try out the final version of her cream, get out one of the new vibrators Gaby, one of the inventors, had wanted her to test, and squeeze a sliver of pleasure out of this crumby night.

"I'm going out tomorrow," she told the dog who had followed her to her bedroom. "You're not watching. Out you go." Sorrel closed the door after the grumbling dog and stripped off her clothes. After a quick shower, she retrieved the test vibrator and the relevant paperwork from her handbag. Then, with a pen and the test questionnaire close at hand, she opened the tub of dream cream. The perfume of carnations filled her lungs, sweet and fragrant.

Unexpected, yet perfect. Maybe not everyone's choice of scent, but she delighted in it. They'd tested citrus and discarded the scent in favor of the more unusual.

She dipped her forefinger into the tub. The product was thick in consistency and almost solid. Body heat softened the cream, helping it to disperse and produce the wonderful tingles and stimulation.

Her forefinger trailed the outer edge of her areola, and the effect was instantaneous. Her breath caught, prickles of pleasure streaking across her breast.

"Yes," she whispered. She stroked her body, coating a little cream on her other breast and working it in until her nipples stood to attention, taut and aching. Taking her time and cataloging every sweet sensation, she parted her legs, the cool air against her swollen pussy ramping up her excitement even more.

Languidly, she dipped her finger into the tub again. Her digit slipped across the surface of the cream, and a whiff of carnations hit her along with a hint of her own musk. Sighing, she ran her finger down her folds and back up. She could feel the silkiness of her arousal, the tightening in her belly as excitement built.

The cream worked its magic. Sometimes too fast if the user took a liberal amount and applied it to the clitoris. Her eyes fluttered closed to better concentrate on the buildup of enjoyment, the quickening of her breaths.

She rubbed lazy, languid circles around her clit with the odd sweeping path across to make the swollen bundle of nerves sit up and pay attention. Oh yes. This was perfect. The only thing that would make it better was a man.

Jake.

Not gonna happen.

She might as well do what Alice suggested and stop putting this part of her life on hold. She fumbled for Gaby's newest vibrator design and switched it on, thankful for Gaby's foresight in providing batteries. Turning it off again, she spotted a few dots of the cream along the shaft of the device since rigorous testing had shown internal use worked well too. She slid it languidly in and out, enjoying the sense of fullness, the stretching. The initial coolness of the shaft warmed to her body temperature.

She could feel the coil of excitement in her belly tighten, and she closed her eyes again. She thumbed the power switch of the vibrator, and moaned as the clit tickler came into direct contact. "Yes."

Nice and quiet. Oh yes. The vibrator was excellent. It was perfectly shaped. Just perfect. Sorrel bit her bottom lip, her hips lifting off the bed. She moved the vibrator a fraction, and a streak of pleasure shot down her legs. Mentally she reached for her orgasm, but the coil tightened even more. Her pulse raced, and another groan escaped. The sensations tugged at her almost painfully. She didn't know if she could bear the direct contact any longer, yet she thought stopping would kill her. Balanced on the precipice, her body fought for release, struggled for satisfaction.

A hoarse breath squeezed past her clenched teeth.

A sharp yank on one nipple zapped the coil of tension with pain and she toppled over into orgasm, sharp, hard waves of pleasure rippling through her pussy.

She gasped, fighting her lethargy to open her eyes. A man stood by the bed. Tall. Dark. Hungry brown gaze fixed on her.

Pretty. He was familiar yet not.

"Jake?"

"In the flesh, sweetheart."

Still spasms of pleasure rippled to her womb, the combination of the vibrator and the cream drawing out her release.

"I thought..." She swallowed and tried again. "I thought you—"

"Didn't want you?" His words throbbed with emotion. "There hasn't been a day go past without me thinking of you, wanting you in my arms. You kept me going." While he spoke, he lost his clothes. His shirt came off, his movements awkward and jerky. A snow-white bandage covered one biceps.

"Are you all right?" She removed the vibrator, switching it off at the same time. Her cheeks turned red, now that she could think properly.

"I am now." He stooped to remove his boots and peeled his jeans and underwear down his legs in one move. His lips came down on hers, cool from the night air, but his first hungry kiss went a long way to shoring up her confidence. "God, I missed you so much."

She stroked his bare cheek and decided he was right. He was pretty without his beard. Stars, she'd missed him, was so glad to see him, touch him. "You didn't email me."

"I couldn't. The assignment they gave me went to crap. Before I met you, our team was ambushed, and Greg, one of my team, died before we could get him out. We had the chance to round up those responsible for his death, but it took a lot longer than I expected. My team was caught behind the lines."

She fingered the edge of his bandage, concern rippling through her. "You're hurt."

"A flesh wound. My vest saved me from the worst. We did what we went for, and that's all that matters." Satisfaction shone on his face, and he seemed more relaxed—if that was the right word—as if avenging his friend's death had closed a chapter for him.

He kissed her again, his tongue stroking deep, twining with hers and pushing a spark of desire alight in her. Her hands wrapped around his neck, holding him close, savoring the solidness of his body.

"Do you have to go back?"

"I'm finished. I'm here for good—if you want me."

"Jake," she whispered, the one word saying so much more than she could articulate at present.

She heard a car outside and Janaya and Luke talking as they walked inside. The dog barked a lot, and she wondered why it hadn't barked at Jake's arrival. The noise ceased, and footsteps sounded in the passage outside her bedroom.

"That your car out there, Jake?" Luke asked through the door.

"It's me."

"All right then," Luke said. "Good night." His footsteps faded as he walked back to the kitchen.

"Why didn't the dog bark at you?" Sorrel asked.

"I don't know. She must've recognized me."

"I never heard you. How did you get in?"

"Luke told me where he puts the spare key." He brushed a lock of blonde hair off her cheek. "I'm not surprised you didn't hear me. You were moaning."

Heat flooded her face again. "I was testing out some Fancy Free products." She strove for dignity. She missed by a country mile, her voice emerging breathless with a side note of huskiness.

"Can I help?" He shifted a fraction, allowing her to feel the hardness of his erection against her leg.

"Now?"

"Yes," he rasped.

"Condoms are in the side drawer. Try a little of the Dream Cream. Rub a smidgeon on the head of your cock before you roll on the condom. Not too much." She slid her finger across the surface of the cream and showed him before applying it to her clitoris.

"This first time might be quick," he said. "I haven't touched a woman since I left."

His words were a gift, his expression serious and without guile.

"I can keep up. The cream will take care of me."

Jake grabbed a condom and applied some cream under her direction. A shudder racked his large frame, and he swallowed audibly. "Maybe I should have waited to test your product."

"We have loads of time. This one is for you." And with her words came the sense of freedom, of flying into a new phase in her life. She realized she'd allowed her fears to multiply into doubt and distrust. He'd come back for her just as he'd promised.

Jake rolled her under him, pushing into her with one seamless thrust.

"Feels way better than the vibrator."

Jake laughed. "Good to hear. No man likes to think of a machine replacing him. God, I've missed you."

He made love to her, tender touches morphing into urgency, and then she was flying apart, Jake's arms keeping her safe.

"I love you," he said. "I wanted to tell you before I left, but I worried about things happening too quickly. I want a future with you. Marriage. Children. The whole works."

"Jake," she whispered, the weight she'd dragged around on her shoulders for the last months falling away. "Yes. I want that more than anything."

"If it's okay with you, we'll make a home here in Sloan. I'll get a job with one of the building companies based here, and you can keep working at Fancy Free. Will that work for you?"

"Oh yes. I love you, Jake." And it was true. They mightn't have known each other for long, but sometimes the heart knows. Jake was strong, but he allowed her to be her own person. "I can't think of anything better."

"Okay," Jake said.

And they didn't do any more talking for a long, long time.

· ♥ · ♥ · ♥ · ♥ · ♥ ·

THANKS SO MUCH FOR reading Safeguarding Sorrel. Reviews, as always, are very welcome and appreciated. Please turn the page for a recipe for chocolate bath salts, a recipe from Sorrel's treasured book. And if you're interested in reading about how Luke and Janaya became a couple, read on for an excerpt from Janaya.

Sorrel's Chocolate Bath Salts

1 cup Epsom salts

1 cup sea salt or kosher salt (coarse grain)

3 teaspoons cocoa powder

1 teaspoon vanilla extract

½ teaspoon cinnamon

1 tsp oil (almond, olive or sunflower will work)

Combine all the dry ingredients in a clean bowl. Add the vanilla extract and oil. Mix well to ensure oil is completely blended. Transfer to small clean jars or cello bags and close tightly. Sprinkle 1 – 2 spoonfuls in your bathtub, lie back in the water and relax.

Sorrel's Notes:

Sometimes I add baking soda to my mix to make my bath salts fizzy. To vary my recipe, I omit the vanilla extract and add 5 drops of peppermint essential oil. The Epsom salts and sea salt is good for soothing sore muscles and aches and pains.

These bath salts make excellent birthday, Christmas, or thank-you presents for family or friends.

Make sure you read the recipe properly. I let Jake make a batch and couldn't work out why his chocolate salts were more chocolatey than they should be. At least until he confessed he'd misread the requirements and put 3 Tablespoons of cocoa in the recipe instead of 3 teaspoons!

As always, do a patch test first before use in case one of the ingredients disagrees with your skin.

EXCERPT — JANAYA

THIS IS AN ACCOUNT of Luke and Janaya's first meeting...

Janaya squinted through the sunlight at the tall figure who climbed from the vehicle and tried to ignore the spark of anticipation. Totally weird. Phrull it, she couldn't wait to leave this god-forsaken outpost. Had to be a twenty-four-hour bug. Her body ached all over. "What are we going to do? We haven't had time to hide the ship."

"I hope he has food," the little dog said, cocking its head to survey the approaching man.

"Is that all you can talk about?" Janaya demanded, eyeing the creature with disfavor. "Aunt?"

Unbidden, her gaze slipped back to the male. He was tall, and even from this distance she knew he would tower over her medium frame. Dark brown hair, tousled and untamed, touched on his collar.

Janaya sucked in a deep breath. The same clean scent she'd smelled before bubbled through her senses like a sparkling tonic.

"Rather nice specimen, isn't he, dear?"

"Humph," Janaya said, trying to ignore the pounding of her heart and the flip-flop of her stomach, the sudden moist dampness between her legs. She ripped her gaze from the Earthman and tried to quell her aunt's smart-ass remarks with a frosty glare.

"I bet he has a nice tush. That would be rear end to you."

Heat suffused Janaya's face. "I have no interest in the man's front end or his back end. I have an agreement with Santana."

"Santana!" Hinekiri's mouth firmed to a straight line. "That male was a horrible child and he hasn't improved as an adult."

"You're not the one joining with him," Janaya snapped.

"Praise Lord Julian. If I were merging with a male, at least I'd check out the merchandise first."

Janaya whirled away from her aunt to stare at the approaching male. Unbeknown to her aunt, she'd already checked out the merchandise. She cringed as she recalled the fiasco. Then her shoulders squared. Next time she'd get the mating procedure right. Santana would have no complaints on that score. It was true that Santana wasn't as imposing as this male but he bore good qualities. And she liked his family.

Longing seeped into the region of her heart when she thought of the empty spaces that only family could fill. Once she'd secured her captain's bars and completed formalities with Santana everything would work out with her father. He'd realize she loved him and would recognize her worth. He'd finally accept her as a blood daughter instead of calling her a nuisance.

"How do we hide the ship?" Janaya asked, changing the subject to forestall the fierce argument building within her aunt. Hinekiri could debate all she liked. Janaya had chosen Santana and her decision was final.

"Oh, didn't I say? There's an emergency camouflage button. The ship will appear invisible for as long as the power source lasts."

"Why didn't you—never mind. Do it. He's nearly here."

The little dog sniffed and sighed loudly. "He doesn't have any food."

"You're right. I don't smell any."

The dog wagged its tail. "You scent better than most humans."

Hinekiri pulled a small control box from her low-slung

Earth trousers. Jeans, she'd called them when she'd handed a similar pair to Janaya. "Camouflage on."

Janaya glanced over her shoulder. The ship was still visible. "The system's failed," she whispered in a terse voice. Was nothing going to go right on this mission? Irritation with both herself and her stubborn aunt shot through her body, finding vent in gritted teeth. Her right hand slid to the weapon at her hip, ready to defend her aunt.

"No, wait. Don't shoot him. Watch."

The man she'd seen earlier strode into the clearing where they stood. He didn't hesitate or even blink on seeing the ship, but continued toward them with a loose-limbed gait that reminded Janaya of a two-toed tigoth—sleek and muscled. Confident that he'd catch his prey. Janaya's skin tingled. The sensation crawled through her body, across her lips, tugging her nipples to tight peaks and finally settling low in her belly. She slid her weight from foot to foot in a slow fidget then froze when she caught the grin on her aunt's face.

"Something wrong, dear?"

"This damned G-thing you gave me to wear is right up my—"

"Hello there." The man's voice slid across her skin like soft, satiny monterey petals, drawing her body tight with unexpected sensual need. Fascinated by the Earthman, her gaze drifted down to the column of tanned flesh showing in the V of his blue shirt. An urgent need to slide her tongue across the same path her gaze had taken gripped her mind. She took half a step forward to complete the action before her brain jerked into gear and screeched to an appalled halt. A soft choking noise drew her gaze northward to gleaming dark brown eyes. Hot eyes that simmered with an answering passion.

Janaya took another half a step to close the distance between them.

"Down, girl," her aunt murmured, placing one bony hand on her arm in warning.

The clear transparency with which her aunt saw her need brought a blush of hot color to her cheeks and that too, flowed down her body, converging in one achy spot.

Janaya opened her mouth but all that emerged was an undignified croak. Instead of interrogating him, her mind drifted to wonder what his dark hair would feel like as it slid between her fingers, if the passion that arced in the air between them would translate to hot, uninhibited mating. There had to be more to the process than what she'd discovered so far with Santana.

Aware of his laughing eyes scanning her face, her body, Janaya tried to dislodge the huge lump in her throat with a dry swallow. The throbbing silence stretched. Luckily, her aunt came to the rescue, interrupting her frantic thoughts by taking the initiative.

"Good afternoon," she chirped. "And it's a great one, too. I'm Hinekiri Jones. And this is my niece, Janaya Smith."

False names, Janaya noted with silent approval.

The man halted in front of them and nodded politely. "Police Constable Luke Morgan," he said in a husky voice that plucked at Janaya's nerve endings. He grinned, showing dazzling white teeth, and shared the grin between both of them before stooping to pat the dog on the head. Straightening, he said, "I know this is going to seem like a weird question, but I've had reports of an unidentified flying object. Did either of you see anything strange in the last hour?"

Janaya gasped. Her croak of denial turned into a cough. Did he really not see the ship parked right in front of him?

"A UFO?" her aunt demanded, her violet eyes widening in excitement. "How exciting. If you find it, holler 'cause I'd love to meet one of those little green men."

The man chuckled. "Personally, I'd rather not come face-to-face with an alien but I'll keep your request in mind." After a brisk nod for Janaya and a wide grin for her aunt, the man—Morgan—strode past them, a mere two feet away from the ship.

"He didn't even glance at the ship. How come he can't see it and I can?"

"There is a scientific explanation, but I don't have time to explain. Your unauthorized presence on my ship has created a little problem," Hinekiri said. "You shouldn't have stowed away on my ship."

"I had to protect you. What sort of problem? The crash wasn't my fault." Indignation dripped from Janaya's voice. Someone had to protect her aunt from the Torgon, and she didn't trust any bodyguard except herself. Apart from her estranged father, Hinekiri was all the family she had left and Janaya didn't intend to lose her to a butt-ugly Torgon.

"You didn't have travel inoculations before you left."

Janaya hated the smug tone her aunt used. Every survival instinct rose up and shrieked of danger. Her eyes narrowed. "What haven't you told me?"

"Earth's atmosphere varies from ours on Dalcon."

"The oxygen content is the same. I checked."

"Ah, but did you check the trace elements?"

The smugness had grown to a smirk. Janaya was beginning to loathe that smirk. "Tell me."

"The trace elements on Earth act like a booster to our systems. Inoculations counteract the effect."

"What? What effect?" It was like drawing teeth from

Dalcon's national bird, the fodo.

"The senses are amplified."

"Hearing, sight, you mean?" A relieved sigh eased through her lips. That didn't sound too bad. She could live with enhanced senses especially if it helped to keep Hinekiri safe. Janaya glanced at her aunt again. The smirk had turned toothy. Very toothy, and it stretched from one side of her aunt's angelic face to the other.

"What else?" she demanded.

"Sexual desire."

"You mean..." Janaya turned to study the figure of the retreating Earth male. Even with the distance between them Janaya saw how well the man's trousers cupped his buttocks. Her palms itched as she thought about fondling.

"Yeah, like I said before, nice tush. Pity Santana isn't here with you. He could take care of the emotional...ah...overflow."

Janaya wrenched her gaze from the Earthman's butt with difficulty. Her heart beat faster, and her breath wheezed from her lungs as though she'd only just finished a heavy training session. Her eyes landed on her aunt's face. The smirk hadn't lessened any. She bit back a groan. She may as well hear the worst of it now. "Out with it," she said. "Tell me everything." To enforce her request, she took two steps toward her aunt and set her face in a threatening scowl.

"No need to hurt a little old lady," her aunt chirped. "I'd like to point out that this is your fault for jumping before checking the consequences."

"You're not old." Janaya took another step, and this time she didn't have to force a glare. "Tell me the worst."

"There's no need to shout, dear. What I was about to say is that even if Santana were here, he couldn't help. I'm afraid you've imprinted on the Earth male." Her aunt beamed. "Nice choice, dear. If I was a little younger… Perhaps I'll meet a nice Earthman while I'm here. We could double date."

Grab your copy today
(www.shelleymunro.com/books/janaya)

ABOUT AUTHOR

USA Today bestselling author Shelley Munro lives in Auckland, the City of Sails, with her husband and a cheeky Jack Russell/mystery breed dog.

Typical New Zealanders, Shelley and her husband left home for their big OE soon after they married (translation of New Zealand speak - big overseas experience). A twelve-month-long adventure lengthened to six years of roaming the world. Enduring memories include being almost sat on by a mountain gorilla in Rwanda, lazing on white sandy beaches in India, whale watching in Alaska, searching for leprechauns in Ireland, and dealing with ghosts in an English pub.

While travel is still a big attraction, these days Shelley is most likely found in front of her computer following another love - that of writing stories of contemporary and paranormal romance and adventure. Other interests include watching rugby (strictly for research purposes), cycling, playing croquet and the ukelele, and curling up with an enjoyable book.

Visit Shelley at her Website
www.shelleymunro.com

Join Shelley's Newsletter
www.shelleymunro.com/newsletter

OTHER BOOKS BY SHELLEY

Fancy Free

Protection

Romp

Buzz

Festive

Friendship Chronicles

Secret Lovers

Protecting the Bride

Alien Encounter series

Janaya

Hinekiri

Alexandre

Milton Keynes UK
Ingram Content Group UK Ltd.
UKHW040619200324
439767UK00005B/195

9 781991 063458